Dear K

Have fun reading a
book that isn't about
your nipples

Alexx

CONFRONTATIONS
OF THE THREE

First Published in Great Britain 2012 by Mirador Publishing

First edition: 2012

Any reference to real names and places are purely fictional and are constructs of the author. Any offence the references produce is unintentional and in no way reflects the reality of any locations or people involved.

A copy of this work is available through the British Library.

ISBN : 978-1-909220-01-0

Mirador Publishing
Mirador
Wearne Lane
Langport
Somerset
TA10 9HB

Confrontations Of The Three
The Second Part Of
The Broken Chamber Trilogy

By

Chris Gallie

Mirador Publishing
www.miradorpublishing.com

For Rachel

Come say 'Hello' on Facebook:

In the Chamber.

As the knife cut into the boy's heart, the division began. It was everything Vericoos had expected and more. He strained as he felt the three falling into nothingness. They did not want to act. They wanted nothing.

He willed Shabwan or, as he had now become, the *Shabwans* forward. *Remember,* he thought. *Remember what you must do.* For a moment they stood like drunkards, motionless and lost. Then, slowly and tentatively but still as one, they took a step forward and laid three hands on three handles.

There was a click, one solitary click, as the impossible became reality, and the God chamber, the prison that Lubwan had created and which had held an unimaginable force of evil for all this time, opened.

The three Shabwans stepped forward and were immediately swallowed by blackness. Behind them the doors swung shut, and delivered their same little click but in reverse.

Vericoos the sorcerer opened his eyes and sat.

He had won.

Prologue.

Making worlds.

She was beautiful but it mattered not to him. What mattered was the troubling news she brought.

'You say that Veo was on this world of Svin all along?'

She nodded. Her face betrayed little emotion, yet she must have felt something. It was her and her kind who could have lost the most. He knew this to be false as quickly as he'd conceived it as a thought. They all would have lost. How had he not seen this?

'His goal appeared to be to kill all the sorcerers, thus unifying the power.' Again, she gave little away as she said this. Yet there was something, a slight twitch in her face, which betrayed the absolute repulsion she felt at the idea. He needed to be careful. Their relationship had always been fractious, and now, at the moment when she trusted him least, he needed her more than ever.

'And this prison…you believe it will hold?'

He tried not to appear like he was studying her as he said this. It would not be in her nature to lie. Her loyalty was to the natural world and to the magic within it. Veo's work had threatened to destroy all that she held dear. Yet still he did not feel that he could trust her, nor she him.

'I believe it to be capable of containing whatever Veo has become.'

This he did not understand, nor did he truly wish to. He should have.

'What I must ask of you now is of gravest importance,' he said.

She looked at him. Their eyes, for the first time, met.

'Can you destroy the flow on Svin?'

Her eyes flashed, but only for the briefest of moments. Then, once again, she was the picture of dignity.

'We can halt it, yes. Though the process…'

'I have complete faith in you,' he cut in. 'Go back to Svin and do whatever you have to. I want no magic to flow through that planet.'

She nodded.

'And Sheeba, you personally are to stand guard. If anything out of the ordinary is happening, I want to know. It seems Veo was trying to assist…him.'

Sheeba, empress of the guardians, couldn't hide her surprise and fear, and of course he noticed. How could it possibly be? Veo, a God, in allegiance with...

'Do you understand me Sheeba?' His voice was threatening and she knew why.

'We will do as you ask.'

'Good,' said he, and well he might, for he was king of the Gods, and he had been there since the beginning.

2.

The king of the Gods had a name. His name was Gask and he had been king for as long as he could remember, which, technically speaking, is as long as there is. He had been there at the great battle which shaped the universe, one part of which Sheeba the guardian has just been sent back to protect. So, before we return to that same corner of the universe, albeit at a very different time, let us journey right back to the start. To a place outside of all conventional concepts of space and time, a place where the two greatest imaginable forces are at war, and where things are not going well...

3.

It's difficult for us to conceive what it was like before the creation of our universe for obvious reasons. Our experience of the world relies on our senses and they would have recognised little. But that isn't to say that there weren't similarities. The space, if you like, in which the Gods and the force resided was vast. Vaster than can be comprehended by the human mind, which, unless you're reading this in some distant future, is probably what you're using. There was land and there was air, yet neither obeyed any of the rules we would now associate with them. Mountains, larger than planets while simultaneously smaller than an atom, spiked suddenly upwards and great oceans, composed of something like-but-oh-so-unlike water, crashed upon them. In short, it was a pretty hostile environment, and it was like this for one simple reason; it was a war zone.

The Gods, who knew not why or how, had come into existence in (or perhaps on) what it is probably best to think of as a blank canvas. They knew it was their duty to create, although, again they knew not why. There may have been something more than them, some kind of creator of creators but that's really their concern, not ours.

Their job would have been fairly easy; Gask was king, they all knew that, and his vision of green and blue planets, illuminated and warmed by gaseous giants, was one that they could have carried out together. The task was enormous, yes, but they were Gods. They had time. At least they would have as soon as they got round to creating it.

Things were made a hell of a lot more difficult by the fact that they weren't the only artists to have sprung into existence and, just as clearly as Gask had his vision, there was another who held one just as firmly, and his name was Rez. The canvas, upon which Gask and his people were poised to paint, was set to be torn to shreds before the first acrylic could fall. There certainly wasn't room for compromise. For Rez was not like Gask, not in any way. He was a being of magic. A being who would stop at nothing until all the Gods were slain, and he could create the universe as he saw fit. As he was to lose, we have no way of knowing what this would have entailed. In a way

2

he embodies the ultimate example of history being written by the victors. To modify this phrase ever so slightly and say that universes are created by the victors seems dramatic, but in this case it was true.

Gask's army met with Rez's in the maelstrom that was nothing, but into which something must become. The fight was one of divine power against ultimate raw magic, and amidst the explosions, the size of supernovas but which could also have fitted inside the nucleus, Rez and Gask found one another. As they fought, energy, which would blow our world to dust like bones removed from a forgotten sarcophagus, danced between them. They ripped each other's forms to the very limits of existence, which, considering that nothing really existed at this point, takes quite some doing. In a moment when all seemed lost, Gask threw the last of his thoughts and power at his enemy and, in doing so, realised something that Rez had not. Until that point, they had both seen each other as something that must be removed before the creation could begin. Rez continued to think like this, Gask did not. Why could their creative abilities not be used as part of the fight, rather than just as a reward for the victor? He acted without thought and unwittingly created the universe. All that there was, which was also technically nothing (I know...it confuses me as well) he clove into three. One part was prison; Rez and his armies were instantaneously trapped in a place the size of a universe, yet one they could not escape from. The victorious Gods found themselves in the universe in which our tale takes place, and between the two was a barrier, a land of nothing which served only to separate.

Having won the battle and simultaneously created their home, the Gods now found that they had form. Before and during the fight, they had been nothing and everything. Movement, sound, mass, none of these words allow us to envisage anything really, but perhaps they are as close as we have. The battle had been mental, physical, and elemental, and had taken place throughout dimensions of nothing and without any laws of physics or nature or any of these things which came later...or now, as it were...or is. To try to imagine it would perhaps be futile, and, in a way, it is not something we need concern ourselves with. The results are really where our tale begins.

For what Gask and the other Gods discovered, as they set about creating the planets over which they would rule, was worrying to say the least. While there were now three layers and Rez was indeed imprisoned, they had not isolated his magic. They could feel it. As soon as they had created the forests and mountains, as soon as they'd heard the lapping and crashing of their first oceans, or heard the ground sizzle in barren desert.

They felt it flow.

At first there was fear; what would happen when they brought life into this world? Was Rez perhaps breaking through? Would the two walls between they and he hold? Would all become chaos again? Such questions needed an answer and one that could be trusted. Perhaps predictably then, Gask turned to his most trusted lieutenant, a God named Veo.

Veo set out on this perilous journey and was not seen for some time. Although to be fair to the Gods, this was still a concept they were working on. When he returned, he knew everything and they did not ask how. It was his business if he ever chose to speak of that time. He explained to the assembled Gods, who since taking on physical, individual forms now numbered about eighty, that Rez was trapped in a universe which was all red, the colour of his raw power. Yet in this place, said power was useless. Without nature it seemed, magic was only superficial, all lightning and explosions, visually terrifying but practically redundant. Hence why Rez was unable to leave. Of the second dimension he spoke very little, although he did say it was the most terrible of places.

'Here magic is living,' he said. 'There is nature but in its most barren form. An ugly terrible place, yet one that the magic can flow through. There are things there, things born of this flow, yet there is no path for them from there to here.'

'You're sure of this?' asked Gask.

Veo only nodded.

'However,' he continued, 'there is, it would appear, some kind of channel between that dimension and this, and while the beasts that I saw may not transcend it, the power that flows from Rez's prison does continue on into this world.' The Gods exchanged worried looks. 'But it feels different here,' Veo finished.

'How so?'

Veo seemed to consider this question for some time. The assembled Gods waited and then waited some more. Just as the waiting was beginning to verge on the edge of tediousness, Veo spoke.

'Here it cannot harm.'

Muttering around the circle was inevitable and, for all his authority, it took Gask a moment to stop it. Later the humans of his creation would, in turn, create a device for this. One which would have the added bonus of being able to knock nails in.

'Then our decision is made; we continue as planned. Although I charge all of you with the responsibility of keeping an eye on this. Clearly a link exists between here and Rez and, while he may not be able to transcend the divide himself, anything coming from there needs to be treated with suspicion.'

There was much nodding. He was the king after all.

Later they created life in their own image and eventually that life started harnessing the flow in ways the Gods could not. It led to much conflict and to the birth of the sorcerer. Yet Rez remained trapped, and while the Gods were no longer invulnerable against their human charges, they continued, to some extent, to rule in their third of all that was. When they were forced from a planet, by magical battle or otherwise, they weren't especially bothered. It was a matter of pride more than anything, as there were always other worlds to rule. They did, however, feel uneasy about leaving these flowing planets

4

unchecked, and thus created the guardians. And this, you'll be over the moon to know, is a story to which we must later return.

Upon leaving a planet, take for example the world of Svin, they would charge these beings to remain at certain points. Points where the magic flowed in at its most raw and unchecked. This would allow the guardians to keep a watchful eye over that world, and to protect it from any unwanted force. It also meant that were Rez to break through, he would not carry the element of surprise with him.

The guardian's loyalty was to the Gods, but there was a flaw in their design. Gask, in his perhaps not-so-infinite wisdom, thought it would be pragmatic to forge, not only a love, but also a deep dependence on magic in these beings. Hence keeping them to their posts with a need to satisfy themselves constantly.

It worked but, like so many hastily assembled plans, it had side effects.

The guardians did the God's bidding and stood guard over their planets, but they held an uneasy relationship with their masters, and often did not report things that should have been reported. As time went on, there was less and less liaison between the two groups, and Gask sometimes wondered whether they were, in fact, no longer loyal to him at all. The God's reign was constantly threatened by this cursed flow, and now it seemed that even those they'd (or, to be more accurate, *he'd*) created to aid them could not be trusted. The kingdom of the Gods became fractious, and infighting was inevitable. Some left and began tyrannical reigns over smaller planets, some fought and killed each other, some returned to flowing planets to wage war; more often than not unsuccessfully.

Gask, in an effort to restore peace, created a kingdom. A kingdom unlike any of the planets on which the Gods had always lived amongst their subjects. This place was removed from these worlds, away from the flow. A place where the Gods, or what remained of them, could live in isolation. For, despite all that had happened, their duty was of both creation and protection. And, while many of the others had turned their backs on this, preferring lives of war and tyranny, he would always strive to look after this universe, which they had fought so hard to make theirs. While he knew that Rez was still there, he would always remain alert. For if that red force were to crash through this place, then all would be lost.

Book 1

The Romantic vs. the Fool.

Chapter 1.

Lost.

1.

Shabwan landed with a bump and immediately he thought of Kayleigh. He could not remember what had gone before, only that now he was here. And she was not. This thought felt like it would tear him to pieces. Indeed, it did somehow seem as if his internal grief was spilling out of him, plucking at the air around him, colouring it and then painting pictures. He could not yet see beyond this initial bubble, and he did not care to, for within it was her.

Yet she was not completely how he remembered. There was change. He hoped against hope that this change did not affect how she felt for him. Such an idea would have been enough to make him turn his own head around. Confused and disorientated, he stumbled and almost fell. Then a thought came to him, a thought accompanied with pain. Not the emotional, heart-wrenching pain that the swirling images of his beloved were delivering, but a physical pain. Something which had been sharp and cold and had only lasted for the briefest of moments. As he tried to reach back into his memories, unconsciousness took him. He hit the ground, which seemed to be made solely of little mirrors, all showing the same face. A face which did not belong to Shabwan.

2.

Veo the fool could not believe what he was seeing. There was much madness in this universe. Much existed that he could have never conceived when he was whole. Much of what was around him he had no control over anymore, and much of it was to be feared. But now, for the first time since he had been imprisoned in this God-forsaken (or perhaps God-inhabited) place, he saw something that he had not created.

A man.

Thoughts raced through his mind, thoughts which were oh so difficult to pin down. Indeed, just controlling his mind enough to see straight was a skill which had taken him a long, long time to master. He was aware of what a fool he was, and aware of the damage he had done. Yet now he saw opportunity; an opportunity he had not believed would ever come. He tried to conceive what it could mean but was unable to. As quickly as he'd seen his salvation, it dissolved, leaving an angry nothing, which could only be filled with the insanity around him. As the familiar wave of madness enveloped him, he would not let the image of the man leave his mind. He clung onto it amidst the storm of noise and colour. As long as he could hold onto this one little thought, the one that was now clinging on like seaweed against the might of the tide, then he would have a chance.

7

Like the young man who had now become his obsession, he too now fell to the ground. They both lay as if asleep, neither truly comprehending the significance of the conflict they must now see through.

3.

Lubwan had done a good job and, like many who do a good job, he'd paid a price.

The chamber had done exactly as it was asked and imprisoned Veo's divisions. There was no way they could have broken out of their confinements. Yet, beyond the three doors in the worlds where the three Shabwan's were now drifting in and out of consciousness, they had complete control. Not that the world, in which we just left the first Shabwan, had been in any way deliberately crafted into its current form, but it had been crafted none the less. The insane portion of the God, which the chamber had dubbed 'the Fool', had been granted the same authority over his surrounds that he had fought so hard for alongside Gask.

Just as when he and the other Gods had been victorious over Rez, the universe had been his to create, only this time he had not been *he*. He had been a slice of himself; completely at the mercy of the way the knife had divided him. Veo the fool had spun into this empty space and, as his emotions and thoughts flowed freely, the world was formed.

Such a concept is infinitely more complex than the simple business of creating an ordered universe. When he and Gask and all the others had painted the worlds upon which Shabwan, Vericoos, Lubwan and all the others later walked, they had created order. Nature, physics and countless other nameless things were all bound by sets of rules. Hell, even the magic that flowed into their universe completely unwanted was still governed by these laws, at least to some extent. In the three spaces beyond the doors, there were no such laws.

When Veo had first entered, a simple thought or outburst of emotion was enough to send the terrain warping off into the distance, where before there had been nothing. As a tear fell from his eye, an ocean sprang into being. Yet, to call it an ocean would not do it any kind of justice. When the Gods first made the universe, they laid foundations. Things would grow and evolve and, of course, things would change. But what they created, they created to stay. In the worlds beyond the doors, anything could pop in and out of existence as quickly as thoughts could pop in and out of Veo's slice of a head. His head was, of course, whole; I'm talking about what was inside it. For who knew how long after he'd entered, this was the case. The blank canvas, which wrapped around and constrained him, was painted a thousand different shades of every conceivable colour. It was ripped into more pieces than could be counted by armies of generations. For so long Veo lived like this; terrified, unable to comprehend the madness that was now both him and his.

Then it began to change.

8

That which was once transient began to be less so. Things: buildings, people, animals and demons, which were flung into existence by the mind, which their creator had no control over, were suddenly not so easily displaced. The ground became solid, and that which had life, kept it. After such aeons of turbulence, Veo was finally creating the foundations of his prison. And it was into these arenas that the three Shabwans now plummeted. Three universes so different, yet all essentially created by the same being.

And so it was with Shabwan.

His three divisions were now far removed from one another. Only the physicality would make one draw any kind of conclusions that they were connected. Yet still they were all *Shabwan*, just as the prisons were all *Veo*. And so on we must go, into three worlds where three separate confrontations must take place. For only can the victors leave the places they now find themselves trapped together. At this stage, the six divisions have varying degrees of awareness of this fact, but they will all come to know it eventually, some not until it is much too late.

One man who was completely aware of it, a man who was lucky enough to still be all in one piece...as it were, was sitting on the ground in, as he called it, the God chamber. His name was Vericoos.

4.

The three Shabwans had entered the doors and Vericoos' work was, for the moment at least, complete. Holding Shabwan together had not been easy. As soon as the knife had punctured the young man's heart, the divisions had taken place. The sudden existence of three minds had been startling to say the least. Vericoos had, of course, envisaged the moment a thousand times over, and was as prepared as he could have been.

Yet still it had shocked him.

The momentary glimpse of the raw insanity that the knife had created made him fear for Veo. He had never doubted for a moment that his master would have the capability to return, yet when he felt what the Shabwans had become...

He had plunged all his mental energy into the three that now stood before him. They'd fought hard to reject him, internally trying to rip themselves to pieces. But, despite one proving much more difficult than the other two, he had taken control of them still. He had reached out his own hand, and they, as one, or as three, had done the same. More than anything, he'd wanted to try and glimpse what lay behind the doors, to gain some idea of what his master's divisions had created. But, when the moment came, his eyes had been firmly shut. The effort involved in driving the three panicked, unwilling Shabwans through the three doors had taken everything he had, and to have let his concentration waver would have been disastrous.

Now he was sat there, just looking at the three doors. It had taken him a few minutes to realise that more writing had appeared on the silver plaques. It chilled him deeply to think that the chamber would have such self-awareness.

For if it did, it was surely not the least bit pleased with his existence or what he had done.

The three plaques now read:

The Romantic and the Fool.
The Fool and the Trickster.
The Reluctant Hero and the Conqueror.

'That last one should be interesting,' said Vericoos to himself. There was, of course, no one to hear him, but there was someone to *feel* him. In the place Gask had created to protect this universe from Rez and the magic, Lubwan shook with rage.

5.

Shabwan awoke and this time felt some clarity. Memories sparked, but they sparked as instantaneously and uselessly as flint in the rain. He could not hold onto them. He knew that his goal must be to find Kayleigh, and he would get to that as soon as was humanly possible. But first he needed to take in his surroundings. He appeared to be on a hill, not unlike the one that overlooked San Hoist and this one, like that one, also seemed to overlook a town. Nothing unusual about that, he thought. What was more unusual was that the sky was a mix of violet and lime green and that huge orange shooting stars seemed to be clumsily criss-crossing their way overhead.

A long way into the distance he could see what looked like a castle, but it was difficult to tell. For now the town would do as a first port of call. Maybe somebody there could explain to him what the hell was going on, and, more importantly, where the love of his life was.

As he set off down the hill he began to weep. The thought of her was oh so raw. Every moment they were apart physically cut him. There was some music coming from the town, which suggested an inn. No doubt filled with kindly souls, who would be able to help him with his quest. Such was his single mindedness that the horrific nature of the music failed to set any alarm bells ringing.

6.

Veo was sitting in the top of his tallest tower, surveying his lands. There were a lot of them, and the young man was a long way away still. Whoever this boy was, he would soon find out. For now he was happy to observe him. Let's see how he does in Farsville, thought Veo, and laughed manically before exploding into voice.

'I'm sure he'll like it just fine…fine and dandy! Hahahahahahaha.'

Next to him, a creature, not unlike a monkey, snarled and breathed fire. Veo looked at it disapprovingly and then laughed some more. He may be a fool but he was sure as hell no damned monkey. And once he'd worked out why this man had been sent here, then things were going to get a whole lot better! Of this, even if nothing else, he was completely sure.

7.

Shabwan, still weeping, was getting nearer to the town. He had, in fact, passed a couple of buildings. They were Strange places; odd little huts with no sign of life but lavishly decorated. One had all sorts of horrible faces painted all over it, and another had been covered in words, which, while clearly painted on, seemed to have the ability to move as they wished. He was pretty sure that the letters had rearranged themselves to read "wHo Is hE?" as he passed. There were birds in the sky but they were not like any birds he'd ever seen. He tried again to cast his mind back, but came up against the same brick wall that seemed to adorn the point just before he'd woken up in this odd place. It seemed that no memory was available, no memory other than her face and the feeling that accompanied it. And this was enough to drive him on...to whatever ends.

The town's entrance was marked by a looming arch, upon which what could only be the name of the place was announced in lurid green paint. It seemed though, that this paint, like that which he'd just seen on the small dwellings, had no real concept of remaining true to any particular message. As he got closer to the arch, the letters seemed to tremble as if shaking off some kind of deep sleep, before taking up new positions. The words they now spelt were unfamiliar to him. They read "SaN HoiSt."

As he rounded the corner, he saw a person. His heart leapt for a moment as he thought it was Kayleigh, and then sunk back into the depths upon the realisation that it wasn't. It wasn't even a woman.

'Good morrow young sir,' came the call. 'What brings you to our little town on such a day?'

Shabwan wasn't completely sure how to answer this question. Should he tell this fellow the truth; that he was searching for his long lost love? Perhaps it was better to hold back on that for a moment or two, and instead try to get the measure of this shambling figure.

'I'm just looking for a place to stay,' said Shabwan.

'Ah! What a wondrous idea my boy. Follow old Marty as he knows the way!' Shabwan was in no condition to argue with such logic, so he set off after the old man and soon found himself in a much busier street, which could only have been the centre of the town. Marty was moving quickly through the crowd and Shabwan was struggling to keep up. He didn't have time to glance at the faces around him, which was probably a good thing.

For they, without exception, were glancing at him.

For ten minutes more, Shabwan followed the accelerating figure ahead of him. It would have been more difficult were it not for the fact that Marty was singing at the top of his lungs. The song, horrible as it was, was not without a hint of familiarity. Yet it was familiarity which bred no comfort in young Shabwan. Suddenly, without warning, the old man stopped and Shabwan crashed into the back of him. There was nothing strange about this in principle, but Shabwan was fairly sure that old Marty had been a good fifty yards ahead of him just milliseconds before the impact. How fast had they been moving through this place?

'Welcome!' said Marty and, as he did so, Shabwan saw his face clearly for the first time. Memory came rushing back to him like a freight train, but, before it could reach the platform, Marty's surprisingly strong arm thumped him through the stable doors of the inn. It took his eyes a second to adjust to the bright, colourful lights and once they had he wished they hadn't. For every patron of the aforementioned inn was stood in complete silence, staring directly at him.

Shabwan felt a rush of cold fear. For the first time since his arrival, he thought of himself. He'd blindly rushed into this place with no idea where he was and now it seemed like he was in deep, deep trouble. He turned towards the exit to find that the suddenly much burlier frame of Marty was blocking the door.

Just as his discomfort was peaking, the whole place burst into rapturous applause. Immediately he was swallowed up into a throng of people, all clapping him on the shoulder and shouting their welcomes. The frustrating feeling of memory, ever so slightly out of reach, prickled around his temples once again.

Then it was shattered by noise.

A roar, unlike anything Shabwan could recall having ever heard before, shook the inn to its very foundations, and the patrons, who had previously been giving Shabwan such a warm welcome suddenly looked panicked. Silence fell over the bar once more. Then there was a voice, cold and high. It spoke in a language which Shabwan could not understand, unlike those around him. They looked at one another, muttering urgently. Shabwan could not get a handle on what was going on; everything was moving far too quickly.

'He knows you're here,' said Marty, clearly intending to provide some kind of explanation for what had gone before.

'Who?' asked Shabwan, proving just how unsuccessful Marty had been.

'Never mind about that now.'

'They're outside!' yelled a male voice.

Shabwan had had enough. There is only so much confusion one can take, especially when one is actually one over three.

'Shut up! Can everyone calm down, and can someone tell me what's going on?'

They obeyed the first two parts of his request, and once again he was confronted with that agonising frustration. He felt as if he knew the people he was looking at, had perhaps known them all his life, but when it came to actually placing a single one of them…it was in that moment he realised he had never been so alone.

'Shabwan,' said a woman of middle age who appeared to be bleeding from her head. 'We are here for you.'

And even though she bore a perfect resemblance to Anika, he recognised her not. Then a crash from the road outside drew his attention. He ran to the

12

doors and peered over the top. Out in the cobbled street beyond were…his first reaction was to say people. But these things were no more people than they were pari, though some of them shared the same heinous colour scheme as the latter. They did not walk towards the pub, they lurched. From their disfigured heads protruded great bulbous eyes. Some of them seemed so tall as to be ridiculous; others barely reached their knees. Indeed, some didn't even reach their own knees, as they were bobbling above their heads in the same way that spiders do.

The overall effect was a parody of humanity. Like someone with access to limitless amounts of clay, a big oven and little or no sense of beauty or symmetry, had set about creating their own army.

As one they were advancing on the inn.

Shabwan looked back at the people (by the Gods it felt good to call them people) assembled behind him. He could not begin to comprehend what was happening to him. No amount of stonk in the previous life, of which he presently has no memory, could have prepared him for what he was going through. Yet none of this mattered. All that mattered was that these people were here, and that meant that there was a chance that Kayleigh was here too. And if he was ever going to live long enough to see her again, then they were going to have to fight these things.

'You say that you're with me?'

They nodded. He turned back to face the saloon doors. There was no noise coming through them, only an eerie stillness which betrayed nothing of what he'd just seen. Then, without being truly aware of why he was doing it, he raised his hand. Thankfully for the dignity of all involved, the assembled crowd did seem to know why he was doing it. They readied themselves, grabbing beer bottles, chairs and anything else that looked like it could effectively bash, gouge or sever. The division of Shabwan, completely unaware of the fact that he was surrounded by things which looked exactly like the people he'd spent almost his entire life with, threw his erect arm forward. As one, they charged out of the inn's doors.

8.

Veo, in his tower, could see it all. He was pleased the boy had chosen to fight and interested to see what creations he had added to the town. Much as he was excited at the prospect of the ruck, he did not want any harm to befall this new wanderer, and therefore it would not. At least not at his hands, or the hands of those which owed their existence to him. He was testing the boy as he himself had been tested on his arrival. Had he passed the test, he would have known much better how to play the current situation, but he had not.

Veo the fool had failed.

But this conflict, which he was forcing upon his new cellmate, was not *his* test it was just *a* test.

The true test can only be designed by the self, and until Veo had seen

13

what form it took for this young man, he would just sit back and enjoy the carnage.

9.

A long, long way away, four friends were sat around a campfire.

One of them was the reason that Shabwan the romantic was now throwing himself, along with momentarily created shadows of his old, unremembered life, into a conflict with a farcical representation of humanity, created by a sliver of a God in a vain attempt at escaping the hell he was trapped in.

But if you had told her this, she probably wouldn't have believed you, even if she'd managed to understand such a clumsily cobbled together sentence. Having said that, the amount that she was willing to believe had grown dramatically since she'd seen the reanimated corpse of a magician drag himself from his funeral fire and bellow a message that could only mean that her love was still alive, after she'd believed otherwise.

It was fair to say that she'd been through a lot recently.

As had the three boys she was travelling with. Yet, despite it all, they were in fairly high spirits. For where there had been despair there was now hope. Riding along the main road that must eventually lead them to the forest and the mountains, they had been talking and laughing with an ease they had not felt since Laffrunda; an event that now seemed a lifetime ago. They had been riding hard, although Lewhay was turning out to be a complete disgrace to the noble art of horsemanship. Every time they managed to get up a bit of rhythm, his stubborn mount would decide to either slam on the brakes, or veer off dramatically into the surrounding farmland. He had thus far managed to stay on the horse, but there had been a few near misses. The others, who had formed much better relationships with their steeds, had watched all this with varying degrees of amusement and frustration. They found it annoying to have to stop, but loved watching the increasing rage and indignation of their friend. They also delighted in listening to how many new excuses he could find for why he wasn't taking to it as naturally as they were.

Still, much as they were getting on better with the art of riding, there is no way to prepare your body to go from no horse riding to being in the saddle for a solid eight hours a day. As they sat around their campfire, waiting for Lewhay, whose hunting skills were apparently second to none, to return with some rabbits, there was much groaning and general lamenting of aches in places that had no business possessing anything that could ache.

'I'm gonna be in no condition to climb any mountains after this,' said Coki and Leeham and Kayleigh laughed.

'Yeah, I hope Shab isn't too far over them,' said Leeham. 'Or at least that they have something more comfortable than horses on the other side.'

'Whatever they have, I'm sure Lew will have a nightmare trying to make it go in the right direction,' said Coki with a smirk, just as the object of his mirth wondered back into the orange sphere which, until the sun returned,

14

was their world. Lewhay was clearly none too pleased with Coki's attempts at lightening the mood, and the latter found out what it was like to be hit in the face with two rabbits, which had, ever so recently, been part of life's great tapestry.

'What was that mate? I thought you were saying something.' Coki spluttered and the other two laughed.

'There you go! I caught them, so you can cook them.'

Lewhay accompanied this proclamation with a little celebratory dance that instantly made him wince in pain. 'Ahhh my legs,' he groaned.

'Sit down and stop crying,' laughed Kayleigh. Strangely, the hard lifestyle they had embarked on seemed to have made her more beautiful.

'Honestly…the triumphant hunter returns with a feast for his lazy companions, and these are the thanks he receives. It's almost enough to make me hang up my bow.'

'I wish we had a bow!' added Liam causing Lewhay to look even more aggrieved at the lack of credit he was receiving.

'Yeah, well you don't need one. Not with me around.'

'How far away do you think they are?'

Kayleigh's question came out of the blue, or, as it currently was, the black, and no one knew quite how to answer. The dynamic since they'd left had been strange in this way. What they'd seen at the funerals had been more than enough to convince them that there was hope for Shabwan. Why or how he had got so far away, they could not and did not know and this, coupled with the fact that they knew nothing of where they were headed, was a daunting prospect. Their intentions to follow Shabwan's trail were as shared as they were crystal clear, but when you know so little of the logistics of your task, thinking ahead brings only discomfort.

'Well, they can't be that far,' said Coki. 'And anyway, as long as we're all comfortable it'll seem like no time.' He lay down on the hard earth upon which they would sleep. 'Ahhhh! Doesn't get much better than this.'

Their laughter was non-committal and it wasn't just because his joke hadn't really been a world-beater. They all knew that his quickness to make light of the situation was an attempt to mask what was painfully obvious; they really didn't know much about what they were doing.

Still, what they had was a lot. They had each other, they had direction and they had a goal. And, for all the doubt in their minds, they all knew one thing for sure: that they would continue searching for Shabwan until all hope had been truly lost.

Chapter 2.

Durpo.

1.

In the city of Durpo, the flow was increasing and, as well we all know, this can cause problems.

And it was.

The mood was electric around the narrow streets. Those who had previously had next to nothing, now had something, and that something was absolutely delicious. Magic fizzed through the air, magic most raw, magic most untrained. The atmosphere was one of a carnival; one where jobs had been forgotten and employers cared not, for they too were out enjoying the fun. By night, the sea in front of the city was illuminated by flashes of every colour, as people set about magically doing things for the simplest and most noble of reasons: because they could.

Yet there was an undertone to all this fun. Not everybody was enjoying the party. Although, wandering through the narrow cobbled alleys of the old town, you'd have been forgiven for thinking so. High up in the tallest tower overlooking the glorious bay, the powers that be were quaking in their boots.

The powers that be were in fact more a *power* that be. For, although there was a council, Mayor Louie controlled pretty much all that went on in Durpo. A lot of dictators make the mistake of concentrating all their efforts on the higher echelons of society, believing they are keeping themselves favourable by rubbing shoulders with the great and the good. Louie wasn't like this. Louie understood that a city, while appearing to be pyramid structured, was anything but. Those who distance themselves from the criminal underbelly of a place, and yet seek to control, are those whose control will always be both superficial and transient. Louie had absolutely no aspirations of transience and even less of the superficial. His control was deep rooted and affected absolutely everyone, everywhere. If you weren't paying Louie directly, and only the lucky few were, then you were paying one of his associates. And if you weren't paying one of his associates, then you were taking your life in your hands.

Taking control of the city in this way hadn't been a particularly easy task, but Mayor Louie had done it none the less. His keen mind and nose for money had seen him rise through the ranks of the council as a very young man. He had a knack for getting those around him embroiled in sticky situations and then offering them salvation. The victim would feel like Louie had done them a massive favour, and be eternally in his debt. Rarely realising that he, who had got them out of this mess, had been the one who'd cunningly manipulated them into it.

Soon the whole council moved nervously around this young man who, despite appearing as nice as a cold slice of Durpoian pie, knew something about pretty much all of them that they were very happy to keep out of the public domain. Without anyone really realising it was happening, Louie took control of the council. And once he'd got the council, mayor Vars' days had been numbered.

Which was ironic as it was the numbers which, on that fateful day, Vars charged Louie with keeping tabs on. The young councillor clearly had something about him, a bit of flair and passion which stood him out amongst the other dry, old relics. Vars wanted to keep someone from the main throng a bit closer to him. The councillors could, if left unchecked, become unruly and a bit too sure of themselves. Vars often found that, when he had been away on official business, he would return to a roomful of men, all with slightly chippier shoulders than when he left. All suddenly a little more assured of their own positions and authorities. It was nothing he couldn't handle, but having someone like Louie, someone who was clearly well liked among the others but full of ambition, would make things a hell of a lot easier.

For Vars, like so many who later came to regret it, began his friendship with Louie thinking that it was he who was playing games. He who was controlling the situation. Use the young man's own ambition against him, he thought. Give him slight prestige by entrusting him with some fairly important business. Let him see what a bright future he might have, if, and only if, he plays his cards right. For if one such as he believes that the path to his ambition lies with you, then anything you ask will be done. The inner workings of the doddering group of men, who he could not afford to relax around, for a tired, old lion can be the most dangerous, would be much less of a mystery to him if he could call this young man his friend.

And so it was, at least for a while.

Louie balanced Vars' books and then some. The shady accounts of the mayoral office of Durpo had never had it so good. Nor had they ever been quite so shady. The boy was a born extorter, yet he did it with such charm that, more often than not, people seemed to be glad to be doing business with him, no matter how much they were losing out. He could put spin on a boulder, and Vars began listening to him more and more. Soon, not a decision was taken in the office of power without the say so of the young man. A young man who lived in the shadow of the mayor, yet burned so brightly he threatened to extinguish it completely.

Vars did not realise that complacency was being bred in him. For, with every little part of his day that Louie took, handled and then presented his master with the profits, his wits got just that little bit blunter. The same instincts that had served him so well and kept him alive for all these years, found themselves out of practice. Every situation, in which they would have been called upon, was now being taken care of. Every time Vars would have needed to wile out what was really going on around him, would have needed to read what was written in the lines created by the crinkles of fake smiles, he no longer needed to. He was the oblivious turkey; not questioning why his meals had suddenly become so much better throughout the month of December, but just enjoying the cordon bleu experience. And, in truth, things had never been better for him, and when things are getting better of their own accord, you don't question. Success is a wave that doesn't slow, it only breaks, and Vars' wave was getting ever so close to the pier.

One night, the old man called Louie into his office for a conversation of the sensitive variety.

'Louie, my boy, Vars began. 'You must have noticed that our success of late is breeding even more contempt than normally dwells amidst our peers.' Vars laced this last word with sarcasm and Louie allowed himself to smile. How much this old man trusted him.

'And what would you have me do about it?'

Vars looked out of his window at the beautiful view of the bay. 'A little bit of discipline is needed with the council.'

Louie's eyes widened. Vars had never made such a bold statement to him before, and he smelt the opportunity that came with it. For all their extortion and assertion of authority among the upper echelons and business people of Durpo, Vars had never dared to go directly up against those immediately below him. Louie had served him well by keeping him informed of the dynamic within the group and, until now, Vars had apparently been satisfied that information was power. Apparently this was no longer the case.

'I get the feeling that councillor Reed, even more so than all the others, fancies himself as something of an up and comer.'

Louie waited patiently for Vars to give him what he needed.

'I'd like you to...deal with him,' said Vars, seemingly choosing each word very carefully. 'Councillor Reed, as you have informed me, has been speaking frequently with the others about my various business interests, and seems to feel that he could do the job much better.' Vars turned and looked at Louie. 'Wouldn't it be unfortunate if...information about the councillor were to come out?'

Louie smiled, 'I like your thinking. You're suggesting something is leaked.'

Vars nodded at this and turned back to his view, 'I leave the details to your discretion.' This was a sentence which had become something of a catchphrase of late. Louie, despite the obvious expectation that he would, did not leave the office. Vars was dimly aware that the younger man was, for the first time, not doing what he expected him to do.

'Was there something else, Louie?'

Louie was tense and he was a man who didn't do tense. But he was also a man facing the opportunity which he had been patiently biding his time for. An opportunity which needed to be handled with absolute perfection. An opportunity which would only come once. Normally, words came to him with such ease and speed. Now it felt like they might not come at all.

'There might be a better way of dealing with councillor Reed.'

The moment was one of tension. For a while, Louie had been interpreting Vars' orders in any way he saw fit, but he had been doing this privately. Whatever the mayor had asked of him, he had carried out in the way he personally felt was best for the situation. As long as the results were equal to or better than Vars had expected, then what had gone before was of little or no importance. Ends beat means hands down, and always will for people like Vars. What Louie had never done was question his boss' orders to his face. And with this kind of thing, there was no way of guessing how people will react. The moment seemed to go on for some time, enough time for Louie to see his own failure, to see how he should have held his tongue.

'You have a better idea?'

It could have been a threat, but there was no going back.

'Yes, I believe that I do,' Louie felt a surge of confidence as he listened to his own words.

'Leaking information about someone can be effective, it's true, but then, information is always open to interpretation and,' he swallowed before continuing, 'Councillor Reed is a popular man.'

Vars did not turn around, but it was not difficult to notice his silhouette tense up against the moonlight. Louie needed to play this next part very carefully.

'And even if he is held in high esteem by idiots, it is still high esteem.' Vars was unmoved by this so Louie ploughed on. 'And to ruin a reputation of one who is well liked, then one maybe needs to approach the situation slightly more...creatively.'

'I'm listening,' said Vars, who was telling the truth.

'Me spreading some filth might cause some problems for Reed, and ultimately lead to his expulsion from the council but equally...well, there are no guarantees. However if we were to arrange a situation where he could be seen, rather than just heard about, then it would be safe to say that Reed would not be long for this position.'

This was what Vars liked about the boy. Just when he thought he was at his most ruthless, then Louie had an idea that was just downright...better. What he could not have realised then was that the very quality he was admiring was about to come and bite him right on his nethers.

'What do you have in mind?'

It was now laughable to Louie that he had felt nervous such a short time ago. 'I think that I could help Reed along his way into a fairly compromising situation, and then perhaps you and a couple of the others might happen to stumble across him.'

Vars smiled. There was no need to know details with this boy. He trusted his ability and his ingenuity.

'Sounds good Louie, just tell me when.'

Louie smiled as he left the office. He smiled because the name carved into the ornate brass plaque on the door suddenly had an awfully temporary look to it.

2.

Alexander Reed had no idea why the young councillor had asked him to go for an after work drink. There had been very little previous friendliness between them. He, unlike the others, did not buy into the hype around Louie. All the others, men much shorter of sight, seemed to think he was the next big thing and a man to be kept on side at all cost. Reed saw what they did not, a snake in the grass, who should be trusted no further than he could be thrown...preferably from the top of a tall tower.

Still, better the devil you know, and hence why he found himself going to a shady nightspot, a place he would never have dreamt of frequenting in a million years, an hour past his normal bedtime.

Inside another bar just down the street, Vars and three other members of the council, equally as bemused with their present company, sat around a dingy table in the corner. The drink had been flowing for some time, unlike the conversation. Vars was biding his time and kept glancing towards the window, waiting for Louie's signal that it was time to relocate. He did not realise that he himself was also being glanced at. As a new round of drinks was delivered to their table by the beautiful girl, who, upon noticing the status of the clientele, had been very keen to stake her claim on the table, not one of the four men, whose eyes had all wandered towards her low neckline as she placed the drinks on the table, noticed her slip something into one of the glasses.

3.

'We should go to a place down the road,' said Louie. 'I know the owners and they'll look after us properly.'

Reed looked unsure, 'I really should be getting home,' he started.

'Ah come on! One more drink.' Louie's tone was measured. Reed hated it. Yet somehow, going home when the boy wanted another drink seemed less dignified than staying. Much as he hated to admit it, he didn't want this young rat feeling like he had one up on him, however petty the stakes.

'Alright then,' said Reed. 'One more.'

They swerved their way along the road towards the bar where we just left Vars. To look at them you would think both were inebriated. You would be wrong.

As they left the street into the warmth of their next stop, Reed was surprised to notice three people he knew sat around one of the corner tables looking slightly worried.

'I'll be damned,' he barked as he went over to the table to join them. 'I didn't expect to see you three in here.' Reed's drunkenness was more apparent in the relative quiet of their new surrounds.

'Likewise,' said one of the councillors. Then they noticed Louie and greeted him respectfully. He had information on all of them, which he had been graciously keeping under his hat.

'Well I guess we shall join you then,' said Reed and sat down heavily in the seat that Vars had previously occupied. The chair had barely finished creaking when there was a shout from upstairs. The bar at large ignored it, but the three councillors immediately exchanged worried looks.

'Something going on?' asked Louie. Nobody responded. Reed looked from face to face inquisitively.

'It's...' the councillor trailed off nervously.

'It's Vars,' another chimed in. 'He went upstairs with a girl. We told him not to be so obvious about it but he seemed so drunk, he wouldn't listen. The last thing we need is for him to be causing public drama.'

'Going with a whore isn't exactly going to bring the tower down,' said Louie as his look said, 'as you three should know better than most.'

'She was no whore,' said one. 'She was Silvia Aran.'

Reed almost fell off his chair.

'He must be out of his mind!' The other three nodded nervously. Silvia Aran was the wife of the man known to them only as Arbelo. Durpo's most wanted. Murderer, kidnapper, robber...pretty much anything unpleasant with 'er' at the end, plus a whole lot more. He was one of the few people who even the mayor didn't have the guts to mess with. He had his business and the council had theirs, and they were more than happy if the two never crossed paths.

'He's a dead man,' said Reed. Nervous nods were exchanged. 'And so are we, just by association.' More nodding, this time with much more feeling.

They couldn't have been sure if it happened at that moment or not, but, thinking back, it seemed that it was at that very second that they heard the last thing they wanted.

'Arbelo!'

It was the barman and he was greeting the gangster like an old friend. Arbelo, however, did not stop to chat. He was tall, and fairly thin, yet his movement radiated strength. Besides, what he lacked in size was more than made up for by the two huge lumps now blocking the door, (or, as our four friends now saw it) the only exit from the bar. Arbelo bounded up the stairs muttering something to himself and disappeared from view. There was the sound of a door being flung open and then a brief scream followed by silence.

The silence spread all across the downstairs area of the bar, which suddenly felt very much like Arbelo's bar. All eyes were on the table in the corner. The man himself soon came back into sight, wiping blood from his knife. No prizes for guessing whose (answers on a postcard though, if you still want to try). He came over to the table where the five councillors sat and asked them a question.

'Do you know who I am?' They nodded like they already had their death sentence. 'I just found your boss lying with my woman.' He appeared to feel little emotion as he said this. Reed saw his life flash before his eyes. 'Perhaps you'd like to give me a reason why I shouldn't kill all of you?'

No words came, there was only terror and true terror is not accompanied by screaming but by a grim vacuum where sound seems as far away as salvation.

'Perhaps I can give you a reason,' said Louie, his voice trembled as he spoke and the two giants at the door laughed. The other patrons watched on expectantly, some had hungry looks across their faces. Blood lust. 'But I will ask that you let my four friends go, so we can speak about this alone.'

The others glanced around in disbelief. What the hell was Louie doing?

'Ah, bravery!' Arbelo laughed, seemingly enjoying himself too much for someone who had just found the love of his life in bed with another. 'Not something we often see in our ruling body, eh?' The bar burst into laughter as one. Not laughing at an Arbelo joke was clearly not to be recommended. 'Alright then, young buck, get your friends out of here and we'll have this out, man to man.' Again there was more laughter. The four councillors looked at Louie with disbelief. Was this youngster really sacrificing himself to save their tired old hides? It certainly seemed so, and they were in no mood to argue with such a proposition. As they went to leave, however, Arbelo stepped across their path.

'One word of this night to anyone and it's you, your families and everybody else I feel like...UNDERSTOOD!?' He roared this last word like a lion and drew newborn whimpers from the four grown men. 'Excellent!' He continued, suddenly the picture of politeness. 'In that case, I bid you the best of evenings.' He sank into a mock bow as the men literally ran from the premises. Arbelo slowly returned to Louie's table and sat down opposite him. The two men looked at each other for a few seconds then both burst out laughing. Arbelo clapped Louie on the back.

'A fine performance!'

'Thank you very much,' replied Louie. Silvia came down the stairs and embraced Albero.

'And well done to you my sweet,' he said, looking fondly at her. 'How's our friend?'

'Still asleep,' she replied. 'What are we going to do with him?'

'I'll deal with that,' said Louie.

And he did.

The next day, Vars, completely disguised in a travelling cloak, boarded a carriage for Hardram. He'd woken up in the bed with no memory but Louie had told him what he'd done. He had almost burst into tears at the mention of the name Silvia and genuinely had at Albero. The old mayor had decided, in close to blind panic, that fleeing the city was his only option. He was as good as dead if he stayed. He barely had time to write the letter handing over control of his office to Louie before he left. He was never seen in Durpo again.

There were a few raised eyebrows when Louie presented the letter to the council, but a unanimous vote, lead especially enthusiastically by four members, confirmed his new position.

That had all been some time ago and Louie had been getting more and more powerful ever since. His allegiance with Albero, the head of the criminal underworld, had been a fruitful one, and for two men with enormous egos, they had clashed very little over the years. All had been well until the flow started to increase.

Now, as Louie sat in the same office that Vars had once inhabited and looked out over the city, which he had oh so recently felt was his, he saw a threat bigger than anything that had come his way over all these years. He saw a power that threatened the very nature of control. He also saw something that, while it seemed to be happening for just about everyone else, was not happening for him. He idly waved his hand but knew that little or no magic would come. Outside his window lights danced and flashed and, for the first time in his life, Louie had absolutely no idea what to do.

Chapter 3.

Fighting and Fish.

1.

As Shabwan and the others charged out of the door of the inn, lights exploded all over the sky. Cloud formations, which could not conceivably have been caused by evaporated water, danced and span. Lightning reached out to thunder and clutched it to its breast as sound and light erupted together. Below, on the streets of a small town, which was half Veo's and half San hoist, the two forces clashed.

Shabwan had never been in a battle before. He had fought and he had killed once, but he had never been involved in anything of this scale. He soon discovered that he was not very good at it. Or perhaps it was just that those around him were so much better. Had he been capable of remembering his life before he arrived in this place, he would have found the feeling rather familiar.

He had armed himself with a leg from a barstool. Smashing the seat off had left him with a rather substantial lump of wood, which looked like it could dish out some punishment. But every time he moved towards one of the atrocities, arm raised, stool leg cocked and loaded, one of his newfound friends would leap in front of him and take the thing on themselves. Battle raged around him, yet he might as well have been stood miles away. Nothing moved to attack him and every time he took the initiative, someone else would intervene. And a fine job they were doing of it too. For the things which lurched and lumbered into attack were taking quite a pasting at the hands of his troops. Hideous heads were batted from deformed shoulders like balls. Yet there was no blood, instead there was fizz. The broken and dismembered body parts, which thickened the air, seemed to begin to dissolve as soon as they'd left their owners control, and within a few seconds they were only coloured mist, heading upwards to join the visual cacophony exploding above them.

Shabwan, like a disgruntled toddler at an older sibling's party, stopped trying to take part in the fight and soon found that it was over. As the last of the smoke fizzed into the air around them, the battle was quite clearly done. Happy faces turned as one to Shabwan and then said nothing. They just looked.

'Enough of this!' he yelled. 'Why do you keep staring at me like this?'

As he said it, something changed. The people, who had previously seemed a gormless extension of Shabwan himself, sprang into life. They shook their heads as if waking from the deepest of cross-dimensional sleeps. Then finally they began to speak.

'They are gone!'

'We are victorious!'

Other celebratory sentiments were expressed along with much hugging and cheering. For the first time since his arrival in this odd place, Shabwan felt a wave of normality. He was finally one in a crowd, instead of a bizarre figurehead. Amidst the celebrations, Marty, looking old and withered again, made his way over to Shabwan.

'They fought for you,' he said.

'But why?' replied Shabwan.

'That is for you to work out.' replied Marty. 'But in the meantime, there is something you could do for them.' Shabwan nodded, then thought of Kayleigh and felt like his heart would explode. The image of brightly coloured red mist popping out of his chest and then swirling on up to join the clouds above didn't bring him much comfort.

'There is something they can help me with also.'

'Then let us talk,' said Marty. Turning to the crowd at large, he bellowed, 'People of San Hoist, Shabwan can help us!' There was more cheering as they made their way back inside the inn. Above them the sky seemed finally to have resolved its conflict.

2.

In his tower, Veo was shocked. His creations had been disadvantaged by the fact that they were not allowed to harm Shabwan, but even so! They had lost the fight awfully quickly. The people, or shadows, or whatever the hell they were, that had been created upon his opponent's arrival had made quick work of Veo's subjects, and now the town was very much Shabwan's. Veo could only hope that, if it came to a fight between the two of them, what had gone before would not serve as a prediction of what was to come.

Yet, he reminded himself, the boy had not yet been tested. Until he had, there was little or no point speculating about what might be coming. For when Veo had failed his test it had changed everything. And whatever happened with the boy's test would doubtless have similar results. Now that the young man had the town at his disposal, it seemed natural that he would become the architect of his own challenge. Veo's game was still very much of the waiting and watching variety. He had his castle, he could still create, and time was not an issue. Despite losing the initial confrontation, Veo the fool did not feel panicked. His memories swirled and disappeared like mist in the fog, and he struggled sometimes to find a coherent thought amongst the hatter-esque madness, but panicked? No chance. He threw back his head, covered by a wooden mask, the expression of which was twisted and contorted into a grim, sadistic gurn, and roared at the sky. The clouds interrupted their peaceful dance and formed a huge twister. This then spun directly into the mask. Veo's body glowed and crackled as raw divine power escaped every pore.

The knife had decided that this part of Veo, the fool, would occupy this dimension. But on his arrival, he had not been consumed by foolishness. He had been in limbo, as it were, but then had come his test. And the failure of this test had condemned him. He had been consumed by the identity that the knife had selected for him. Doomed to a life of insanity and mayhem. The hideous beings, which Shabwan's people had oh-so-easily destroyed, had been his attempts at creation. He could form nothing of beauty or logic, he could only wave his brush like a man possessed. The canvas was not his to manipulate but to attack. And often that which he poured onto it attacked him back.

Such was the nature of these three dimensions. You arrived as a division, yes, but that division was not fully formed. It seemed only upon a test, created by the self, would one find out what one would truly become in this place. Had Veo passed his test, he would still have been the fool. But it would not have been so all consuming as to render him like this. Foolishness was the knife's choice, but Veo had been the master of the extent. And now young Shabwan was facing the same part of the process. The knife had decided what element of his character would be dominant, but whether his romance would consume and devour him, or whether he would have a measure of control over it, was still to be decided.

Why the dimensions worked in this way was anybody's guess. Remember that both the knife and the chamber had been flawed in the moment of their creation. Haste had ruled Lubwan's hand, whereas lack of skill and thought had given birth to the knife. As a pair, it was not difficult to see why they'd kicked up a slightly odd set of circumstances. But then, order does have this stubborn way of finding a path through chaos.

What was for certain, even to what was left of Veo's mind, was that his cell mate must face what lay immediately ahead. And once he had faced it, then he could plan his next move. Regardless of which way it went, this next move would almost definitely involve *her*.

3.

The Inn was raucous with the sounds of celebration. Shabwan was perplexed with it all. No one had given him any indication as to why there had been a fight, or as to whom they had fought. They all just kept cheering and singing. Victory was victory at the end of the day. And it did feel like the end of the day. Yet the day would not end, this he knew, for he could not sleep until he had found his love. Whether or not these people could help him was what he needed to ascertain, and this was proving difficult.

Mainly because they kept going on about a fish.

'The fish holds the heart of the town, it holds our happiness,' Marty, apparently the town's official spokesman, was saying. 'And without it, we cannot be truly content.' It was difficult not to fall into the gaping chasms in the logic, but Shabwan diligently listened on. 'Not two days ago, it disappeared from our shores you see. It used to swim just off the coast, keeping an eye over everyone. Breathing happiness into the bay. But now it has disappeared and we think we know why.'

Shabwan's head was awash with images of his beloved, but he strove to cut through them. Whatever they were asking of him would be his only bargaining tool when it came to his search. So far, it seemed that they had done him all the favours, smashing those horrible monstrosities to fizzy pieces as they had. And he got the feeling that this fish was damn important. Were he to return it to its bay of happiness, ludicrous as that sounded even to him, then he didn't doubt that all hands would fly to the pump, and his search would become infinitely easier.

'The fish has been taken by one who would use its energy all for himself,' continued Marty, 'and he will be in no mood to give it back willingly.'

'Where does he have it?'

'In a cave just around the coast. We have a boat which you can take and these three will accompany you.' In the same way that Shabwan had instantaneously crashed into Marty's back as he'd travelled through the town earlier, there were now three men, of similar age to Shabwan, stood around the table. There was no way that they had been there previously.

'These are three of our finest fisherman, and they have a superb boat to match,' said Marty. Shabwan found it difficult to focus on the three faces but nodded all the same.

'When do we start?'

4.

They started the next morning and what a morning it was. The night before, the sky had been a blazing mass of purple, green and fiery clouds. This morning it was so empty as to be perfection. A flawless, baby blue stretched from one horizon all the way back over the land and doubtlessly on to the invisible other. The glorious, white orb of the sun warmed Shabwan's face and said nothing of dangers to come. Shabwan's three companions had woken him early from his slumber at the inn, and, after a quick breakfast, they had made their way to the harbour. The three others had not spoken all that much, but they were much easier to make out in the glorious light of the day.

The tallest was exceptionally thin and had a mop of tousled black hair, which he kept running his right hand through. He walked as if the word 'rush' would have tasted sour in his mouth. The smallest had a more comedic gate. He walked confidently but bumbled. In a crowd he would have caused severe discomfort to all around him. The third had not spoken at all and seemed the most focussed. He was of medium height with dark features and a strong frame. When he looked at Shabwan, the latter could not help but feel like some kind of evaluation was being made. The stranger seemed to want to know something before they hit the water.

The other two seemed far too busy criticising each other's sailing ability to take much notice of Shabwan. Both seemed to feel that they were not just superior to each other in this field, but superior to all who had gone before.

'So…do you feel ready for this?'

The question seemed friendly enough, but it still made Shabwan feel slightly uncomfortable. How could he be ready for something that he did not understand?

'I think so,' he lied and the other young man smiled, thinly masking his doubt. 'Well… to tell the truth, perhaps I'm not,' said Shabwan. 'Is there anything you think I should know?' He tried to think back to the conversation he'd had with the evasive Marty at the bar the night before. It felt like a long, long time ago and details were difficult to pick out. He was going to rescue a fish, that was the gist and the gist was all he had.

'We'll get a much better measure of things when we're out on the water,' said Coki and Shabwan wondered what had made him think of that name. It seemed to fit quite well.

The boat that they were to take was a thing of beauty. Sure it was essentially a rowing boat, but what rowing boat had ever looked like this? What rowing boat was made of the darkest mahogany and had a prow of glinting steel that looked like it could cut any swell in half before so much as a drop had entered the boat itself. The oars, while light as a feather, were strong and sturdy, and their blades cut into the water as if it was air. Soon, the four young men were making excellent progress across the glassy surface, and such was their speed that their hair flew out behind them, even though there wasn't a breath of wind. For a couple of hours they continued like this, hugging the coastline, whose emerald green grass came to an abrupt halt as it met the smooth rock face of the cliff. Shabwan was really beginning to enjoy himself and thought little of what was to come. The four men spoke as they had in the real world, laughing, joking and goading one another. And while Shabwan was getting more and more used to the nagging sense of familiarity that followed him around this strange place, he could not think where he had seen any of these three young men before.

5.

The four friends who travelled together in the land of the real had almost reached a town, and it was a town that was in good spirits, having recently been liberated of its tyrannical magician. Not long ago had they burned the great black house to the ground, yet the memory of it already seemed so distant. Life had returned to normal in Payinzee…well, almost normal. Just like in Durpo, the flow was increasing. Unlike Durpo, however, this did not carry a threat. For the people of Payinzee had seen first hand just how horrible magic could be, and, as excited as they were to use it, they understood that it was not to be trusted.

Those who had acquired the gift were using it only for practical purposes, the fields had never been so well cared for, but the flashes and booms that illuminated the skies of Durpo were completely absent. Paynizee had all it needed and wanted no more. The memory of Lomwai saw to that.

The excitement amongst the travellers when they first saw the town was considerable. Coki shouted something incoherent over the noise of the horse's hooves. The only distinguishable word, repeated several times, was 'bed'. It was a simple sentiment, but one they all shared. The thought of a night in a bed of any description, after the time they had spent in the dirt, was enough to induce stonkette like euphoria. They rode hard into the town, only slowing as they reached the buildings. They attracted a few worried looks from those working around the fields next to the road. They must have looked more like a very small invading army than excited guests.

They tethered their horses outside the inn and entered. The welcome they received couldn't have been more different from the one Vericoos and Shabwan had received in the same place. It turned out that the inn had two rooms free, which they took without question and settled in for a heavy night of drinking.

They discussed lots of things as they sat around the table, the ride and the horses, the sun and the moon, the Hoist and what lay ahead. But they did not mention Shabwan, as had become customary. Yet as drink flows and inevitability takes over, the things that you try ever so hard not to mention have a tendency of popping up.

'I wish he knew we were after him,' said Kayleigh. Her initial laughter and enforcing of drinks upon the others had ebbed into quiet weepiness. The others had tried to lift her spirits, but she had gone deeper and deeper into herself. The tone of the evening had taken a sharp u-turn, and the initial jubilation they had felt at the sight of the town had faded away.

Coki took the initiative, albeit in a fairly clichéd way, 'To Shabwan,' he said, rising to his feet and almost falling in the process. The other three glanced at each other and then rose to join him.

'To Shabwan,' they said with much more enthusiasm, banging their glasses together and frothing ale over their already dirty table. As they sank back into their seats, a voice rang out and the words it carried caused a collective leaping of hearts.

'Did you say Shabwan!?' The burly figure of the barman was making his way over to their table as he said this. They glanced at one another, thoughts racing in different directions, not daring to believe. They could not be hearing what they thought they were. 'Well, did you say it or not?' It was difficult to tell how this man felt. The obvious excitement could have been born of rage, love or any number of things. It was Lewhay who broke the silence, always one to rise to a situation with a hint of confrontation.

'Yeah, that was what we said. What of it?' The barman looked slightly put out. Clearly this was not the reaction he had expected.

'Slightly odd looking fellow, travelling with an old man?' The speed with which Kayleigh jumped to her feet made the others doubt she'd ever really been sat down.

'Yes that's him!! Have you seen him? When was he here!?'

29

This was what she meant to say. Unfortunately it sounded more like, 'Yeshimuvyousinimwhenwzeeere.' The barman chose not to answer her directly and instead turned to the rest of the bar.

'Oi, you lot! These are Shabwan's friends.'

The patrons as a whole rose to their feet and the barman turned back to the table. He was more than a little surprised to find Kayleigh's small but strong hands grabbing him by the lapels.

'Tell me what you know.' It was an imperative in the purest sense of the word. Those who had been enthusiastically making their way over to the table, halted.

'Erm, perhaps if you unhand me, we can all have a drink and a sit down, and I'll tell you what I know.' He nodded over to the bar, where the barmaid began filling up five tankards. The barman, whose name they did not yet know, but who had information they could not bear to wait another second to hear, sat at their table and began his story.

As he talked, others joined the table and took up different parts. They explained all about what had happened with Lomwai, and how Vericoos and Shabwan had ridden into town oblivious to what was going on. As they spoke, the four friends made excited eye contact but spoke not a word. They did not yet know how the story ended, but they did know that their friend was alive. The madness they had observed in the Hoist had proved to mean exactly what they'd thought. The dream, which had felt so fragile that they dared not speak of it, was becoming harder than granite in front of their very eyes. Excitement, unlike anything they'd ever known, was building in them. Kayleigh dared not blink for fear that this glorious reality she was now confronted with might prove to be anything but.

'Hang on…He did WHAT!?'

'He killed Lomwai.'

The looks they'd been exchanging stopped. All eyes focussed directly on the barman. Coki felt numb. The unbridled joy, which had been so evident on Kayleigh's face, evaporated.

'He…killed someone.' Lewhay said each word carefully, as if by working through them slowly he could erase the meaning. The barman, noticing the dismay he had caused, quickly came to Shabwan's defence.

'What he did, he did bravely in the service of people he had no loyalty to. It was one of the bravest acts I have ever seen.'

There was no dealing with it now. They would need time to come to terms with this new information. And quickly as the shock of the news had come, it was gone, replaced once again with euphoria.

He was alive, he had been in this very place recently, and they were on his trail. No news in the world could taint that feeling.

6.

The cave came into view and, before any of his three companions spoke, Shabwan knew that this was where they were heading.

'He is in there,' he said and the other three nodded. Whoever had captured the fish had taken it away from the beautiful crystalline ocean, where it swam about spreading waves of love and happiness, and imprisoned it within a jet-black cave. A cave that looked ominous even from this far away. Their boat swung in a wide arc until its razor stem was pointed directly at the black hole. They would soon enter, and Shabwan knew he needed to be ready for anything.

He felt a chill as he entered the cave, and the glorious heat, which they had enjoyed throughout the boat ride, melted away. Shabwan struggled to adjust to the darkness. For a moment he felt all alone in the boat. But if he concentrated hard he could hear three sets of lungs working away. He would not call out for fear of letting the others know he was scared. He remembered how the one he called Coki had looked at him as they'd walked down towards the boat.

There was something terribly eerie about the cave. Noise seemed conspicuous by its absence. Then Shabwan noticed the flashes. Had they been there all along, or had they only just appeared? Either way, they were making it much easier to see. They made him think of blood being pumped through veins, as all the lights seemed to move in unison, temporarily illuminating the tunnel through which they were travelling.

'We should follow the lights,' said one of his companions and Shabwan knew he must be right. Whoever had taken the fish captive was somewhere in this tunnel and these little streams of light, rhythmically accelerating along the walls before vanishing into temporary darkness, would lead them on.

As they rowed, Shabwan suddenly became aware that the boat, which had amazed him with its speed and power out on the open water, suddenly felt unsteady. The dark mahogany wood, which had seemed so indestructible, now felt rotten and waterlogged. The oars no longer drove them majestically through the water, but flapped and struggled to get a grip. Shabwan waited for another flash, or pump, of light and glanced at his companions. They were all staring straight ahead, eyes focused and unchanging. He wondered if they would fight as bravely as the others had the night before. The memory of the monstrosities they'd destroyed troubled him. It was easy to imagine such things lurking in the darkness down here, and this time they would bring the element of surprise with them.

As they rounded a corner in the tunnel, they were presented, for the first time since they'd entered, with a choice. Their boat came to a halt against the rock which made up a fork in the tunnel. Shabwan turned to look at the others, expecting some kind of help. They offered none. This choice, like every choice he must make from now on, was his and his alone.

Before he had to toss the proverbial coin, a laugh rang out from the left hand tunnel. A cold high laugh, followed by a childlike shriek. The flashes of light, which had been flying down both tunnels with each pump of the heart (Shabwan only now realised it was his heart they were synchronised with), set off with much more vigour and illumination down the left hand side of the V. The boat followed as they dug in even harder with the failing oars. It creaked and crunched with each row and threatened to break completely. Shabwan did his best to ignore it and found it was no trouble. Every time he relaxed his mind it was overrun with images of her. Her running, her laughing, her smile. It was more than enough to get lost in. Indeed, he had to work hard to haul himself back and wasn't sure how long he had been absent in everything but body.

The laugh came again, colder and higher and was followed by the shriek, which sounded even more distressed than before. They rowed harder and the boat re-asserted its threat of sinking. Shabwan believed it would get them there, but the journey back would be another matter. As he was about to lose himself in another wave of Kayleigh, their little boat drifted out of the narrow tunnel into a much larger cavern. The lights, which had continued to burst along the walls to the rhythm of Shabwan's heart, seemed to feel they'd reached their final destination, and took up permanent residence like creepers hugging the damp walls of the cavern. The now undying light they cast showed a large lake, which surrounded a central island like a moat. Although, unlike most moats, it was much more spectacular than that which it defended. Atop the island was a shack, made of what looked like soaking black wood, the same that their previously glorious boat was now made of. An oily, dirty orange light glowed from within, accompanied by a sea shanty.

Shabwan tried to catch the lyrics but could not. He strained to hear but was almost immediately distracted by another colour that had hitherto gone unnoticed. Gold. A golden fish was swimming lazily around the circumference of the lake. As their boat drifted on, the fish did not change its course and passed almost directly under them. Shabwan saw it clearly through the illuminated water. It was injured. It's fins looked ragged and, like their oars, barely seemed sufficient to propel it. It had a long thin body of flawless gold but deep scratches crisscrossed its sides. It was singing. It took Shabwan a while to realise this. Mainly, he supposed, because fish, much as they can boast many achievements, are not known for their singing voices. The song was a sad one and, although Shabwan didn't understand the language or, for that matter, which part of the fish could be emitting it, he understood the notion. Trapped, unable to escape, missing others, all sentiments he could relate to. Although his 'others' was actually one other.

As the fish swam in its endless circle, a kind of golden mist flowed upwards from it, arcing across the empty space above the water and disappearing into the shack. It was the loss of this energy that caused the fish such obvious pain. Its life force, a beautiful energy with the potential to bring happiness to so many, was being brutally and endlessly harvested by one. It made Shabwan angry, the selfishness of it! How dare this individual harm the fish and take for himself that which was designed for so many?

As their little boat neared the island in the centre, it followed the popular philosophy of parenting, i.e. that all threats must be carried out, and promptly sank. They clung to the broken shards of saturated wood and kicked their legs, arriving soaking wet on the rocky micro-shore. The four men walked up towards the shack, water dripping from their clothes and catching the light that radiated from the walls.

Shabwan glanced to his left and right. His three accomplices were staring straight ahead. They didn't say a word but looked ready. He trusted them to do what was right, trusted that they were with him. But then, he thought to himself, of course they're with me, they're my best...

Before he could finish the thought, a man came stumbling out of the shack. Physically he was in a very bad way, though mentally he was evidently flying. He wore only a baggy old smock and some loose fitting shorts. His skin was covered in tattoos showing a range of horrible beasts and sailing knots. His bald head was covered in scars and one eye had been put out for good.

The golden ribbon emanating from the poor fish was connected with the man's shining dome of a head. It appeared to be massaging him and soaking into his temples. His one good eye was spinning around and occasionally rolling backwards, as if in pleasure, as more of the gold dust reached his brain and blood. His breathing was deep and heavy, as if his heart was working much faster than it should have been. He lurched barefoot across the rocky surface towards the four young men. Fixing Shabwan with a one-eyed, thousand-mile stare, he began to speak, 'Well, well, well,' he said.

Shabwan was in no mood for repetition and responded abruptly, 'That fish you have taken prisoner is not yours to keep. You will release it now or you will suffer.'

The old fisherman breathed in, his good eye temporarily only white. As he did so, the golden band intensified and the fish gave the same screech they had heard twice before. When the eye returned, the pupil was bigger and blacker and the owner was more aggressive.

'You believe you have the right to do this...you of all people!?' With this he burst out laughing. 'Shabwan, you and I are not so different. I would have thought that you, at least, could have understood what I am doing here.'

'That fish's love is for everyone to enjoy and for the fish to freely give.'

The old man moved closer towards him as he said this, his muscles tensing. For all the damage he had clearly done to himself, he seemed to possess a core strength, which was still something to be reckoned with.

'Unification is not your game it's true...but you enable, don't you Shabwan? That's what you've always done.'

Memory prickled and pumped but could not be grabbed.

'You enable a good time, and if others abuse that, how can it possibly be your fault?' He cackled and spat. Shabwan looked at his three friends, suddenly seeing them for what they truly were. Shock raced through his veins as he tried to make sense of what was happening to him. Then a fist hit him hard in the mouth, he fell back smashing his head on cold, wet rock and darkness leaked across his vision until there was none.

7.

Coki and Kayleigh lay in the room together. Leeham and Lewhay had taken the other. It had been a long time before the appreciative locals had allowed them to go to bed. Neither could see straight and thinking straight was causing all sorts of problems.

'He's alive,' said Coki, which, considering the endless confirmation they'd had of this fact, didn't really need saying.

Kayleigh beamed at him, tears streaming down her face. She had cried for most of the evening, but had been assuring everyone that they were tears of joy.

'He's with the old man,' she said. This was the one fact that they hadn't discussed. Shabwan was alive, which was the most joyous news she had ever heard, but he was willingly travelling with the old man who had fought the three in the plaine. The same old man the boys had told her all about in the wake of his disappearance. It was too much to take in. Had Shabwan allied himself with this destructive force willingly? If so, for what possible reason? It troubled her deeply, but, as with the news that Shabwan had apparently become a killer, it did not stand a chance of surviving long in the sea of delirious joy washing over the previously troubled shoreline of her mind.

Coki looked at her. They had grown so close over the time they'd travelled together. They had shared a lot with each other, more so than with the other two. As he looked at her now, he felt something that he could not feel. Immediately he felt disgusted with himself. How, in this moment of such happiness about their friend, could he be thinking of this girl as he was now? He looked away awkwardly. She noticed but said nothing.

They'd both been through enough that evening and, despite the cocktail of alcohol and emotion, they both knew that sleep was not far away. Tomorrow morning would be different. Tomorrow they would not be setting off on their trail powered only by blind hope. Tomorrow they would set off towards the forest, safe in the knowledge that Shabwan had gone that way before them.

Morning came, bringing with it the promised headaches. Lewhay needed to slap Leeham hard in the face to wake him up...well, that wasn't strictly true. He didn't have to, but it was always fun. He felt like anything was possible today, despite his head exploding every time light reached his eyes, nothing was beyond him. His friend was ahead of them and, as far as they knew, was alive and well.

'Get up and stop bitching!' he barked at Leeham, enjoying the sounds of impotent rage it brought from his friend. He left the room making sure he slammed the door as loudly as possible. 'You'd better be downstairs in five,' he yelled back through the door. Leeham shouted something unprintable back at him and Lewhay chuckled to himself.

Just at that moment, Coki and Kayleigh emerged from the adjacent room. Both looked terrible but grimly determined. Lewhay thought about delivering another friendly slap in Coki's direction, but as he was about to administer the fatal blow he caught a glimpse of his friend's expression. There was something serious there, something that put him off an unnecessary act of mild violence. Together they traipsed down the stairs and were soon joined by Leeham.

'You won't be able to ride with your eyes closed you know,' laughed Lewhay.

'I know,' said Leeham. 'But I don't plan to open them until I absolutely have to.'

They bid their farewells in the bar, stocked up on some supplies for the road including, the most glorious of sights, four travelling sleeping mats. The townspeople were very willing to give them good deals. Word had travelled fast that they were affiliated with Shabwan. As they mounted up, preparing for their exit, people yelled to them.

'Say hi to Shabwan for us!'

'Tell him to come back and visit.'

They smiled and waved like royalty as they departed.

Amongst the wreckage of the big, black house, something moved. It had been lying low for some time, only coming out to feed on scraps by night. Its miserable existence had been nothing to envy, and many times it had wished for death. But now it had something to live for. It had heard a word. A word which represented that which it most hated.

'Shabwan,' it spat and moved around the charred, jet black wreckage to get a better view. The four people on horse back were not Shabwan, nor were they that damned other one. But there must be a link, otherwise why would the people be saying it?

It had very little energy left, but it had enough for invisibility. It scuttled out into the crowded street. There was far too much noise for it to be heard and, as the four horses got up to speed, it charged on after them. The pace was difficult to keep, but when your blood is full of the fire of revenge, anything seems possible. As long as it kept these four riders in its sight, then there was a chance of being led to Shabwan.

And then he would rip that murderous swine limb from limb.

8.

Shabwan's consciousness came back to him, beginning as a narrow point and rushing forwards. It gave him the impression of diving out of darkness, perhaps through an open window, and back into the real world. He could not dive far, however, as his hands were tied to a beam in the old fisherman's hut. His captor realised he was awake and then laughed. He took another deep breath and the dark interior was temporarily lighter, as the golden band of energy flourished again. The fish screamed and the noise tugged at Shabwan's heartstrings.

'Where are my friends?' he asked.

The old man with the scars looked surprised, 'Is it them you care about?' he asked. As he spoke the grimy surface of his oil lamp moved and painted a picture. Shabwan saw Kayleigh's face and strained against the beam. Try as he might, it would not budge.

'WHAT HAVE YOU DONE WITH HER!?' he bellowed.

'That's more like the Shabwan we know,' laughed his captor. 'We all know what the real concern here is, and it's not your friends, nor is it my little fishie…' The man paused and studied his prisoner. 'Yet there is something else here, is there not?'

Shabwan did not know what he meant by this.

'You are here to find your woman. Your act of "selflessness" only serves you Shabwan. Yet I must say, I'm surprised to see there is another force within you…could it be that there is something better than her?'

Without warning, he punched Shabwan hard. The young man dropped, his full weight was taken on his wrists, fastened above the bar, and he cried out in pain. The door of the hut flew open and the fisherman turned. Coki, Leeham and Lewhay stood in the doorway. The old man smiled at Shabwan and drew a rusty old knife from his pocket. Shabwan saw the immediate peril facing his friends and strained harder than ever, but the beam and rope held fast.

The fisherman had not yet turned. His advancing friends did not see the knife. Shabwan opened his mouth to try and cry out but could not. He felt power, a power he had seen but never felt in his own body, surge up his arms. The fisherman turned, hiding the knife behind his back. The rope that bound Shabwan so tightly fizzed and burned. A few seconds later it was no more.

Shabwan watched the knife drawn back and saw Lewhay's arms wide open, his torso unprotected. The knife would cut through him like butter. Shabwan tried to throw his fist out, but there was no time. Besides, if he connected, he would just force his enemy into his friends. He was at the point of despair when the realisation came.

The hut exploded. Shards of rotten timber flew into the air landing with soft plops in the lake. When the light from the explosion faded, he saw the old fisherman lying on the floor. Shabwan's three friends stood unharmed, though they all wore the same bemused expression. The golden ribbon, which had been connected to Shabwan's former captor's head, had vanished. Shabwan himself was stood, taller than he'd ever stood. His hand was still crackling with the same light that adorned the walls, the same light that had led him here.

The fisherman, for the first time, appeared scared. Without his golden ribbon, he now had to face the reality of the situation, and his odds weren't looking great. He looked up at Shabwan's glowing hand and spat blood onto the stones.

'So,' he said. 'That's what it is.'

9.

Up in his tower, Veo grimaced. A horrible sight it was too. Splinters jumped out of his wooden mask as it cracked into its new position. Sap, like blood, flowed out of the cracks.

'Well, well, well,' said Veo, largely to himself, though his voice rang out across the land.

10.

'So,' said Coki. 'Shall we stop for the night?'

It had been an invigorating day's ride since leaving Payinzee. They had covered almost as much ground in a day as they previously had in two, and they were all more than happy to stop.

After ten minutes bickering, it was eventually decided that Leeham and Lewhay would hunt together. Both claimed not to be too tired to the point where they had to go and prove it. This left Coki and Kayleigh making a campfire together.

'I can't believe we've got mats,' she said. Her beautiful but tired eyes glistening as the fire licked the dry timbers.

'I know, things are looking up,' said Coki. 'Shabwan's alive and we can sleep.'

She laughed, so did he, but they did not make eye contact.

Sat outside their circle of light, it watched and it waited. The days sprint in the wake of the horses had almost killed it. But when you have but one wish, dying in the pursuit of it is not something which concerns you.

It listened to their conversation, feeling a surge of hatred every time it heard Shabwan's name. It would need to eat soon it knew. But before it had even begun to hunt, it collapsed, seemingly dead, into the deepest of sleeps. It dreamt of vile images, blood and gore, which it would visit not only upon Shabwan, but upon these four who seemed to hold him in such high regard.

11.

The fisherman was suddenly up and mobile. For such an old bag of bones and sinew, he moved at an unbelievable pace. As he ran, seemingly across the water, towards the back wall of the lake, it opened up for him. A gash appeared in the wall of the cavern and the old codger disappeared through it. As it began to close, Shabwan acted without thinking. Leaving his three friends behind, he leapt into the air and stayed there. He flew like a bird though his body did not move. Just before the gash sealed shut, Shabwan, moving like an arrow, travelled through it.

He pursued the fisherman who, while not airborne, seemed to be able to scrabble through the narrow rocky tunnel with the speed of a downwards-travelling mountain goat. As the tunnel narrowed, Shabwan was forced to twist and turn his body into all sorts of shapes to avoid decapitation. Just as it seemed that the tunnel could not get any narrower, he reached out a hand and took hold of the old fisherman's smock.

They were no longer in a tunnel. They were in the centre of a town. The buildings to either side of the road looked oddly uniform. Shabwan looked down at his hand, there was a rock in it. He was kneeling on the chest of his enemy, who was watching him with interest.

'That's right,' he said. 'This was how it happened.'

Shabwan suddenly couldn't see. Flashes of memory sparked in his mind's eye. The rock felt light in his hand and he fought not to beat it against the fallen man's head.

'That's the thing see,' said the man whose face was becoming different, dark hair was growing and the eyes were becoming greener. 'It's not her you want anymore...' Images of Kayleigh flooded his mind, but for the first time since he'd been there, he found them difficult to cling onto. The same feeling, which he'd felt racing up his arm before he'd freed himself and destroyed the hut, was driving the pictures away. Much as he didn't want it to.

Lomwai looked up at him, '...It's me!' As he said it, he grabbed the dagger, which the old fisherman had dropped; and, quick as a flash, thrust it towards Shabwan's midriff.

Shabwan was too quick for him. As the knife neared his flesh, it appeared to slow and, at the same ratio that Lomwai's arm slowed, his accelerated. The rock connected with a soft thud and the magician's hand, still clutching the rusty dagger, hit the dusty earth.

Shabwan watched as, just like the monstrosities outside the pub, the body began to fizz and evaporate. This did not bother Shabwan, but then he realised that there was a difference between what had happened then and what was happening now. The smoke, or mist, or whatever it was, was not on its way up to the heavens. Instead, it was going into Shabwan. His every pore seemed to be taking it in. He jumped to his feet and tried to brush it off himself, spinning around the road like a madman. It made no difference, the substance continued to bind with his body. Shabwan cried out. He did not want either the energy from the fisherman or from the magician Lomwai to become his. Then, just as quickly as it had begun, it was over, and once again he was in a town. Although, it was no longer the same. He had returned to the town where he had been with his three friends that morning, and there were many people around him. The townspeople were cheering and running up to him, clapping him on the back and kissing him. He nervously glanced around the crowd, looking for those he now remembered as his best friends and found them quickly.

'The fish brought us back,' one shouted by way of explanation. Seems logical, thought Shabwan, displaying, for the first time in this place, a sense of humour.

He looked round towards the bay, where the energy from the fish could be seen clearly flowing back into the town. Whereas the fisherman had been enjoying a highly concentrated beam of stolen energy, the fish was now allowing a beautiful mist, which touched all, to flow back into the town and the people were basking in it.

Shabwan had saved them.

He had also passed his test.

12.

Veo would not allow himself to panic. That would help him not. It was difficult, however, as he now knew that the young man had a huge advantage over him. Not only had he passed his test, he also had...the other form of power. No longer was he relishing, in any way, the idea of the confrontation.

Veo did not know exactly what the effects of passing the test would be, for he only had experience of failure. But he had his suspicions, and they did not bode well...

13.

Shabwan did not need to speculate about such things as he was now experiencing them. Kayleigh was still at the forefront of his mind, and he still burned to reach her. This had not changed, but now he had control. Before, these thoughts had, at times, all but consumed him. They had forced all memory from his head, even rendered him blind as he struggled to think of anything but her.

Now it was different. Not only was he stronger in his own mind, he also had memory.

Not much but some.

He knew that the three people who had accompanied him to the cave were his three best friends, and he knew that the people around him were those he'd grown up with. He also knew that he had a mission. A mission to destroy.

He could not remember how he knew any of this; only that it was his task. For there was another in this world who threatened them all, one who must be destroyed. And therefore, in Shabwan's newly organised train of thought, it seemed only reasonable that this was the person who had Kayleigh.

He bid his farewells to the town, amidst much cheering, and set off. His three friends offered to accompany him, but Shabwan knew that he must go alone. He must find his enemy whose name he did not know. He must defeat him, and he must find his beloved.

For the first time since he'd been there, he had true direction and it was a glorious feeling.

Though there was another feeling which, despite everything else, was troubling him. The man he had killed had seen something in Shabwan. Something which had allowed him to defeat him in the first place. Not only had he seen it, he had identified it as the only thing which could force the images of Kayleigh out of his head.

Much as Shabwan hated to admit it, the relish he felt, as he recalled the surge of power rushing up his arm, was indeed able to hold its corner amongst all the beautiful images of Kayleigh in his mind's bedroom. Whatever it was had saved him and, for that, he was eternally grateful, for in salvation he could now find his love. 'But,' said a tiny little voice in the back of his head. 'Let's just hope you still care as much about her when you find her.' He looked down at the hand, which had glowed with that unforgettable raw energy, wriggled his fingers and hoped against hope that he could control that which had flown from it.

Vericoos would have understood how he was feeling.

Chapter 4.

Civil unrest.

Working in kitchens isn't fun. Well, at least that was how Marie saw it. She was sure that some people probably got a buzz out of working with food, but it was difficult to feel that way in her position.

An orphan, she was told. Lucky to be taken in off the streets, she was told. Privileged to have a roof over her head, a (meagre) wage and her (very rare) own time, she was told.

Told she was, but feel she didn't.

What she felt was used, exploited and, more than anything, trapped. Trapped below ground for fourteen hours a day like a mole. The intense heat of the kitchen, the steam, the smell, the shouting when she did the slightest thing wrong, she hated all of it.

She worked like a dog so those upstairs could live like kings.

Maybe she would have had a better time of it if she were more outgoing. Perhaps she could have joined in with the banter and got something out of her time down here. But Marie was shy and shyness is a prison. Her societal position dictated that she must work hard and remain in the kitchen for *most* of her life, and her personality dictated that she was trapped for *all* of it.

Sometimes, when she went upstairs and saw how the others lived, it brought a sick taste to her mouth. The injustices of the world didn't even have the decency to try and conceal themselves. The Hutchinsons were one of Durpo's leading families, an interest in importing and exporting, combined with a below-board control of the docks had seen them rise very close to the top. There were some who had more wealth and power, but not many.

Even Mayor Louie was keen to keep a cordial relationship with the Hutchinsons, so they said, but who could trust 'they'. Marie didn't personally believe that Mayor Louie cared what anybody in this world thought about him.

Marie did not remember being taken in by the Hutchinsons, and she was not the only one. There were a few like her in the kitchens, orphans who would have stood no chance. They would have ended up living on the streets, trapped in an endless cycle of theft and drug abuse. Sometimes, on the glorious occasions where she was sent out of the kitchen to get supplies, she would see them hanging around the bridge down by the market. Terrible they looked, nothing in the world to live for. She supposed that she was, or at least she should be, grateful for not ending up like that. Or at least that was how she used to feel, before he started visiting her.

2.

She remembered the first time like it was yesterday. She knew it would never be forgotten.

Her duties, as she was one of the younger ones, included making sure the kitchen was beautifully clean after dinner had been prepared. It was a duty she didn't really understand, as they had to be back in the kitchen the next morning anyway. She knew it made sense to put everything away in the right place, but why did she have to get it all so shiny when they would be making the same inevitable mess in it a few hours later? It seemed to Marie, that this particular duty was much more about massaging the ego of the head cook, Mrs. Baker, than about the proper running of a kitchen.

'Mind you girls get it perfect down here, or there'll be trouble,' she would say as she and all the other staff left noisily up the stairs. And trouble there often was. Marie had been thrashed on two occasions. Both times it had not been her fault, but, nice girl that she was, she couldn't bring herself to tell Mrs. Baker who had left the slightest of smears on the slate work surface. The pain had been awful but she would not let the tears flow. For she knew that even the slightest of trickles would be like a gourmet dinner to the sadistic Mrs. Baker. It had made the beating worse, she knew that. Any slight admission of defeat or display of pain would have probably been enough to bring an end to it, but that was not important. For when you have nothing, what you do have becomes so much more important and Marie had her pride.

There were three of them responsible for the after work clean up. Marie suspected that, under different circumstances, the three of them would have become friends. Sharing a common enemy and being forced into the same situation every night certainly seemed like enough to create a bond. The problem was that they were all so exhausted after the hard day that conversation was difficult. They always smiled at each other and Marie felt a connection of sorts, but there was little opportunity for the forging of true relationships.

When they finally finished, they would leave the kitchen, walking quickly and quietly passed the merriment that was usually going on in the living room. Mrs. Baker saw disturbing the masters as an offence punishable by belt or worse, so heads would be down and steps fast. Then they would cross the gardens over to the tiny servant's quarters. Marie loved that little walk, short as it was. She would hang back slightly from the other two and crane her head backwards. The skies over Durpo were clear, more often than not, and the stars entranced her. For those few seconds she was any normal girl, a girl not constrained to a life she hated, surrounded by people who didn't care. To Marie, the stars spoke of possibility and she loved them for it.

This had been their routine for some time. The more senior members of the serving staff took them for granted more and more. The better job they did of the kitchen, under fear of beating, the more of a mess the others left it in. So the three girls worked later and later. Marie burned inside with raw hatred, but knew that the little flame had years to go before it would give her the strength she needed to open her mouth. She did not really fear the pain of the beating. That she could take. But the idea of opening her mouth in front of all those eyes, of saying something strong and right without stuttering, without breaking eye contact…it was enough to bring her out in a cold sweat just thinking about it.

The night began like any other, with cleaning and lots of it. As per usual, there was a lot of noise coming from up the stairs. The majority of the Hutchinsons had no reason to get up in the mornings and celebrated every evening accordingly. The noise was slightly different this evening, however. There seemed to be some kind of heated argument. The male voices became louder and more forceful, squashing the more rational sounding females. Marie tried to ignore it all and carry on with her cleaning. The noises got louder and then came sounds of things banging around and glass breaking. The three girls glanced at one another nervously, it sounded bad up there.

For a few minutes this continued, until they heard the huge front door creak open on poorly oiled hinges and then slam shut. There was still noise, crying and shouting, but it seemed that the situation had calmed. One or more of the conflicting parties must have left. Marie heard more people leaving then a woman running up the stairs in tears. Then there was silence once more.

She didn't really think anything of it and went back to her cleaning. They were on the home stretch and her bed was in sight. She set hard about her scrubbing.

She wasn't sure how long he'd been standing there before she noticed him, but she got the idea it had been some time. As soon as she looked at him she knew something was wrong. Daniel Hutchinson was the brother of Marn, the patriarch and head of their business interests. Rumour had it that he was madly jealous of his brother's position, both within society and the household. He was often mocked by the serving staff, albeit in the hushiest of hushed voices. For he was a horrible greasy little man who, when seen stood next to his brother, seemed to share little or nothing with him. Marn was tall and dashing with a fine deep black moustache, every bit the Durpoian gentleman. Daniel was every bit not. Short, hunched and unfortunate of facial profile, the only heads that he turned were those wondering what the smell was.

Marie did not know much of what went on upstairs, but she had often noticed how sad Daniel's wife looked. A woman much younger, closer to Marie's age than his, she often had eyes that looked like they'd been shedding tears. The expensive powders she wore on her face didn't do enough to cover the bruises. Marie had caught herself thinking on a couple of occasions that, bad as her lot was, it was not as bad as it gets.

'Jobs finished for tonight girls.' He wasn't looking at the other two as he said this, only at Marie. They looked at her, wandering what to do, sensing the danger. Noticing that they hadn't moved he wheeled round angrily. 'I said get out!'

The two girls hitched up their skirts and made for the stairs. Marie did likewise, hoping against hope that his command had been aimed at all of them, though she already knew this not to be true. Her two companions reached the stairs slightly before her and, as she made to follow them, Daniel put his arm across blocking the way.

'Not you,' he smiled the most ghastly of smiles. 'There's one last job.' The other two girls stopped on the stairs. Marie reached out to them wordlessly. Please don't leave me here with him! She knew they could not hear her mind but perhaps they could sense it...

'Get out of here before I have you flogged you little sluts!' he screamed and raised his walking cane as if to strike. The two girls ran off. Would they say anything? Would they alert Mrs. Baker? It was a grim testament to Marie's situation that her hope for salvation lay with Mrs. Baker. The old witch would probably enjoy knowing what was happening to Marie, and none of the others would help without her say so. Odd that one of the lower rungs of society was its own little microcosm of Durpo as a whole.

Daniel pushed Marie back against the great wooden table that ran down the centre of the kitchen. The impact hurt her back but she did not cry out. Fear was clenching her throat shut.

'Take off your dress,' he said.

She could not speak but she could shake her head. He smashed his walking cane down on the table next to her with enough force to kill.

'I said take it off!'

Not really believing what she was doing, she began unbuttoning her front. The true horror of the situation began to take hold. Tears welled up behind her eyes. She didn't want it to happen, it wasn't fair. She wanted to be away from this horrible man. She wanted her mother, the mother she had never known.

Excitement was building in the hideous being that stood in front of her. His eyes were locked onto her breasts, his fingers drumming a hideously agitated pattern on the top of his cane. He reached out towards her.

As he did so, Marie felt something she had never felt before, something that would change her life forever.

A surge began at her shoulder and flowed all down her bicep and along her forearm. The first thing she noticed was the tingling and the gloriously warm sensation, then she noticed how she felt in her mind. Moments ago there had only been pure terror, now there was control. This vile creep had no right to touch her and she had the power to stop him. She did not know how exactly, but she knew it as surely as she'd known anything. Her hand felt full, yet there was nothing in it. The power that coiled around her fingers had no substance but, at the same time, it had more than she could ever have dreamed of. Her mind felt clear and cool, as if the breeze, which came in off the ocean, was going straight through it.

She looked at Daniel. He clearly hadn't noticed. All he had noticed was that she'd stopped unbuttoning. He moved his hand towards her breasts and she prepared to let him have what he deserved...

The huge oak doors above them crashed open.

'Daniel!' Came a booming voice.

The hideous little man in front of her looked panicked. His hand poised in between the two of them, preparing to do unspeakable things, retracted like a snake. Without looking at Marie again, he scuttled off up the stairs to meet his brother.

She heard the kitchen door shut and the two brothers begin talking. Clearly they were not going to start fighting again but neither had the argument been resolved. Their tones still sounded angry as their footsteps continued into the living room and that door too was shut.

This was all that Marie needed, she ran up the stairs, throwing the kitchen door open. She had not finished her cleaning and would doubtless be flogged for it the following day, though right then that seemed like the smallest concern she'd ever had. She ran through the great front doors into the garden and didn't stop until she reached the servant's quarters.

'Where the hell have you been?' barked Mrs. Baker.

'Sorry miss.' She did not say another word but headed straight to bed. Her two cleaning companions tried to make eye contact with her but she wouldn't, she couldn't. It was not their fault, but they had left her. They were probably the closest thing she had to friends and she wasn't sure of their names. But this thought bothered her not as now she knew she had something more. Something she could never have imagined having. She didn't know what it was but it was glorious.

She lay in bed recalling the feeling in both her arm and her mind as she'd realised that, for the first time in her life, she had power.

The next day it was gone and it broke her heart.

She lay there in bed after a terrible day in the kitchen staring at her arm, willing something to happen but it did not. What had this gift been? This wonderful thing that had saved her but, in her mind, had no name. She could not bear to think that it was gone and she would not feel it again.

For weeks nothing happened, either with her arm or with Daniel. She had walked past him a couple of times in the house and felt a knot of fear twist within her stomach. Putting her head down she had hurried past him. Praying that he would say nothing and, thank the Gods, he hadn't.

For the first time she had truly spoken to her two cleaning companions. It turned out their names were Elsie and Jen.

'Did he do anything to you?' Elsie had asked with a scared look in her eye. Marie supposed that she must have felt terrible for leaving her.

'No...his brother came home.'

It was the truth but not the whole truth.

'You should say something to Mrs. Baker' said Elsie. 'Maybe she can help.' They both knew that this wasn't true but Marie appreciated the fact that her friend was trying to help.

'Anyway', said Jen. 'We'll just get it clean as quick as we possibly can every night, and make sure you're not down here any longer than needs be.'

Marie smiled. It was strange that she had gained friends at the very time when she had lost so much.

Usually she never really listened to the daytime gossip in the kitchen, but this particular day something was said that she could not ignore.

'....so this woman Rachel, they say that she has the power.'

'What power?' said a listener. Her gormless tone irritated Marie immensely. The storyteller looked pleased.

'The magic!' she said in a whisper.

'Collywocks!' exclaimed Mrs. Baker. 'Everybody knows there's been no magic in this world for as long as anyone can remember.'

'There are magicians,' put in someone, indignantly.

'I means *proper* magic,' said Mrs. Baker. She was not a woman who took kindly to having her semantics criticised.

'Well, word is,' continued the first speaker, eager to bring all eyes back on herself, 'that this Rachel has power that no one's ever seen before. Apparently Mayor Louie has asked to see her.'

Glances were exchanged. If Mayor Louie had indeed summoned this woman then things were worth listening to.

'But, thing is, she refused to go.'

There was a collective 'oooooh!' And these are always the best kind so everyone involved felt pretty satisfied.

They began muttering about it amongst themselves, swapping theories of what this could mean. Only one person was completely silent. In the corner, Marie was soundlessly trying to make sense of what she'd just heard. Was that what she'd felt?

Over the next three weeks talk grew, as did the flow. The rumours of this one woman, Rachel, were eclipsed. People weren't just talking about what others could do, but what they could do. It seemed everybody in Durpo was feeling the surge. Those in the house above were feeling it and those in the kitchen below were feeling it. Kitchen work became much easier as the staff realised that the knives, pots, pans and cleaning apparatus could all be dictated to. Life got a whole lot better for those who had always had it harder. And Marie's lost gift was back.

She knew that she felt it more than the rest. She knew when they spoke about it. She knew when the idiots said things like, 'ooh yeah it does tingle a little bit if you use lots of it,' that they could not possibly be talking about the same raw energy that was flowing through her.

Yet she did not speak of it. Much as she did not understand this new gift, she knew one thing for certain: it was hers. And, for the moment, she had no desire to tell anyone else about it.

The cleaning duties were still theirs, though the task was a hell of a lot easier than it had been before the flow. The work of hours had become the work of minutes, and the friendship between the girls had grown as the time had shrunk. One night, after they had finished up, they were all walking along the garden together when Marie felt a sudden strong desire to have a few moments alone.

'I'll catch you up,' she said to the other two, and as they entered the door of the servant's quarters she lay back on the grass. The grass was cold and crisp and she enjoyed the feeling of it on her skin. As she let the magic flow out of her, the grass seemed to dance and sway, enjoying the energy as much as she was.

Then, without warning, hands grabbed her shoulders and a foot kicked her hard in the ribs. She let out a scream and the boot returned at jaw level. Her vision went blurry, the stars swam in and out of focus. Then she lost consciousness.

When she awoke, Daniel was on top of her ripping at her clothes. Another much bigger man stood above them. Daniel was grinding his body against hers and panting heavily. She tried to move her arms and realised they were tied. Daniel's hand was travelling across her belly down towards her undergarments. She felt sick. The big man was grinning at her. Then there was a flash and the stranger was sent flying into the air. The rope around her wrists shrivelled and died like old flowers. The energy flowing through her was at its peak. She felt like she could conquer worlds or destroy mountains. She could most certainly take care of the nasty little specimen trying to force himself on her.

She looked at him; his eyes were full of fear. He seemed to be filling his hand with some kind of drizzly orange magic. Some kind of *nothing*! She could sense his power and it was nothing to hers. A drop of black ink in a glorious crystalline ocean. Yet he was trying to kill her. The look in his eyes had gone from fear to hate, and clearly he felt that the force he was brewing in his palm would do the business. For all she knew, it would, but he would never get his chance.

'Have this you whore,' he screamed thrusting the orange ball towards her. Her hand moved quickly but decisively. It drew a thin white line through the air, through Daniel's body and out the other side. The orange in his hand evaporated. He looked at her for a second with confusion on his face then dropped lifelessly to the floor.

She lay there for a few moments, breathing deeply. The exhilaration she felt was like nothing she had ever experienced. Yet at the back of her mind there was discomfort. She had become a killer. It had not been her choice and she had been completely justified in her actions. But she had killed nonetheless. Even the absolute joy of using magic could not cover this fact.

She could hear footsteps and shouting coming from both directions. Then people surrounded her. She could not compose herself enough to stand, let alone speak.

'They're dead!' screamed someone.

'Call the guard,' said another.

'Grab her!' said a third.

She tried to explain, tried to shout over the chaos that they had attacked her, that she had been acting in self-defence. She saw faces as they picked her up off the ground and restrained her. She saw Jen and Elsie, their eyes red and teary. She saw Mrs. Baker wearing a cruel sneer, making no effort to disguise how much she was loving the situation. She saw the face of Daniel's wife, though this expression she could not read. They tied her up and put her back on the grass. She knew she could have escaped and killed all of them if she'd wanted. Even collectively they did not have power to match her. She could have escaped but she chose not to. As the excitement faded and the reality closed in, she began to take stock of the situation. She had killed; the thought of it brought sick to her stomach. She had terminated human life. Even the thought of what would have happened had she not acted did not make her feel better.

She had killed and she would not risk killing again.

She would, instead, let them take her. Surely she would be given a fair trial, even as a lowly serving girl. Surely she would get her chance to explain to everyone what had happened. For the first time since the attack, she felt a pang of fear.

People would listen, wouldn't they?

When the guards arrived, they listened to a brief and wholly inaccurate description of what had happened, then they took Marie away. That night she lay in her cell which had no window, wishing she could look at the stars, unaware that her actions were about to split a city down the middle.

3.

Some rooms are designed for a purpose and this was one of them. The thick walls and lack of windows, combined with the oily orange lamp light told you one thing: what happens here stays here.

Whereas some rooms are designed for the purpose of entertaining or perhaps creating, this one was made so that people could conspire. And conspiring they were.

A group of about twenty men and women sat around the heavy table. A lot of them had left their hoods up, for even in this most secret of places, far from the prying eyes of the mayor, they still felt unsafe. For the business of which they spoke was enough to see you swinging from a rope.

Thon had not left his hood up. He wanted to be seen. For people like Thon, to be seen is to live. People have often speculated about whether a falling tree makes a sound in an empty forest. Well Thon cared not for any trees, but in the same way that sound may or may not exist if there is no receptacle, egos of a certain type fear that their very existence might cease to be if there is no one looking at or talking about them. Not that he would ever have admitted to any fear.

Raised in the kind of household in which Marie had oh so recently been trapped, Thon had never wanted for much. At least he shouldn't have. Often you find the greatest want amongst the group who theoretically shouldn't. Attending the best parties, being seen with the classiest of classy ladies, the thought of soon taking over his father's empire, none of it was enough to satisfy young Thon. For he knew and understood all too well that, for all he had, he was still the proverbial small fish. And Durpo was the biggest of ponds.

Thon saw it, you see. He saw it in their eyes as they greeted him. He was a passenger, and, while the great and the good of Durpo would always shake his hand and meet his eye, true respect was never offered. That was reserved for that special little club, and by the Gods were they a clique. New members were taken on very, very rarely, and the work involved in forcing yourself in was considerable and not something that anyone of Thon's age had ever achieved.

He would often watch them, Mayor Louie and the rest, exchanging their niceties with all and sundry, and he saw it all. Saw their complete contempt for the world outside of their little group. For while the upper echelons of Durpoian society were numerous, those who actually had any kind of influence, any kind of *true* influence, could be counted on one hand. A hand which was a closed fist to the likes of Thon.

At least that was how it *had* been.

Times were changing and for Thon, unlike Louie, change was as good if not infinitely better than the rest. Power was a commodity carefully hoarded and exclusified by those with it. But the nature of that commodity, much like the times, was changing. And the time for action was upon them. For economic influence and political weight were nothing compared to the raw energy that Thon now held in his hand, and he had a hell of a lot more of it than anyone else.

Like Marie, Thon had started noticing his new abilities before everyone else. At first he hadn't known what to do. He sensed the opportunity ahead of him but he also sensed the danger. As one man with this power he was still vulnerable. Much as he hated to admit it, he was not ready to take on a whole city. The seat in the Mayor's office was his to claim, but doing things by force is rarely preferable when you seek to carry public favour.

Thon was facing a dilemma. Exposing himself would doubtless put him in a position he could work with. If people knew of his magic and what he could do then what possible motivation would they have to keep Louie in office? Yet Louie was nothing if not sly, and Thon had no doubt that the old man would do everything in his power to squash this new threat. As he often repeated to himself, he was not ready to take on a city, but that might be exactly the position he found himself in, if he didn't play his cards right.

He could see the 'Wanted' posters now. Plastered all over the city they would be, as Durpo sought to flush out this dangerous terrorist. The margins between glorious new leader and the hangman's noose were ever so fine, and thus Thon bided his time. It wasn't something he was used to nor something he in any way enjoyed, but he did it. His moment would come and his young age was, for once, on his side.

His moment, or at least the path towards it, had come and not in the way he had expected. It had come in the form of others.

Durpo had awoken and suddenly everyone was using the power. Now all they needed was a leader. Thon's dilemma had come from not wanting to take on the authorities of the city alone. But as the leader of the uprising…well, that was a much more attractive proposition.

Slowly he had begun searching, seeking out like-minded people. Though he had to be careful. One misplaced word in the wrong ear and his uprising would be over before it had begun. So, careful he was and here they were. Those who shared his idea but not his power. Those who would stand up against Louie and lead Durpo forward. Those who looked to him as leader but, he suspected, trusted him not.

For now it did not matter. Trust could be won later. For now he needed them only for their magical abilities. Relationships could be forged later, once they were running the show.

'So,' he began. 'We are poised and ready.' This was not greeted with the enthusiasm he had hoped for. Instead, nervous glances from within hoods bounced around the table. Frustration burned within him but pragmatism burned stronger. He needed them, and despite all of their non-committal reluctance and worries, he must keep them on his side.

'Mayor Louie is scrabbling around trying to keep control, and word has reached me that he has, only this morning, declared the use of magic illegal for everyone outside of his guard.' There was a much more satisfactory reaction to this news. 'So it seems that our new found abilities are to be taken from us.'

He paused, allowing time for the murmurs to spread. It was, after all, a ridiculously audacious move by the mayor and one that played straight into Thon's hands. The old man must be losing his touch. By attempting to squash the magical revolution, he was dangerously alienating himself. The siege mentality currently being employed by the mayor's office was not going to win him any popularity and things would only get worse, as whatever it was that was giving them this power increased. And increasing it most certainly was.

'What do you plan to do?' asked a man sat three places down from Thon. His name was Lars and Thon suspected that Lars was going to be important over these next few weeks. He had more power than the rest, nothing like Thon of course but still a considerable amount; and, more importantly, he was a man of action.

Since he had assembled this little group, admittedly not very long ago, there had been much talk...*so* much talk, but action had been hard to come by. Thon was hoping that this latest push by Mayor Louie would be the necessary catalyst. He had been savagely frustrated to learn just how damp an apparent tinderbox atmosphere could be. But finally, he suspected that the oil had arrived.

'Tomorrow...' he began, but he did not finish. For he was interrupted, and the news which this interruption brought changed things.

'What are we going to do about this Marie girl?' came the interruption, as promised.

There was much of the murmur but none of the substance.

'Who is Marie?' asked Thon, confused yet interested.

'The serving girl who they are to hang tomorrow.' replied the interrupter or, to use his proper name, James. It seemed that this was common knowledge and Thon sensed the tension. Clearly this was something he *should* know.

'She has been tried and will be hung tomorrow for using lethal magic.'

'Lethal!' Thon could not hide his surprise and instantly regretted his tone.

'They say she was attacked by a member of the house where she worked, horrible rat of a man, and she acted in self defence.'

Thon's mind was racing. For while he knew he had the power to kill, he strongly suspected that the majority, the *vast* majority, did not. If this serving girl had killed, then her power must be considerable.

'Her trial was yesterday, not that you could call it much of a trial,' continued James. 'It was over in five minutes. It seems that her pleas of self defence fell on deaf ears.'

A plan, beautiful and seemingly flawless, was forming in Thon's mind. A public arena, where the mayor was executing someone for a magical crime. Someone who had been acting in self-defence, or so they (and it was the 'they' who were the important ones in all this) said, and who would look wonderfully innocent up on the gallows. The fates could not have designed a better arena for their takeover.

Just as he was about to speak, a woman entered the room. A few people jumped to their feet in panic. Thon did not panic, for he knew who this woman was. He had never laid eyes on her but could feel the raw power that emanated from her filling the room. He had wanted to meet her for some time.

'Welcome Rachel,' he said.

4.

History has an annoying habit. One which all those who unwittingly fall into the same careers and marital mistakes as their parents wish it wouldn't: repetition. Clichéd as it may be, you can't get away from it. Mayor Louie was about to find out that even the most cunning have a tendency of eventually repeating the mistakes that they profited from in earlier life. Perhaps it is born

51

of arrogance. Even when we have seen something play out in front of our very eyes, the tendency is still to think, well, it won't happen to me.

The form in which Mayor Louie's biggest mistake was currently residing was his aid Luc. Unassuming to look at and quiet of voice, Luc was not the kind of person that many people noticed. That was all about to change.

Luc had noticed, of late, how dangerously Louie was playing his game. The old man wasn't adverse to a bit of risk, but risk that was heavily calculated and rarely backfired. The way he'd been handling the city since people had started gaining the power had been erratic and rarely well thought out. Normally the old fox was at least three steps ahead of the game, now he seemed to live in a world of reaction. Luc, as Louie had all those years ago, saw opportunity. For within the quiet young man, ambition burned hot and white. Slipping under the radar is a skill not to be discounted within the world of politics. Making a name for yourself by being loud and public is, of course, the preferred method, but it was not for Luc. Luc preferred to watch and learn. Let the brash ones battle it out and destroy each other, let them make their amateur mistakes and bravely spit words that will inevitably come back and haunt them. He would not get involved in such things, as him game was of the long variety.

Getting close to the mayor had seemed like the natural thing to do and had proved surprisingly easy. From this position, Luc watched and Luc planned and, like the hapless Vars all those years ago, Louie did not see it. He barely spared a moments thought for his young aid but, to be fair to him, he did have rather a lot on his plate at the moment. And this brimming plate, full of magical nuisance, suited Luc right down to the ground. A well-liked mayor in a firmly established and fruitful state of corruption makes for a difficult coup. A mayor lashing out wildly, like a wounded animal, does not.

The girl would be the final straw, that much he knew.

The previous day, Louie had summoned an emergency meeting with the full council and the most important business and legal figures in the city. It had been a bad move, bringing so much power together had made it as plain as day just how much he was losing the city.

'This must be stopped!' he had barked at the assembled.

They had not shared this belief.

'But Louie,' said Losh, the head of the guard. 'How do you expect us to police it? If everyone has the ability to use it how are we going to stop people? especially when it's so...' Louie looked daggers at him.

'So...what?' he asked.

Losh looked nervous, '...so useful.' He trailed off and looked at the floor.

'It's not my job to figure out how you do it. That's what you're paid to do, damn it!' the old mayor roared.

Others had protested, they must embrace this new phenomenon and incorporate it into their existing structures. It came as a very real threat, they said, and would change everything. They were absolutely right and everyone could see it apart from one. Unfortunately his opinion was the one that mattered.

'What we need,' he continued. 'Is a scapegoat. A nice public example of just what happens if you use magic in my city.'

There was a pregnant silence as everyone present thought about the same two letter word: my. Such a small word with such vast connotations. Luc smiled the thinnest of smiles to himself, the beginning of the end, he thought.

'Has there been anyone arrested who we could use?'

Losh looked even more uncomfortable than before, 'Well, there is this one girl who we currently have in our custody, she is soon set to be tried.'

'Tried for what?'

'For murder.'

Louie's eyes lit up, for the first time in a long time he looked happy.

'Are you telling me that this girl used magic to kill someone? Why the hell didn't you tell me?'

Amazing how quickly happiness can become anger.

'Well we thought...' Losh began and then stopped. He needed to choose his words awfully carefully. Durpo could burn or flourish depending on how he sold this idea to the mayor. 'The issue is a very sensitive one. The serving girl in question claims she was attacked. By a member of her house no less. The lethal magic she used was only to protect herself.'

'And?' came Louie's sharp retort. 'I fail to see the problem.'

Again the room was united, this time in worry. The man who had called the city his own was showing a worrying disregard for those who had put him in such a position. It doesn't matter how big you get, you are nothing without your people.

'Well Louie, if we are seen to execute a girl for defending herself against rape, by using a power which people have just discovered and are becoming very attached to...It doesn't exactly look good does it?'

Louie seemed not even to be listening. Losh pushed on, 'The potential for uprising in the wake of this is huge. There may well be riots. People will not be happy and, I'm going to be completely honest, I don't know if the guard can contain them.'

Louie sneered. 'If you're having trouble fulfilling your duties Losh, you are easily replaceable.' Losh fell silent. 'I'll tell you what we'll do,' continued Louie. 'We'll execute this girl as soon as possible, give her a trial but don't waste much energy on it. Then we'll make such a spectacle of her death that all these would be rioters, who have Losh quaking in his boots, will think twice before using their magic.'

The matter was clearly settled. There were more protests. Arguments that magic, if controlled, could benefit the city. That schools should be set up in order to use the power properly. Louie didn't listen to a single world. His old mind was made up and, with it, his death warrant had been signed.

5.

Rachel's presence had a dramatic effect on the dark little room. Where there had been a lack of enthusiasm, and indeed fear, there was now confidence. The assembled had struggled even to make eye contact with Thon, now they were all gazing at Rachel.

It was difficult to take your eyes off her.

She wasn't tall but she seemed to tower. It was an odd effect, somebody towering from below your line of sight. Her hair was dark and her skin fair. Her eyes twinkled, big and green. But, physically attractive as she was, this was not what drew the attention. What drew the attention was felt rather than seen, and what a feeling it was. Just to be near this woman was enough to make you feel that anything was possible.

Thon was powerful but this was something else, something glorious.

It was difficult for him to know how to react in those first few moments. On the one hand, he was happy to finally meet this woman who he'd heard so many rumours about. There was no doubt that with her as an ally, their task suddenly became infinitely easier. But on the other, he couldn't help but notice how quickly he had gone from leader to second in command. Reassertion of authority was imperative.

'Please take a seat Rachel,' he began. She smiled at him, the picture of courtesy, and then sat down.

'I hope my presence here is not an intrusion.' This was greeted with varying degrees of word and noise that suggested that this was, indeed, not the case.

'Absolutely not,' said Thon loudly. He was keen to create the dynamic of a meeting between him and her, with the others as spectators. He did not like the idea of her coming in and addressing the group as a whole. 'We were just discussing what we plan to do about the hanging tomorrow.'

'Ah yes, of course this issue is of the upmost importance,' she replied. 'This will not be allowed to happen.' They all nodded at this. They had not nodded when Thon had suggested things. He was losing control of this situation all too quickly.

'We plan to kill the mayor at the hanging.'

Thon said it without thinking. The truth was that this had not been planned at all. He wasn't completely sure why he said it. In his panic when faced with the changing dynamic that this new individual had brought with her, he had sought to regain some credence and a big, bold statement seemed like a good horse to back.

Big, bold and stupid. That was what the looks told him. Rather than winning back his subjects, he had pushed them further away. For all their conspiring and whispers of revolution, it seemed they lacked the willingness to actually get their hands dirty.

'There will be no death tomorrow. Not the girl they plan to hang but not the mayor either.' She could say things with such finality. It angered Thon.

He felt like he was being told what to do. Whatever power this newcomer had, she was still in Thon's house, as it were.

'The mayor has to go,' he said making direct eye contact with Rachel, trying to entice some anger out of her. She offered none, only an unmovable calm.

'Agreed,' she said. 'Mayor Louie has made his stance on this position very clear. The fact that he is stooping as low as public murder is a clear testament that his time in office cannot be allowed to continue.'

'If he is willing to kill one of us, why the hell should we not respond in type?'

'We will not become murderers,' said Rachel. 'It is as simple as that. We are making a bold statement tomorrow and we are asking for a lot of trust from the people of this city. We are saying that we believe we have the right to remove control from the mayor's office. How do you think the people of Durpo will feel if they think that one corrupt killer has been replaced by another?'

He knew he had lost. Much as it ripped at him to admit it, he knew he was no match for this woman. Continuing this battle, especially in this setting, could be disastrous for him. Ever the pragmatist, Thon buried the hatchet.

'You are right of course,' he said. 'No death tomorrow.' She smiled at him, apparently instantly forgiving.

'Tomorrow we will go to the hanging and we will put a stop to it. Then we shall tell Mayor Louie that his services are no longer required by the people of Durpo.'

'And after that?' asked a member of what used to be Thon's and was now unanimously Rachel's.

'And after that we will see what the people want.'

Thon grimaced. He had been hearing rumours of this woman whose power was said to be so great. His desire had, of course, been to make her part of their secret society. The more power the better. What he had not imagined was that once she arrived, the society would be no longer his. His dream of ruling over the city was not lost but it had become a lot more distant.

Thon was going to have to be very clever, very clever indeed.

Chapter 5.

Travel and meetings.

1.

Shabwan was on the road and had been for a while. It seemed pretty obvious where he had to go. The big castle was hardly inconspicuous. It was a long way away though and didn't seem to be getting nearer at any great speed.

The landscape swirled up into impossible shapes around him. Hills curled over like great waves and trees seemed to grow upside down, their roots snapping at their neighbours as they jostled for space. It seemed that the landscape was very much alive and wanted to get a good look at Shabwan without getting too close.

Kayleigh drove him on and all that he saw reminded him of her. Sometimes he saw her face in puddles of water, other times leaves swirled in the wind and painted her face. But, as omnipresent as she was in his mind, there was another. Another that Shabwan could not quite fathom.

The longer he walked the less he enjoyed his own company. His own thoughts irritated him, yet he seemed powerless to demand any kind of silence. The winding road was just that, ands sometimes he wondered if he was indeed moving towards the castle at all. Still, there was no other option really. All he could do was follow and hope.

It was evening and he wanted to stop. His legs ached from all the walking and his stomach, always quick to empty itself, was grumbling at him. Before long he was sat next to his standard campfire. The natural world, still keeping its watchful eye, began to calm and settle.

He awoke with a start and immediately knew something was different. The feeling of isolation, which had been grinding on his nerves as he travelled, was gone. There was someone else here. Yet there was nothing around him that actually supported this idea. Whatever it was that had awoken him was not within sight or smell, or any of the other senses that would normally alert one to such things.

Shabwan rose to his feet, 'Hello?' he shouted. There was only darkness. His fire was burning very low indeed. Whoever or whatever was out there did not feel like they posed a threat but Shabwan could not be sure. He curled his hand into a fist and immediately the energy started running to it. Kayleigh's face, which moments before had been dancing in the fire, disappeared. There was only fire.

That was when he saw her. She was moving quickly and he had to follow. The glimmer of silver skin that had, for the briefest of seconds, caught a piece of the moonlight, had not been standing still.

Shabwan ran, blind as a bat, but drawn on by something much stronger than sight. The movement of this being left patterns in the air. Unmistakable ribbons that felt like the softest of silk to the touch. He followed, sprinting like he had never sprinted. For this being tugged at both sides of his heartstrings. She might lead him to Kayleigh and then she might also offer...

He pushed such thoughts out of his head. He could not allow himself to be distracted. Ahead of him there was only darkness. Yet every few seconds the moon, orbiting at incalculable speeds, would fly overhead, and as it did he would glimpse the silvery skin.

He fell, landing hard on unforgiving earth that welcomed him not. Instead it seemed to boost him back to his feet, shoving him on like a disappointed parent. The moon came over again but this time, as it passed, he focussed all his energy on holding it. Hand outstretched, he felt the glowing white orb connect, and much as it strained to continue he would not let it.

Light filled his black world, as if the moon had been holding it all back and was now defeated. The silvery treasure which it had selfishly hoarded rolled forth. He saw the path upon which he still ran. He saw the trees, his omnipresent audience, and more importantly, he saw her.

She was no longer running.

Indeed, she was walking back towards him. She smiled, but it was not a welcoming smile. It taunted him, as if to say that he could not hold the moon much longer. Were he to release it, he knew she would flee once more, and if she did then he doubted very much that his blind running would ever catch her. His one hope was his power.

She walked with agonising deliberation, each step panning out across millennia, and as she walked Shabwan began to burn. It started in his hand, for this was where he held the moon, but soon enough it raced up his arm. Retracing the steps made by the power that had felt so sweet as it travelled the opposite way. There was nothing sweet about this feeling. Soon his whole body yearned for him to release. The pressure and tension wrapped and twisted every muscle, every vein felt fit to burst. Yet he would not let go.

He began to scream and as he did the light intensified. It was as if the moon was throwing everything it had at him, in an attempt to break free. *If you can hold me you can hold all of me*, it called and Shabwan did not know if he could.

He fell to his knees, but the ground that had so kindly helped him on his way moments earlier chose not to return the favour. This time it grabbed at him and dragged him down. Roots reached out and clawed at his arm. They sought to break the connection, already so fraught, and he fought back.

Just at the moment where he could take no more, the pressure eased. At first he did not know what had happened, but then he realised.

She had taken his hand.

The moon was no longer straining to get away like some petulant hound. Now it happily sat above them allowing its light to pick out every nook and cranny of the land around them. As she held his hand Shabwan felt her energy flow into him. It was everything he'd ever dreamed of. He teetered on his metaphorical edge (which, as we all know, are the worst kind of edges). Part of him wanted to die in this moment of utter euphoria. Whatever this was that he now shared with this being, whose name remained a mystery but whose essence did not, he would let it take him. The physical world was no longer of any importance, for his mind had reached a utopia. Then a voice within him cried out, and feint as the voice was it carried an edge, an edge so sharp that it cut through the cloud of warmth and goodness that was obscuring everything. The little voice sought to bring only one image and that image was a face.

The face of a girl lying in a field with the grass stroking her face and the sun glinting off her eyes.

Willpower is a commodity which rests upon the edge of a knife. It can slip off in either direction before we even realise any kind of decision has been made. When confronted with a choice where one option is right and the other pleasurable, the moment of making that decision can become an object of fascination once the ramifications are in full swing. Yet curiously, this moment remains ever ready to elude that retrospective grip. 'Why did I do it?' ask so many.

Luckily for us, and for so many others, Shabwan did not find himself in this position. He did not allow himself to be consumed by that which offered instant and eternal gratification, which, when you think about it, does sound pretty good. Instead he listened to that sharp little voice and he looked at the picture it brought. Right and wrong are, unfortunately, never as black and white as the paper and ink of which they are often composed, but in this instance Shabwan truly believed he had done what was right.

He had chosen Kayleigh.

The gorgeous being above him seemed more than a little confused by this choice. She stared down at her hand, which had seconds before been filled by his, as if trying to understand what was wrong with it. Then she looked at Shabwan and comprehension dawned on her face.

At this point it became nigh on impossible to judge her look. Was it one of respect or disdain? One of affection or repulsion? She gave away little, despite being naked from head to toe. Shabwan picked himself up off the floor so that he was stood face to face with the silvery being in front of him.

'What are you?' he asked.

'I am a guardian,' she replied. 'The question is what you are and I'm not sure anybody can answer that, least of all you.' She giggled suddenly seeming childish, despite the awesome power that flowed from her.

'I have been sent,' she continued. 'To find out who you are and what your purpose is in this place.'

'Sent by who?' asked Shabwan, sensing the hand of his enemy. The one who held Kayleigh prisoner. She ignored him.

'I thought I would have an easy task but it seems not.' Her interest in him seemed different now and she stepped towards him, her body arching, highlighting just how beautiful and just how naked she was.

'It would not be the first time one of our kind has…' she trailed off and, instead of finishing her sentence, she moved her face close to his. He pulled away. Having ever so recently given up everything for his love this did not seem so difficult. She too moved away as if she had momentarily lost herself, then she spoke again and this time it was not for Shabwan's benefit, 'He has it, but he wants it not…'

'Listen,' he said, now feeling more confident. 'I need you to help me.' As he said this he looked over her shoulder, and realised that the castle, which had remained frustratingly equidistant from wherever he happened to be, was now looking awfully close.

'And I need you to help me,' she replied. Shabwan sighed, wasn't it always the way? First entire villages left depressed by the absence of some joy spreading fish and now this.

'What can I help you with?' Images filled his mind of more breakneck pursuits down living caves and battles with unhygienic fisher-folk.

'It's nothing really,' she said. 'All I require is your story.' He looked at her and saw not her but another, another with whom his story had been shared. It did not seem like an unreasonable request. Not in the least. Yet just as he was about to open his mouth to begin, a thought swam to the forefront of his mind. And like so much that he'd felt since arriving in this strange place, he did not understand this thought. All it could feasibly do was slow him down. Yet he knew it was right, and what was right was what was right.

'I'm more than happy to give what you ask,' he replied. 'But first you must give me yours.' At this her eyes lit up in a new way, one he had not yet seen. She glanced over her shoulder at the castle and then turned back to him.

'Let us sit,' she said and all the world changed.

2.

Veo cried out in rage. This was not what he'd asked of her. How could she betray him after all he had done? He had created her and not in the way of the tyrant. He had agreed that they should have will and freedom. It had been another who had confined her to a life of imprisonment.

Now she would tell his tale to this newcomer and, instead of Veo gaining the upper hand, the young man would gain yet more power. He must take the fight to the boy right now. But, as he looked down upon the great path that stretched and wound its way over the impossible landscape, he realised that both the guardian and the boy had disappeared.

3.

They were in a new place and it was not a human one.

Shabwan knew he was not truly there. But he also knew that if he had been really there, it would have been no place for him. She was clearly leading him through something which had already happened, and while he was free to move and to look, he was no more there than he was a dog.

The great square, in which they now were, seemed an impossibility. Nothing needed to be this big, nor did the flagstones need to be laid in such perfection. This place had not grown or evolved over time, it was the work of a moment…albeit the very impressive work of a moment.

Ahead of them was a hall, as tall as the square was large and so symmetrical it hurt to look at. Two great columns supported the arch above the great black entrance and upon this arch were carvings, carvings of faces.

'You are looking at the temple of the Gods,' said his companion. 'Where I and all my people were born.' It was all a bit overwhelming but Shabwan fought to keep his head. 'They used to create this place only temporarily, when there was something important to discuss, and this is how you see it now. Later they were forced to make it a permanent fixture.' Shabwan looked at her, wondering if any of this was supposed to make sense to him.

'Shall we go inside? They are just deciding how I shall be made.'

They walked across the square and, as they did so, the chamber ahead became smaller. It was an odd illusion. Things tend to get bigger as you move towards them. Perspective being the stubborn old bean that it is. But in this place it seemed that size was an illusion, one that was easier to create from afar. By the time they reached the chamber, it looked like any normal, large building, far from the towering behemoth it had been on first sight.

Noise emanated from within. Raised voices leading debate into argument.

As they entered, they were confronted with the sight of the full council of the Gods and an impressive sight it was. Two rows of seats of the whitest stone raced away on both sides towards the end of the chamber, where two large thrones stood, elevated above the other seats. Almost all the spaces were taken, and a lot of voices were attempting both to be heard and to sneer at the ideas of others.

Shab's eye was immediately drawn to the three people at the far end of the room, one of whom was clearly some kind of king and to his right sat his queen. The king's long white beard and muscular frame seemed to burst out of his throne, whereas she was completely dominated by hers. Next to him she was tiny.

To the left of the king stood another younger looking man, or God, Shabwan reminded himself. It was interesting that, while all the other minions were uniformly positioned in the parallel rows of chairs, this one figure was clearly required to stand. He did not look different or special. The only thing he looked which the others did not was calm.

There was clearly a fairly heated argument on the go. Something was afoot that all felt passionately about, and it was difficult to pick out what any one individual was saying. The guardian was staring calmly ahead.

'We are being forced to leave more and more worlds!' yelled an enormously fat Goddess to Shabwan's left. There was a lot of agreement expressed in various ways to this. 'The magic is becoming more and more

60

powerful and we are being forced out of our own universe by it.'

'Hear hear,' chimed in a much younger looking God, dressed only in a simple tunic. 'I only got out by the skin of my teeth last time.'

'They are discussing the problem of the increasing flow in worlds,' said the guardian. 'Gods and magic have never mixed well.' As she said the word magic, Shabwan felt a tingle up his spine and his empty hand suddenly felt much emptier.

'Enough,' said the God who was clearly king, rising to his feet and looking even more impressive than before. 'We have talked about this enough and my decision was and remains final. There are many, many worlds for you to rule over and many that need rule that have none. If a world begins to flow and the people rise up against you, you are to leave. We don't know what happens if they concentrate the damn stuff so much. We don't know if it could lead to *him* being let back in.' Clearly there was not much debate on this point, whoever *him* was, it was apparently most undesirable that he should be let back in.

'But, my Lord,' began the fat Goddess again cautiously. 'If we are to leave these worlds then there is no telling how much of the magic might become concentrated when they fight one another.'

'Yes,' agreed another. 'I've seen what happens when they all attack at once. With the sorcerers it's not such a problem, but when you get everyone using it together, there's this sort of...danger in the air. Like the barrier becomes fragile.' The king looked at the God who had just spoken. He appeared, both literally and figuratively, to shrink. Then he turned to his Queen and spoke in a hushed voice, she looked up at him, looked at the assembled and then nodded.

'What we need,' he said, slowly and deliberately. 'Is a new being.' He seemed to be talking more to himself than to anyone else. 'If something were to stay on these planets we have left and keep a watchful eye over what is going on there, then we needn't worry so much.' The assembled Gods looked at one another. Shabwan tried to read their faces, but there were too many and their rapidly changing expressions were too difficult to gauge. 'We will meet again soon,' continued Gask, although Shabwan did not yet know that was his name. I am going now to design this new being. Something which can protect and report on worlds where we no longer reside. That way we won't have to fight so many damned wars, and if anything is happening with Rez, we will be ready.'

The chamber began to dissolve and, one by one, so did the Gods. What the guardian had told him seemed true, there was no real substance to this place. Very soon there was nothing, only Shabwan and the guardian. She looked at him.

'So, you were designed to protect places where the people had forced the Gods away...because the Gods are afraid of magic?'

'Yes,' she replied. 'This was indeed our purpose; to watch over, what they

61

saw as a dangerous entity, and to try to limit dangerous usage on our worlds.' Shabwan looked around at the nothing that surrounded them. 'Is magic dangerous?' he asked. She laughed at this, a wholehearted laugh, like a parent laughing kindly at a child's first attempts at understanding something complex.

'That,' she said, 'is a question.' He supposed she was right. 'Would you like to see more?'

He nodded and a new scenario began building itself around them. Like the court, it did not seem real, only a place for sorting things out. In their previous destination there had been many Gods present, Shabwan hadn't counted but would have guessed close to a hundred. In this new place there were only three.

'Their name's are Gask, Eree and Veo,' said the guardian. 'And what you saw last did not represent the whole story of my creation. This is when I was truly *designed*.' The way she said this last word interested Shabwan. She obviously felt no love for her design.

The room in which they were now stood was much smaller than the chamber. It was dingy and dark and had none of the grandeur.

'They are creators by nature,' said the guardian as if reading his thoughts. 'When something is, as you just witnessed, for the public eye then it's a huge marble chamber with thrones, when their business is of the covert variety then they reside in places like this.' It was curious, thought Shabwan. Gods in a small wooden room sat around an unremarkable little table.

In the large chamber Shabwan hadn't seen any of these three close up, but here in the dim light he could. Gask was what he'd always imagined a God to look like: huge torso, long white wavy hair and beard, a strong hooked nose and heavy dark eyebrows which contrasted shockingly with the white of his hair. Shabwan was surprised to notice a few scars on his face. To his right sat his Queen, Eree. She was small, so slight that she did not appear to be of the same species as her King. Her hair was jet black and straighter than the flight of the truest arrow. Her nose was long and thin and her lips even thinner. Yet, strangely enough, the overall effect was one of beauty. The features should not have worked as a collective, but they did.

Facing them both, on the other side of the table, sat the one the guardian had called Veo. He was younger looking, with shoulder length brown hair. He had a hugely strong profile that also sported several scars. There was much of strength and business about him. Shabwan's first impression was that he was not to be messed with. The other Gods in the chamber had been powerful, that was plain to see, but here sat a true warrior. Shabwan was not surprised that Gask wanted to keep him at close quarters. But was it a case of keeping your friends close or your enemies closer?

'We must act swiftly,' Gask was saying. 'Leaving the worlds unattended may be a bigger risk than we thought.'

Veo's tone was measured and calm as he replied, 'I agree. We need to leave them in the care of someone we can trust. A magical catastrophe has not yet completely consumed any world, but it could and if that were to happen...' Gask was watching him earnestly as he spoke. Despite being leader, he clearly still held a lot of respect for what the lesser God had to say, as did Eree. '...If that were to happen, I believe it could perhaps open a path for Rez.'

'You are the one who has been there,' said Eree. 'So of course yours is the most important say in the matter.' Gask looked for a moment as if he wanted to say something but then did not. Instead he stared intently down at the table. While he was thus engaged, Veo and Eree briefly met eyes.

'We need this new being,' said Gask, not looking up. 'Something that we can trust to watch over these places, perhaps guard the magic and alert us at the first sign of any abnormalities.' He had said almost exactly the same thing in the chamber. Shabwan wondered if he was in the habit of repeating himself. Those who don't care too much if others are listening often do.

Shabwan looked at the guardian but she did not return it. Her gaze was intensely focussed on Gask.

'It seems like the safest idea,' agreed Eree. 'But are you suggesting we create them above humankind?' Gask nodded slowly, well aware, it seemed, of what she was implying. 'We must be vey careful,' she continued. 'For what you are speaking of is like nothing we have ever done before.'

'I am well aware of that,' Gask cut in. 'But these times are unlike any we have ever known and we must react.'

'But you're talking about creating something which could...'

'I know perfectly well what I'm talking about,' roared Gask, slamming his hand on the table with a thump that made the dark room temporarily waver out of existence. Eree looked surprised for a moment and then fell silent, clearly she was used to being spoken to like this.

'If we are to attempt such a thing,' said Veo, his carefully diplomatic tone diffusing the tense atmosphere. 'Then it would be wise to think carefully about it. While time is of course of the essence, perhaps it is not in such short supply as all that.' This seemed to calm Gask. He looked at Eree, who took a few seconds to make eye contact. Then they smiled at one another. Shabwan couldn't have been certain, but it seemed like Veo's broad shoulders clenched for a second as they did so.

'You are right as usual Veo,' said Gask and suddenly the three of them seemed much closer than before. It was a moment of tenderness that seemed completely out of place, but at the same time oh so normal. 'The trick of it will be creating something which has such a degree of power but without the ability to come up against us, or take control of worlds themselves.'

Shabwan felt, for the first time, that he was beginning to grasp where this was going.

'What we need is an element of *control*.'

It was what Shabwan had expected would come next but not the reaction to accompany it. He had expected agreement and the commencement of plans of how to carry it out. Instead of this there was shocked silence. Veo looked uncomfortable and Eree looked rather dismayed.

'We should not...' began Eree but then seemed not to know how to continue. She looked over to Veo, as if asking for help but found none. Gask could not have missed this. He seemed to grow even bigger and more impressive around the small table.

'We will create these beings and we will give them the power they require but we will also give them something else. We will give them dependency. The magic will be to them like the strongest of addictions, and with this will come a need to protect and nurture those worlds through which their magic flows.' Gask seemed to think this was a fantastic idea. Eree most certainly did not.

'But you can't...you mustn't...you're talking about creating something without free will!' Shabwan did not quite understand what she meant by this but he could see the newfound passion in her eyes. In Gask's mind, he was hatching a master plan. In Eree's, he was contemplating the unthinkable. Veo kept his counsel. Shabwan felt he could almost see his mind ticking over.

'Creating a being that is born with dependence on something that is not its mother! You're talking about making slaves,' said Eree.

'I'm talking about doing what I need to in order to ensure not only our survival, but the survival of every being in this universe. It's because I can make these decisions that you answer to ME!' He rose up on this last word, not completely standing but hunched over the table. Eree leant away from him, suddenly fearful. Her eyes flew to Veo.

'Veo...' she began, eyes pleading. Gask, whose eyes were now blazing, smashed his fists upon the table once again. This time the room did disappear and, for a moment, they were five floating in the cosmos. Shabwan had little time to marvel at the beauty but it was enough. Then the room swam back into its indifferent existence, unaware that the future fate of the whole universe was being decided within its walls.

'What he thinks is of no importance,' roared Gask. 'You will do what I tell you!'

For a few seconds there was silence. Eree looked incredibly emotional, as if she could explode into floods of tears or a murderous rage just as easily. Then she broke the silence.

'Not any more,' she said and with a flash of sky blue she was gone. Gask, for a moment looked taken aback, unsure of what to do. Then he composed himself. He turned back to Veo, who was still sitting and still wearing that look which suggested his brain was working double overtime and had no intention of clocking off any time soon.

'So,' Gask continued as if it had always been only the two of them. 'Lets get to work.'

Shabwan's head prickled and spun, and a moment later he and the

Guardian had returned to the real world. At least that was what he thought it was.

'So there you have it,' said she. 'My story.' Shabwan was stunned. He didn't know what to say. In the space of a few minutes, he'd just been shown that Gods existed, created everything but feared magic (a fact which had led to the creation of his new friend) and were not so massively different from people. It was a lot to take in. He didn't feel like his story was really going to match up to hers all that well.

'Now please,' she said. 'I have shown you how I came to be here. Perhaps you can do the same.' Shabwan thought for a second, he did not really know how to begin. Perhaps it was better just to go for it.

So he did.

Chapter 6.

Gallows Day.

1.

Marie was pretty sure she'd never seen so many people in one place. She had also never felt so alone. Which was odd as she was the centre of attention, another first. Well, that wasn't strictly true. Technically she had been the centre of attention in her court case, but only technically. In truth they had barely even looked at her and she had not spoken, save to confirm her name and utter a few feeble defences that were quickly shouted down. They had held no desire to listen to what she had to say.

She was a murderer, it was that simple. Someone who had hijacked what they called 'the power' and used it against her kind master. Her pleas of self-defence fell on the most stubborn of deaf ears and, before she knew it, she was hearing her own death sentence.

The family of the man she'd killed had been present. Marie couldn't help herself from looking over at Daniel's widow. She was attired in mourning black and did not return Marie's gaze. Marie didn't know quite why she wanted to make eye contact with her but she knew that she did. Did she want forgiveness? She didn't think so. It was nothing as simple as that. With all the strange, life-changing things she had felt of late, she now seemed to share some kind of affinity with the woman whose husband she had killed. It did not make sense.

But then, nothing did.

As she lay in her cell after her 'hearing' she felt a million miles away from the garden where she had experienced that rush of energy that had both saved and condemned her. She looked down at her hands, barely able to believe that they had been capable of such a thing. Now they didn't even feel like they could scrub a floor. Marie had been given a momentary taste of something, a taste of something which had rescued her, had saved her from what she thought was her life's depressingly inevitable path. Then it had been taken away, and instead of merely returning to where she had been (although that would have been bad enough), she was now going to die. She was going to swing from the gallows in front of the condemning eyes of the city. She was going to die for refusing to be raped.

The days turned over. She ate when they gave her food but she didn't really know why. In a strange way she found her fate easy to accept. It was as if she had lost so much already that her life only felt like losing a little bit more. She stopped crying after the first couple of nights and instead just stared until she fell into something which wasn't really sleep but delivered painful images none the less. She was not aware of how many days had passed. Just enough to drum up some publicity, she supposed. When they came to get her, the heavy door of her cell creaked open and three men stood on the other side.

'It's time,' said one of them.

Her hand tingled slightly but offered nothing.

2.

Mayor Louie looked upon the girl in her tiny cell and felt no pity. She was not a human being deserving of empathy but a ticket back to civilisation, back to the world as it had been and as it soon would be again. He could almost taste the resolution. He knew the others had doubted him. He knew they had dared to question whether he still had it and, when this damn inconvenience had blown over, he was going to enjoy his revenge. Once again he was about to win, against all the odds he was about to win. And the swinging carcass of this girl would symbolise his victory.

He barely looked at her as they walked down the narrow stone corridor, he, Losh and whatever that aid was called. Odd how it always seemed to be the same one who was around these days. The air was fresh and crisp as they passed the narrow slit windows and the excitement in the air was unmistakable. Nothing woke the city up like a good hanging, especially a nice topical one. Such was the delusion that old Louie had allowed himself, he genuinely believed that his problems would end as the hangman dropped the lever.

3.

There are very few times in the lives of people like Losh when they experience genuine fear. Being the captain of Durpo's guard was not a lifestyle that allowed the weak of heart to flourish. Losh's scars were a testament to the life he'd led, and with the appearance of each new line Losh had lost another part of his fear. He had very little left, but apparently he had some and right now he was feeling it.

He, like Louie, felt something as they passed the slits of the windows, but he shared none of his boss' optimism. Indeed, as the wave of noise met their ears with each passing tear of light, his dread increased a little more. Mobs make a variety of sounds and he had heard most of them. Much of his life had been spent going up against people, not as one but as a collective. And when people lose their individuality then a whole new rulebook needs to be opened. Once the face of the one becomes the sea of the many then the values that might normally govern that individual might as well not be there, they may as well never have been there. Those that would not normally raise a hand in violence would raise a stick, and those that would normally raise a stick…you get the idea.

Yet for all the various tones and choruses of the angry masses Losh had heard, he had never heard anything quite as bitter and seething as this. Perhaps it was the lack of obviously audible aggression that made it all seem quite so perilous. Whatever it was, the foolish, foolish man to his left, who seemed completely oblivious to any of this, might be leading all of them to their deaths and an entire city to ruin.

The guard had been out in full force since long before sun up. It was of the absolute imperative to get as many strategic strongholds on the street as possible. If you could keep large groups of people from forming then perhaps…perhaps you stood a chance.

But perhaps not today.

Losh's men had been clashing with protestors ever since there had been people on the street and, while it appeared not to be of the dangerous variety, magic was being used. And where they were confronted with it, the guard fought back. Scuffles, which would normally have been fought with fist and bottle, were fought with gleaming streaks of colour. Wood caught fire and glass was smashed, but as yet nothing too serious had happened. It had been with immense regret that Losh had removed himself from his commanding position to accompany Louie to get the girl. But he knew it was the right thing to do. The hanging was the flashpoint and whatever running battles were taking place around the city, he needed to be there when the girl was lead out to die.

For he feared that the noose would welcome them all in just as warmly.

4.

Durpo's main square was in front of a large cathedral which was rumoured to have once been an academy of some sorts. Buildings were a commodity not to be wasted in the eyes of the Durpoians. History was not as important as real estate and the religious community believed no different. In front of the cathedral was a mass of people. Hangings were always popular but this was unprecedented. Looking down on it, preferably from a safe height, perhaps keeping one of the cathedral's gargoyles company, you might have wondered if a single of the city's residents was not present. They filled the square and were piling in still from the surrounding streets. In front of the crowd the guard stood two layers thick, the first was doing all it could to hold the crowd back. The second stood, weapons at the ready, waiting to deal swiftly and sharply with anyone who broke through. Flashes of magic were present but only seemed to be coming from further back in the crowd. Those at the front, nearer to the guard and ominously close to the noose, were not yet finding the confidence to use it at close quarters.

Occasionally the guardsmen would glance at one another. They had all faced crowds before and they all knew the golden rule that Losh had continually drummed into them. Control is only an illusion, the moment the illusion breaks then we have lost and we will not recover. There are always enough people to overpower the ruling authorities, but the reason that they don't is for fear of consequences that will doubtless find them. Once the mob reaches a certain size, however, the illusion becomes so transparent, and soon the fact that the guards stand very little chance of making a single arrest is almost impossible to ignore. The more frail of heart amongst the armoured men began to wonder, if they didn't believe in the illusion themselves anymore, then how the hell could they expect anyone else to.

Just as it seemed like the square could take no more, a carriage entered the protected bottom corner and the atmosphere changed. It was an odd transformation, initially it appeared that the square had become calmer, those at the front stopped pushing and shouting at the guardsmen, the magical missiles that had been intermittently flying over the top and bursting upon wooden shields stopped. Then as the 'calm' began to truly descend, and with it the quiet, the real danger became more obvious. As a noisy sea of faces these people seemed like they might, just might, be all bark and no bite. Often the noisiest are the ones who won't actually cause you the problems. The brash and the big talkers are often also the fastest runners and the quickest to disappear. Once the carriage containing the girl had entered the square, you realised just how many of these people actually meant business.

As Mayor Louie began to walk up the stairs to the podium, there began a sound. A low hum almost, the sound of a thousand murmurs and, for the briefest of seconds, it seemed like the assembled thousands would indeed smash, as one, through the protective walls of soldiers and charge upon the mayor and his podium. But it was not to be, for before this mood could become collective action, Losh appeared, leading the girl.

Losh' reputation was well known throughout the streets of Durpo. And while his name did not command respect amongst those of higher houses who had, of course, stayed well away from the square this morning, amongst the regular folk of the city he was known as a man it was better not to test.

5.

It was a bizarre phenomenon to behold, thought Marie. So many people present yet seemingly one will. They shouted and argued as one, they fell silent as one and now they watched as one. Clearly a battle was taking place, an unspoken battle which, as yet, consisted of no bloodshed but was a battle none the less. But instead of being played out between thousands, it was between two. Major Louie was one, the assembled were the other. The impression that her trial had given her was that every man woman and child in the city had been clamouring for her death. That the city could not wait to extinguish her and move on to a better future. Thus she had imagined her hanging would be punctuated with taunts from sneering faces. She had imagined rotten fruit hitting her as she was lead to the noose that would deliver her final rest. They had not been pleasant images, as barely needs saying, and they could also not have been further from the truth.

The city did not want her to die and the message it was giving her was so clear that she doubted even the mayor, who seemed to be taking such a delight and interest in the proceedings, could ignore it.

She could feel the guardsman's hand on her shoulder. It was shaking.

6.

Louie was becoming dimly aware that he had made a mistake. A big part of him had already accepted it and everything that came with it, but this was not the part currently at the reins. That part had slinked off to take whatever fate the world was about to throw at it and be glad when it was over. The part of him that was now running the show was the same part that had made all of his bad decisions of late, and by all the Gods it was ready to go down fighting.

As he stood on the gallows, which seemed to be trying to become his own, he grinned at the assembled and raised both his hands. The calm, which had momentarily arisen when Losh had first been seen, shattered into a million pieces which, if they were not metaphorical, would have then showered the mayor like oh so much broken glass, propelled forward by the roar that erupted. The guardsmen at the front tensed against the strongest and freshest of surges and somehow held. Those behind who had been standing their ground, waiting now rushed in and started delivering serious blows to any unlucky heads that presented themselves in the crush.

'Silence!!!' roared Mayor Louie. His wishes were not respected. On the contrary, flashes of magic began to fly from the middle and back of the crowd, as they had before only now much more numerously. Screams could now be heard from in front of him where the guards were being drawn into armed conflict. Some of them had apparently had more than enough of Louie's ideals and were firing their own magic back at the crowd.

7.

'Get the hell out of here!' yelled the guard into her ear. He pushed her roughly aside and ran forwards, leaping off the platform of the gallows into the fray that was erupting just below it. Marie couldn't believe what was happening. Was she free? Emotions were overwhelming her but she must stay focussed. It was now only she, the mayor and that odd little man who was with him stood on the wooden boards. It seemed that the whole square was about to erupt into untold violence as more guards were pouring in from the road behind her. The sky was getting busy with flashes. They were nothing like what she had produced, but that didn't mean it was desirable to get caught in the face by one. If she was to make her escape then now was most certainly the time.

8.

Louie could not let the situation get out of control. The guards, while suffering heavy casualties, were still holding the mob at bay, and if he could just kill the damn girl and show them what they were facing, then he could put an end to this. The part of him that was now patiently awaiting its fate knew this not to be true but it said nothing. Without thinking, Mayor Louie raised his hand to his throat and, as he did so, something powerful began to flow into it. When he next spoke it came at a deafening volume, and such was the shock that the fighting stopped as all looked to see where the cacophony was coming from.

'RISE UP WILL YOU? PERHAPS YOU'D LIKE TO SEE JUST

WHERE THAT GETS YOU!!'

The girl was making a run for it, that fool Losh having flung himself into the skirmish just below them, but he caught her with no trouble at all. He clasped a hand over her shoulder and thrust her head into the noose. Turning to face the crowd, still momentarily stunned, he put his hand upon the lever...

9.

Marie did not notice the noises, only the visuals. Her own heartbeat seemed to be all she could hear as she felt the rough unforgiving rope against the skin of her neck. Fear seemed to flow and ebb. In the space of a few milliseconds she mourned all and accepted all. She wept inside that she would never feel grass or see stars again and she gave thanks that she had experienced these things. She felt huge sorrow at her soon to be cut short life and immense gratitude that she had even had the opportunity to share a kind word with another human. She looked up and saw that everyone was looking towards her, the guards had turned their backs on the fight and those behind them, many covered in blood, were seemingly as stupefied as she was. She tried to enjoy her last few moments, tried to take in the beauty of the people in front of her who had tried so hard to save her. It was ironic that having felt like such an outsider all her life she was going to die at the very centre of attention. She was going to die against the wishes of so many. She felt the trap door surge under her legs and her weight begin to fall.

10.

Losh couldn't believe his eyes. The mayor had led the city to the brink of destruction and apparently still seemed to be of the belief that killing the girl would resolve everything. Did he not realise that this action was the very reason that Losh's men were dying around him? He saw Louie's hand go to the handle. There was nothing that could be done to save the girl now. No one was within twenty feet of the mayor. It was tragic that she would die so unnecessarily. Her death had been unjustified to begin with, downright immoral and wrong in every sense of the word, but a least it was designed to serve some kind of purpose. This...this was just nothing.

As he closed his eyes, not wishing to see the girl's neck snap, light and sound erupted from everywhere.

11.

Marie's feet were standing on thin air. They supported her weight for a second and the noose fizzled into nothing, then she fell. Her poor brain had been through enough for one morning and took a few precious seconds off.

Slowly she came back to herself. She stood up. There was silence, complete silence. There was also no movement, the square had frozen still as a painting. She looked to her left and saw the mayor, his face a twisted mask of anger, his frozen hand upon the handle, which had reached its zenith. The thousands of people below her, in front of her and back as far as she could see, not one of them moved a muscle. Though there was one who did. A

71

woman, small and beautiful was looking at Marie. She had a calm that matched their surrounds and a power that suggested she could destroy the whole thing in moments. Marie felt her own power. For the first time since that fateful night it rushed back to her hands, bringing joy with it.

She looked at her new friend. 'Are you OK?' the woman enquired. Marie nodded. Then all was sound and light, the world exploded and was white for a second, the crackle and buzz of magical energy snapped around like whips. When Marie could see again, everyone present was still, only not like before. Before they had been frozen, trapped in a world where time was there but did not pass. Now they were moving, just not all that much. They all looked completely stunned.

'Mayor Louie,' said the woman who had saved her. 'As you can see the city will not be requiring your services anymore. If you agree to leave now then I promise you a safe passage out of the city. If you do not take this offer then you sacrifice my protection.'

Her voice was heard all over the square but not in the same way as Louie's. Louie's magical voice had been a harsh invasive sound, like an assault with noise. Rachel's voice reached all ears comfortably as if she were standing next to every single person in that square.

Mayor Louie looked at her, then down at his hand, still holding the lever of the gallows. For the first time, possibly ever, he looked defeated. Despite his crazed actions and his attempt at 'resolution', he knew he had stared death in the face and now he was being offered salvation. He nodded, very slowly.

12.

Luc's moment had come. As this new woman had stood next to him and cast her enchantment over the square, he had felt his own powers multiplying tenfold. As if her energy was such that it could not be contained within one body. After being a man who watched for so long, Luc now knew, clearer than anything, that it was time to become a man of action.

This woman had clearly saved the situation, but she was making the fatal error of misunderstanding the people. They did not want Mayor Louie exiled. They wanted him dead. Only this would sate them and only the deliverer of such justice would be welcomed as their new leader. Luc filled his hand with glowing energy, the type that would smash Louie into a million pieces, and stepped forward.

13.

Thon also stepped forward. Rachel's magic had calmed the situation and all eyes were on her. The fighting was over and he wanted to be remembered as part of this moment. The mayor's scalp was not to be his, but he could still sneer over his departure. The old man looked pathetic as he nodded, choosing a life of exile over remaining in the city that had meant everything to him, that had been his whole world. Thon wanted to get nice and close to him, so the mayor could get a good look at his face. Perhaps he would remember the minimal respect he and his type had shown to Thon and perhaps, in this brief moment, he would acknowledge the changing of the guard, acknowledge that it was Thon and *his* type to whom the city now belonged.

He did not notice the young man until he'd almost reached the old man and, as he turned towards this newcomer, a flash of white-hot energy flew past him. Thon did not know why he was under attack but he did not need to. There was no mistaking the deadly nature of that which had almost taken his head off. Without another thought he unleashed his own stream of power straight into the chest of the advancing assassin. He saw the boy's eyes blink out the moment the force hit him, and then he fell back and lay still. Thon had killed for the first time. As he turned back to face the crowd, he realised he was not the only one. For Mayor Louie's corpse stared gormlessly back up at him.

For a moment there was silence then the crowd, protestors and guardsmen alike, cheered as one. Thon looked out at the crowd...his crowd.

Chapter 7.

The Romantic and the Fool.

1.

They sat as two and Shabwan spoke. Her tale had been given to him and he knew the favour must be returned. Veo too was listening, listening and learning.

Shabwan had begun by recounting what he remembered, how he had arrived at the town and met the people, how they had battled the strange creatures and then saved the town by liberating the fish. She had listened with polite interest but with no more than that. There was something about the way she sat that suggested this wasn't really what she wanted to hear. Yet she did not interrupt. Soon his tale had made its way up to the very point at which they were now sat and Shabwan could go no further. He trailed off and then looked at the guardian, wondering what she would make of it all. The story of hers, the story of her very creation, which involved some fairly influential people, made him feel pretty inadequate now that he had finished his own. But still she just looked. There was something encouraging about the expression she wore but also something which he did not like. Around them, the night was maintaining its traditions of darkness, although the moon was spectacular.

The feelings which had been troubling Shabwan, those that had been distorting his quest and blurring the beautifully defined lines of Kayleigh's face in his mind, were even stronger when he was around this beautiful being. It was strange that it wasn't her naked form which made his mind wander, but the power she seemed to carry.

'What more can I tell you?' he asked, already knowing the answer to the question. She smiled.

'You have only told me what I already know,' said the guardian. 'As well you are aware.' He could not tell if he was being reprimanded for this or not. 'Why don't you cast your mind back and instead of telling me about this miserable little world that I know so well, why don't you tell me about before?'

He knew why he had been avoiding doing so. Thinking back brought with it an intense feeling of discomfort. It was easy to plough onwards, single minded in your quest and your goal. But when it came to thinking about the time before, the time when there was apparently nothing…this was not so easy. How could Shabwan be sure he was doing the right thing? Hell, how could he even be sure this girl, of which he thought so much, wasn't an illusion or a figment of his imagination? The fact was, if he did not know where he had come from or what he had done in his life before, then how

74

could he know anything. People say it is not where you've come from that's important but where you're going. Those people are wrong.

'Shabwan, you must think back,' she said taking his arm, and energy, both sexual and other exploded within him. 'For therein lies the key.'

What damn key? he thought, but it was not a thought that lasted long. For as the guardian had taken his arm, and the flow of power had increased, the change in him had finally come. The immovable wall, which had represented the back end of his memories, was crumbling. And with her power flowing and joining with his, he could see through the cracks. Though it was not easy, it was like looking into a huge wall of light and trying to make out the shapes of silhouettes within or trying to spot a black spot on the sun. He strained with all his might, the wall warped and buckled. Images from the light within flew in front of his eyes, he grabbed at them, knowing they held the key to all he was and all he must do. And as he grabbed he could feel her strength failing. He knew she was giving him everything in an attempt to open his mind. Without her help, the wall would reform in a second and he would be as lost in this world as he'd ever been.

Clenching every part of himself, mental, physical and whatever the hell else, he drove himself at the wall once more. And it broke.

2.

Memories flooded back to Veo the fool, though they came in all sorts of bizarre forms. Pictures and sounds smashed into him like rocks and with each one he cried out. His nature was so damaged that he struggled to interpret what he was seeing and hearing, but interpret them he did. He saw his prison for what it truly was and he saw how he'd got there. He saw Vericoos and Lubwan as they stood in the hall and he saw the knife in front of him. Shabwan's memories came to Veo too, and as they did he saw his escape.

3.

Shabwan could not believe what was happening to him. How had he forgotten so much? As the wall in his mind came down, the world around them changed. The trees and the rocks around them painted the pictures of his last scenes before he'd entered the God chamber. He saw Vericoos' face and he saw Kayleigh's. She was, of course, not here at all. His heart burned with the thought that he wasn't even in the same dimension as his love. He had been charging around on a fool's errand, completely oblivious to the reasons he had entered the damn place. There was work to be done here. Dirty work. He thought of Lomwai and gritted his teeth. It wasn't like he hadn't done such work before. The land behind him rose up as if to offer its support and push him onwards while that which lay ahead seemed to laugh and taunt him. Come and have a go, it seemed to say.

In this moment of clarity, where Shabwan the romantic was almost torn in two by realisation, he had almost completely forgotten that he had a companion, one who had helped him reach this state of enlightenment. Without the guardian he would still have been lost. Now, despite being several dimensions from home with a God to kill, he still felt…well, found.

He turned to look at her and express his thanks, but he did not see what he expected.

4.

Veo was airborne, travelling fast over the land. He was experiencing a similar thing to Shabwan. That which lay behind him seemed to join him as he flew but that in front of him taunted him, painting pictures of his defeat and his stupidity. He flew fast but not true, his line was not a straight one and it was made all the more difficult by the clouds. Those which bore Shabwan's face were attacking him and grabbing at him, he tried to summon some of his own but they were weak and deformed in comparison and easily swatted away. It was going to take him a little longer to reach and kill the boy who Vericoos must have sent. Veo did not know anymore what of the world around him was real, what of it belonged to him and what to the boy. It seemed like all that they inhabited was beginning to battle. Trees whipped at each other, the grass and vines knotted and tugged, yanking each other out of the ground. The world was, quite literally, at war and it told Veo one thing; he needed to weaken the boy. The battle shaping up around him frightened him. Those bits which belonged to Shabwan seemed to be overpowering his and, if this continued, it seemed an ominous omen. How much chance would *he* stand if all his world was already being ripped apart? Then a thought occurred; she was still with him.

5.

Shabwan looked at the guardian and felt desire like he had never experienced before. She was lying naked, clearly waiting for him to join her. But, like before, it was not just her body crying out to him. It stirred something deep within his soul. Something unlike love but just as physically powerful. He knew then that if he were to lie with her, then these troubling thoughts of a power, which threatened to wash his beloved clean out of his mind, would be troubling no more. She offered salvation, for it was magic he had, this he now finally understood. He did not know how but he, like the sorcerer who had led him here, was now a being of magic. And before him lay this beautiful being, offering him her body and her power. If he were to lie with her, then the little surges that he had experienced up to now would cease to be temporary flashes and become a permanent way of life, an existence in itself. Human relationships, the thing which had always been most important in his life, seemed like something he had ultimately misunderstood. The 'him' who had lived all his life, made all his decisions and mapped his path had been the wrong 'him'. That was the only possible explanation.

But in his moment of madness Shabwan, like Vericoos all those years before, underestimated the little things. The part of him which now desired a life of magic was so momentarily caught up in a utopian vision of the future that it allowed another through. Much smaller and weaker was this other, but much sharper also. Sharp enough to drive a wedge into the inferno. It ground around trying to gain purchase, and somehow it did.

As Shabwan looked upon the guardian, moments ago his blissful route to salvation, he did not see her. He saw another woman, lying in a similar way in a field outside the town where he had grown up. A town full of people, a town where his friends lived. One part of his mind screamed for one thing and the more it did the harder the other retaliated. Shabwan was going to have to make a choice, one that would affect everything...

Luckily, or perhaps unluckily (that'd be telling), he never had to make it, as at that moment Veo finally reached him.

6.

Shabwan picked himself up off the floor and for the first time he truly saw Veo. Veo who was to be his mortal enemy across three dimensions. Veo who would see his world burn. Veo who would kill his friends and his love. He no longer thought of his choice, the world was no longer magic or Kayleigh, it was kill or be killed. The God in front of him looked just as he'd imagined. Vericoos was, after all, an exceptionally good storyteller and would have done a much better job of this than I am. The strange contorting wooden mask atop the shining metal breastplate seemed to stare deep into Shabwan without really looking. He knew that his adversary saw the same as he did: escape, salvation, redemption.

Without even so much as a glance at the guardian, he charged forward and the confrontation began.

Shabwan didn't know what was controlling his hands but it was certainly *something*. Perhaps it was him. But if it was, it was a part of him which apparently worked a lot faster than his mind. He thought only of killing the God and his body seemed to respond in turn. They smashed their fists into one another and the world around followed suit.

As Veo had flown across the land, there had only been parts of Shabwan's world around him and likewise as Shabwan had looked ahead towards the castle, he had only seen snippets of what was Veo's. Now all that was around them crashed in on itself. Both the town that had become San Hoist and Veo's castle ripped themselves out of the ground and flew onwards to join the fight. It was a great spinning ball of destruction. All that they had both created, the insanity of Veo and the romanticism of Shab, twisted and fought. Earth battled water which in turn savaged fire but was then forced back by wind. And in the centre of this collapsing micro universe, two figures fought. And Shabwan was tiring fast.

Oddly it seemed to be Veo's insanity which was actually working in his favour. He was fighting in such an erratic way that blows were getting through, and those which Shabwan landed upon the head under the mask seemed to draw more laughter than pain. Without warning, a monstrous blow caught Shabwan in the stomach and he was flung down, not to the ground, as this was busy battling the sunlight...just down.

Veo dived on top of him and began raining blows to his head. The first few felt normal but after that, with each hit Shabwan could feel his life force ebbing away. It was not as if he was being beaten to death in the physical sense of the word, just that their battle, which was really so much more, was taking on a physical manifestation. The blows were not crushing his head but they were defeating him...and killing him.

As he became weaker, he could no longer lift his arms. Instead he slipped his hand inside his trouser pocket. There was something uncomfortable in there, something which seemed to have cut him as he'd fallen. It was strange, as he'd noticed nothing in there until now. It was just as he was musing about how strange it was that he would die wondering what was in his pockets, that he realised what it was. It came accompanied by the memory of a sense of terror before huge relief that he'd experienced under the mountains. He was holding a blade in his hand...not the one he had stabbed himself with in order to get here, another one.

Veo the fool, a God who could almost taste freedom and his reunification with his other divisions raised a fist once more, it became giant and jagged and Shabwan knew this would be the last one. The spherical inferno that contained them now seemed to be almost all Veo, little flashes of Shabwan were bravely holding on, but they didn't seem to stand much chance. The great castle was swatting the helpless residents of San Hoist off itself as if they were flies. The remnants of the town lay crushed under it.

As Veo swung the great fist, Shabwan stabbed upwards and everything stopped. The God's wooden mask looked confused then split down the middle and fell off. Shabwan tried to make out the face beneath but could not.

As Veo fell, he, like everything else around them, the land, the trees, the cliffs...the world, began to dissolve. Within a few seconds there was nothing. Only Shabwan and a wooden door. Shabwan reached out and pushed it open...

Book 2

The Fool vs. the Trickster.

Chapter 1.

The kingdom of the Gods.

1.

Shabwan landed and fell. For a moment he lay there on the stone floor. For the briefest of moments there was silence in his mind, perhaps it was born of shock. Then all hell broke loose. His mind was flooded with all manner of things, some beautiful, some terrifying. He opened his eyes and, in the stone not two inches from his eyes, he saw a whole universe. Within the little glints and crevices, armies marched and herds stampeded. He tried to keep a sense of himself; it seemed the only feasible option when faced with this utter madness. Perhaps if he could find his own parameters then he would have some bearing from which to work. This proved much more difficult than expected. The insanity with which Shabwan had been confronted came on harder and faster. Delirious, the young man struggled to his feet and tried to line up his eyes. He didn't know where, who or what he was but something was driving him. There must be a purpose to all this and, whatever it was, he had to find it.

Walking seemed like a good point to start from. Like a toddler, he experimented with putting one foot in front of the other and found that he could do it. With each step it felt like a thousands winds rushed past his face and the roaring in his ears was only proved not to be deafening by the fact that it continued. Shabwan was truly lost, in every sense of the word. A man so twisted by confusion that he was in danger of losing his very form and disappearing like dust on the wind, and with each step he took the feelings intensified, but he would not stop. He drove himself forward, not knowing what else to do, unable to take in anything around him. This was arguably a bit of a shame, as he was in a place that looked exactly like the kingdom of the Gods.

2.

Vericoos had fallen asleep which was distinctly unlike him. His exhaustion must have been strong indeed. He was still in the little room that owned the three doors and, of course, so much more. The cracks in the room were becoming much thicker now and the light that emanated from them looked all the angrier. Vericoos grimaced, there was clearly a hell of a fight going on somewhere, and if it didn't reach its conclusion before this room exploded then who knew what, if anything, would emerge. He knew that, somewhere, Lubwan would be doing everything he could to reach him and, with this new level of flow lighting up the planet, he wasn't all that confident that it wouldn't be very soon.

The chamber shook again and made a strange, almost human, groaning sound. Vericoos shuddered, wishing beyond anything he'd ever wished that he could see what was going on behind those doors.

3.

Shabwan could see.

It happened suddenly and without warning. The thoughts and sounds that were trying their hardest to rip his mind to pieces were still going at it like there was no tomorrow, but at least his vision was clear. And what a sight there was to behold. Around him were the most beautiful ornate buildings he had ever seen. They gleamed in the light although it was a strange silvery light, unlike that of the sun. It seemed to come from the low-lying mist that hung delicately around the place, rather than from the sky above. In stark contrast to the brilliant white of the constructions, stood trees of the deepest green, their leaves too symmetrical to be real. Rather than see them as a unit, Shabwan fancied that he could see the spaces in between each leaf. There was something enticing about it. He wished he were small enough to get in between those leaves. They looked like they would provide sanctity.

Unfortunately he was not that small, indeed his body felt big and cumbersome. Moments earlier he had been fighting with all his might to keep it together, now he felt like he didn't even want it.

What he wanted was his purpose, or at least the knowledge of what it was. We humans love to believe that there is some reason for being wherever we happen to be. Without it, what would we be? Pointless? Perhaps it is so, but it seems equally arguable that existing is itself the point. Why waste precious moments of being, speculating about the meaning of that being? Easily argued, less easily achieved, for the thought of nothing is a scary one and a lot of what drives humans seems to come from it. Death itself isn't so scary; it's the abyss beyond we don't like.

Shabwan was experiencing a very condensed version of all of this. His very sense of self was fickle in the extreme and his mind, such as it was, seemed to have become his worst enemy. He was on the brink, on the very brink, and yet still he clung to the notion that there must be some sort of reason for all of this. It couldn't just be happening. What would be the sense in that?

It was these thoughts that brought on his test.

4.

Lubwan had to keep on the move.

His spell, which had allowed him to reanimate the corpse of the magician and deliver his message, had knocked him unconscious. When he'd awoken, he'd found that things were coming. He had abandoned his rock, not something that had troubled him deeply, and set off at a kind of lurching run. If the creatures which had sensed his work were to catch him now, then he would not survive.

He had been travelling like this for some time when he sensed the difference. Being trapped in the barrier world, there was always a certain amount of magic flowing through. And while it had none of the beauty of the magic in the real world (as he thought of it), it could be used none the less. It came at a price though; each spell ripped and tore at you. The unfiltered raw flow was a dangerous entity, and humans were certainly not designed to handle it. When Vericoos and Lubwan had first arrived in this place, they had attempted to continue the battle that had brought them there but almost killed themselves, rather than each other, in the process. The magic was like sunlight, a little bit of it coming from a long way away was beautiful, but being too close to it in the full force of the glare was no fun at all.

What Lubwan could not understand was how Vericoos had forced himself through. For all the power that there was here, it did not seem feasible that his enemy had somehow harnessed enough to break through the divide. Possession was possible but to actually traverse the wall…how in the names of all the Gods had he managed it?

At least that was what he *had* thought.

Then the flow increased…savagely. Lubwan hadn't, at first, been sure of what he was feeling. It was somehow different from that which he'd become so used to over all this time. So much hungrier. It could only be coming from the red place. That infernal hell which he would have sent Vericoos to, if the damn boy hadn't intervened.

Lubwan feared it but that didn't mean he couldn't use it. As the flow had increased the wall which kept him from the world he'd once inhabited had begun to feel more vulnerable. Lubwan now saw in it what Vericoos must have seen, that which enabled him to break through.

Upon realising this, Lubwan sat down again. He had a new rock to call his own and here he would make his last stand against this place. Using the flow that came from everywhere, he would attack the barrier like he never had before and he would either succeed or he would die. For if the spell itself didn't kill him, then the creatures hungrily closing in on his location most certainly would.

5.

A lone figure stood on the white road directly ahead of Shabwan. A tall figure wrapped in a black travelling cloak. The figure stirred memories, memories of safety and assistance. Shabwan lurched towards him, hoping against hope that, whoever this person was, they could offer him some help and perhaps an explanation of his current predicament. The figure's face was completely concealed by a hood which seemed strange, even to Shabwan. Why would someone not want to let all this beautiful light play on their face a while? Shabwan could feel the little grains of light dancing on his cheeks and he welcomed them. This hooded figure could have been enjoying no such sensation. As Shabwan neared the stranger, the world around him began to look slightly different. That which had been beautiful began to seem crass. There was no longer any subtlety to the effect. The purity of the white seemed lurid and the odd symmetry around the trees and plants seemed dangerous in its artificiality. This strange hooded figure seemed to bring a degree of truth with him, and Shabwan was all up for a bit of truth.

As he reached the figure, he extended his hand. It seemed an odd thing to do, but then, the whole situation was odd. The stranger looked down at it but did not reach for it. Instead he spoke in a voice which plucked at the memory strings like a kitten plucks at a sofa.

'Shabwan,' it said, which Shabwan supposed, quite correctly, must be his name. 'You have a task to fulfil.' Shabwan's heart leapt at this. It was as he'd suspected. This stranger knew why he was here and what he must do.

'Ahead of you lies a palace and within it lies one who can help you. But you must seek his help because he will not come of his own accord.' Shabwan nodded and as he did so the world around him began to pivot. The stranger seemed momentarily surprised by this and turned to look at their now rotating surrounds.

'You see how fickle this place is? The one who can help you lies ahead and you must reach him as quickly as possible.'

'Can you help me?' asked Shabwan, forcing each word out as thought it were a lump of stone.

The stranger pulled back his hood to reveal an old, bald head and a long hooked nose. Not blessed in the looks department, thought Shabwan, which was an odd thing to think at a time like this.

'My part in this ends here,' said the thing which looked exactly like Vericoos. 'You must go ahead alone.' Shabwan had suspected that this might be the case and as he nodded again. The world began to slow in its rotation. 'But I must ask you one more thing,' continued the now fading figure. 'Do you trust me?' There seemed to be as little sense in this as there was in anything else in this place, and as Shabwan looked up into the startlingly bright eyes of the stranger, it was only then he noticed that they were in a sort of bubble. This, he supposed, was what had allowed them to remain stationary, as the world had spun around them. The stranger repeated his question but this time more earnestly, 'Do you trust me?' Shabwan nodded and spoke a single word. As he did, the world stopped spinning, the bubble was gone and so too was the tall figure to whom Shabwan had given his trust.

And with that, Shabwan the fool had failed his test.

6.

Veo the trickster, on the other hand, had passed his, although it had been a long, long time ago. His trick had been one of the dirtiest, though it had been for the purest of reasons and he was not sorry for it. Indeed, the story of said trick had continued playing itself out in this world he'd created ever since. For years, if there even was such a thing, he'd watched that little chunk of his life story play out over and over and over again. Each time he would will it to turn out differently in some way, but it would not. The past, it seemed, could be recreated but not altered.

Veo the trickster knew a lot more than Veo the fool. The passing or not of your test meant everything in these worlds. And, in the same way that Shabwan was now a complete slave to his foolish division, condemned to the same life of insanity that Veo the fool had so struggled with up until his demise (which, confusingly enough, has not yet happened), Veo the trickster was liberated. That is to say, he was a prisoner but a liberated one, a concept almost as confusing as the previous sentence. He knew that he was contained in this place and knew that there had been something before, something he must get back to. He was also aware that, as a God, he had creative influence over this place and that, to some extent, it was an extension of him.

The arrival of this newcomer, and his almost immediate inception of his own test, had taught the God a lot. The boy had clearly been sent here, and it was on a false errand. His trust in whoever that hooded figure was had been misplaced and now he was going to pay the price. This boy must represent his passage out of here, but he was not sure how. Urgency there was not, so Veo decided to sit back and take a bit more in. He had learned a great deal in a short time, and there was doubtless more to learn. Soon the boy would stumble across the story of his trick. He would see, played out before his very eyes, one of the defining moments of Veo's existence. Indeed, the only one he could remember with any clarity, and when he did, Veo would get an idea of who he was up against.

The boy had failed his test, it was true, but that did not mean he wasn't still dangerous. The more you know the better you fight, thought Veo and, even though every part of his being screamed for action, he took none.

7.

We cannot hope to imagine what life was like for Shabwan's division. Before he had created his spectre of Vericoos, to whom he had once again given his trust, he had been aware that something was wrong. Now everything seemed right and that was so much more dangerous. The old man he'd met had told him there was someone here who could help him, someone who would need to be persuaded rather than come of their own accord. This seemed reasonable enough and, since the world had stopped spinning around him, it was painfully obvious which way he should go. There were signs for God's sakes, and the signs said 'ThIs wAy.' What more could you ask for? The birds were being helpful as well. Great flocks of them forming the shapes of arrows. It was most considerate. Shabwan imagined that they had plenty of other business to be getting on with, yet still they were helping him.

Once again, the buildings around him looked beautiful. The little window of time he'd shared with the old man had given him food for thought in that respect, but it had already been digested and long forgotten. The troubling symmetry of the nature and the lurid brightness of the buildings had all become one beautiful blanket, in which the fool was wrapped and he liked it. There was much of the niceness about this world and he felt in no hurry to find his target. Nor did he think back. Shabwan the romantic strove (or strives, it's important to remember that our three divisions are experiencing their times in the dimensions simultaneously) to remember what had gone before and why he was where he was. Shabwan the fool did not. His mind wondered naively onwards and, while he did see himself working towards some kind of solution, he thought not of escape or anything like that. Up against the most wily and cunning of Veo's divisions, there perhaps wasn't a great deal of hope for him, but lets not prejudge. There is always a chance, however slim, and in a place such as theirs, anything is possible.

Shabwan had not been wandering long when he saw some people. They, unlike the old man who had clearly been waiting for him, seemed to be unaware of his existence. This intrigued him. After all, what was there apart from him? Nothing of any great importance, he was sure of that...still, perhaps he was being a little arrogant and discourteous. These people obviously had a reason for being (again we go back to that old fallacy), and seeing as they were making the effort to be, he supposed he should settle in and see what they were up to. Thus Shabwan the fool, though he didn't quite understand what was happening, found himself seeing what happened when Veo the trickster exercised that part of his nature to the fullest of extents and pulled the wool over the eyes of the king of the Gods.

8.

Veo was not used to seeing Gask show weakness. It was not becoming in a ruler, especially one who was trying to rule over a bunch as untrustworthy as the Gods. Gask sometimes needed to verge on the side of harshness rather than fairness and Veo had, on occasion, been charged with enforcing. It was not a job he relished, nor one he disliked, but one that was necessary. Necessity had always been a big part of Veo's makeup, a God much more of action than words and one who was respected accordingly. Hence why he held such an esteemed position next to their great ruler.

This set up had always suited Veo just fine. He could have been compared to a certain Mayor Louie in another space at another time and perhaps later to his killer Luc. Watching and waiting, all the time he gained more knowledge, and where there are bees there is honey, and power is sweeter than the sweetest of honey. Veo's grand plan had all been going to...well, plan, until he had started having feelings for Eree. They had always spent a lot of time together without really spending any time together. Stood either side of Gask, both of them, in their different ways, to his proverbial right; they spent endless time in the same room as part of the same conversations but never really interacting with one another.

Then one day it had begun. It was strange that Gods, to whom time was not of massive importance, could have feelings which grew and changed over it. For all that they did know, there was much about themselves that they did not.

Obviously having feelings for your king's woman is a less than ideal situation. The history books have many brief cameos from such people, usually ending with the inevitable creaking sound of rope on wood. Veo had no intention of becoming one of those and while he was technically immortal, people usually misunderstood that term. Immortality was more of a right than a guarantee and, as with so many rights, it was often abused and, indeed, removed.

Every time the three of them would meet, usually after Gask had addressed full council, they would hear what he truly thought compared to the public address he had just given, and Veo would feel the burning pull of her eyes. He would try his best not to glance over, try to keep his mind on what Gask was saying, but it became increasingly difficult. It was a strange sensation to be so in love with someone with whom your communication had only ever amounted to small pleasantries, but that was what Veo felt and he would be damned if she didn't feel it too. Then again, he was probably damned either way. The moment he had felt the feelings were too strong to ignore, he knew that something would have to give. And the thought of taking on Gask in a direct contest was not one that he relished.

Yet still he did not act. It is perhaps difficult for us to relate to. When humans fall in love they tend to feel that time is of the absolute imperative. Every wasted moment is a moment when chance or circumstance can conspire against you. Not so when you're a God. When time is not your eternal enemy then your perspective on everything is different, the concept of 'one day' takes on a whole new meaning. One that we couldn't possibly hope to appreciate, and so Veo bided his time.

It was the creation of the guardians, Gask's ill-advised attempt at defending the universe against Rez, that gave Veo his chance. In the immediate aftermath of Eree's departure from the kingdom, you wouldn't have thought that anything was wrong with Gask. He continued about his business much as normal. He didn't say so much as a single word to Veo about her and continued with his plan of creating his new beings. Veo assisted him as he always had done, and attempted to behave as normally as he could. It was difficult when every part of him burned with a desire to find his love but he knew that to do so would be suicide, not just for him but for her also and it was that thought, rather than any other, that kept him in the kingdom. The creation of the guardians interested him not. For Veo had always believed Gask's stand against the use of magic to be far too lenient. Visiting destruction upon the worlds that took it too far would have been his personal preference; they were Gods for God's sakes (he probably wouldn't have used such language), why should they run scared from those they had created? This new idea of creating another being to manage those that they themselves were failing to manage did not seem pragmatic or logical to Veo, who prided himself on being both. There was something about this whole thing that suggested the beginning of the end of old Gask, and this thought would once have excited Veo more than anything. Now, however, it interested him little, for running the kingdom of the Gods, even running the whole universe as they were supposed to, would be nothing without her.

Then, just when he felt like he could bare it no more, his opportunity came. Summoned to Gask's secret chamber, a place they only came when their business was of the type that could not be shared with the council as a whole, Veo could hardly believe his ears once his king began to speak.

'I trust you have noticed that Eree has not returned,' began Gask gravely and Veo couldn't be certain, but he was fairly sure the old man was avoiding making any eye contact. Not something he was renowned for. 'I want you to try and find her, Veo. I need her here.' The God paused before completing his sentence and, in that little gap, Veo heard so much. The pain of admitting his weakness was almost killing Gask. Veo knew that he must have thought long and hard before reaching this decision.

'Have you any idea where she might have gone?' He asked the question carefully. He didn't trust his own voice not to give away the slightest hint of what he felt. For while Gask was losing his touch, he was no fool and never would be.

It now seemed like he was thinking, but Veo couldn't be sure. Was Gask internally debating whether to release anything more or was he just deliberating for deliberating's sake?

'I don't' he finally admitted and Veo's heart sank a little. Things had just become slightly more difficult. There were many words that could be attached to the universe and small was certainly not one of them...kind of goes without saying, but you can never be sure and there have been some tiny universes, although that's another story.

'It is imperative that the others don't know where you have gone. Do you understand me Veo?' Veo did, all too well. Gask's pride was always most likely to be his downfall. Veo only nodded and Gask turned away. Clearly the conversation was over and Veo couldn't have been happier about it.

He left the kingdom of the Gods and began his search. It would take him some time to find her and when he did it was on a world we would find very familiar.

For Eree was on Svin.

Chapter 2.

Decisions, Decisions.

1.

Things had not gone as planned, but that was not to say they hadn't gone. Mayor Louie had most certainly gone. This was confirmed by his still smoking corpse. And with him had gone the Durpo they all knew.

It was an odd moment indeed. A moment where the prize, which thousands had been fighting for, had been won. Yet the reality did not bring a mood of celebration. More one of grim acceptance, or perhaps it was one of confusion. Everything had happened so fast. One minute there had been pandemonium, as they'd tried, as one, to storm the gallows. Then it had seemed like Mayor Louie was going to kill the girl, despite all their protests. But then it was the major himself who had become the victim of it all. He and the other fellow, although few people had even realised that another had fallen. All eyes had been on the mayor. Indeed, most of the people present quite wrongly assumed it had been Thon who'd struck Louie down. It seemed logical and, to be perfectly honest, the vast majority were not in the least bit interested in how the mayor had been killed.

They had won, simple as.

Only it wasn't quite so simple. It did not feel like the job was finished. The city had gone through a bizarre and awfully rapid period of transformation. The patriarch who, despite his various flaws, had kept things running for all these years was gone. Yes, every man, woman and child present had wanted him gone, but they hadn't really had time to think about what would come after. Mayor Louie had forced the speed of his own demise and, in the process, he'd allowed little thinking time for all parties. The city suddenly felt vulnerable, a city without a ruler. Could it work? It didn't feel so. People in the crowd looked at one another. They looked for reassurance. They knew they'd done the right thing. They knew an innocent life had been saved and a tyrant removed of his. But doing what is right is only half the battle. Doing it in the right way is, by way of contradiction, the much bigger half.

One way or another, no one was leaving that square until a decision had been made. Rather inevitably, all eyes were turning to the podium. It was where their last leader had fallen and, well, if this wasn't a day for poetic notions, then when was? There were two figures on the stage, two figures who, in the eyes of the crowd, had saved the girl and killed the mayor. Clearly these were people of some importance, people who, in the rapidly forming new city, could be trusted. People who were worth listening to.

As one, the crowd began to call out and soon the noise was deafening.

2.

Thon was having a great time.

He'd always suspected that, when put in front of an adoring crowd, he would find himself a bit of a natural. He was being proven right. The mob were calling out to him, calling out to the one who'd defeated the mayor, at least that was how they saw it. He stood at the front of the podium, punching the air and loving the response he got from the crowd. Each flex of the arm seemed to increase the rapture. He felt Godlike, but he knew that this was not only due to his newfound fan club.

Thon had felt something, something which only he and one other who currently abided on Svin were aware of. Coincidently enough, the one other was currently sat in a chamber praying it wasn't going to break. When Thon had killed Luc, energy had flown from his hand. What he'd not expected was for it to flow back again...tenfold. At first he hadn't been sure what was happening to him. He'd almost panicked, was the spell rebounding? Was the magic going to kill him as it had killed the other? The panic lasted less than a second, for Thon was not in danger, far from it. Thon was *taking* the power of his victim.

3.

Marie looked at the woman who was now stood facing the crowd. She felt her own feelings mirrored by the thousands who stood in front of her. The man was trying his level best to draw every eye to himself, but he could not do it for more than a moment. All eyes moved to her.

Marie felt the tension. There was still danger here. Not danger like she herself had faced mere seconds ago. Not danger that could remove a life, but danger none the less. Moments ago these people had been violent. The guard and the assembled throng had been clashing and blood had been spilt. The spectacle that her would be assassin had made of himself had been enough to bring a halt to all that was happening. But now there was this noise, a roar of expectation. And, as part of the theatre of it all, she felt the weight of expectation upon them. Something needed to be offered to this crowd. They had risked a lot to achieve this end and they now, quite rightly, expected.

But Marie was not someone who could deliver this. She had not asked for her part in it. Indeed, her only crime had been to defend herself. Suddenly the wave of injustice that had been with her in the cell washed over anew. Why, when all she'd ever done was work hard and accept her lot, was she forced into the middle of this thing? The man in front of her loved it, this she could see. The woman to her right was a different matter all together, clearly nothing would faze her. As quickly as she'd felt hard done by, she felt guilty. The real reason she was up here was because of the fantastic gift she had received, the life affirming energy which had offered her everything, and now it appeared she'd been saved by those who wielded the same thing. How dare she be unwilling to take the place that was being offered to her, in what was fast becoming a bizarre microcosm of an election?

4.

Thon could feel the loss of the crowd, just like he had lost the room when he'd first met her. There was no mistaking it. In the wake of his killing, he had been, for the briefest of moments, the hero. Now he was sinking back to where he knew he must wait. And yet he knew that he now had so much more power. The revelation, that for now at least was only his, changed everything. He had assumed that the level of power you had was something nature granted you, a bit like your height. He hadn't, for a moment, entertained the idea that power could be taken. Was it possible that Rachel had not realised what had happened?

She was not looking at him. She was looking at the crowd and he couldn't be sure of it, but he sensed there might be the faintest hint of indecision in her eyes. Perhaps it was wishful thinking, brought on by his new discovery...for if he could take enough power...he stopped himself. It was not wise to think such thoughts at a time like this. If that time were to come, then it would be a different matter and one that needed to be considered at length and in private. Now was the time for decisions of a different sort.

Rachel spoke again in that perfect voice of hers and, once again, the square listened.

'I stand before you now as a normal person of this city.' This was greeted with uproarious cheers. Rachel looked a little surprised, perhaps even slightly uncomfortable. Despite the fact that, once again, she was running the show, Thon was beginning to enjoy himself.

'We did not come here today to shed blood.' This drew a more mixed reaction from the assembled. Thon looked down at those who had come with them, those he had conspired with in the room. They were looking up at her enraptured. 'We came here today to deliver this city from the tyrant and this we have done.' Thon wouldn't have thought that there could have been more noise but there was. Rachel's voice rose accordingly. 'But now the decision rests with you.'

This was clearly unexpected.

The mob, as is its nature, takes on a very single minded way of thinking. That is to say, all minds present become one. It can react to things and follow others, it can move and fight but it does this almost intuitively. It does not make conscious decisions. No one person had decided to try and storm the gallows earlier, the mob had. Group mentality is a fascinating and dangerous type of psychology. People are capable of so much more but also highly limited in other ways. Bravery comes in abundance and rational decision-making clings on for its life. This is perhaps why when Rachel told the mob it was its or, even more challengingly, their decision, she was greeted with stunned silence. Seconds previously the individuals had been cheering away, blissfully enjoying their complete lack of any individuality. Now, this small, beautiful woman had made it clear that the decision regarding the future of the city rested with them. Not them as a whole, a great faceless rabble, destructive and secure in equal measure, but them as individuals. It was what they call a bit of a wake up...call.

People looked at each other, not for the first time that day. In fact some of them were starting to get cricks in their necks. Not an injury that those at the front with blood pouring out of various gashes would massively sympathise with, but an injury none the less.

Was this woman going to say anything else? they wondered. Surely she couldn't be finished. It was *their* decision...it couldn't be that simple, or that mind-blowingly complicated, for such a notion was both. Within politics it is always a choice but never a decision. Often the choice is for the lesser of two evils and those are the good times. Sometimes it is just which evil will hurt you less if you don't vote for them. Now it seemed they could have, well, whatever they wanted. What the hell did they want?

Like so much that happened that day, it seemed to happen organically. No one present would ever claim to have started it. Indeed, as impossible as this notion was, the majority of the Durpoian's began their chant at exactly the same moment.

'You, You, You, You...' they began.

5.

Marie agreed wholeheartedly with the notion. Whoever this woman was, she was more than willing to pledge her support to her saviour. It was strange though; for all her charismatic presence, the woman who stood on the front of the podium did not seem completely comfortable. It was as if things were not playing out quite as she'd expected, or perhaps hoped. Moments before, she had been the picture of unflappable confidence. Now, confronted with a ringing endorsement from a vast crowd, she seemed less so.

Marie moved up next to the man, the one who had killed the mayor's murderer. Clearly he'd forgotten all about her as he jumped slightly when she moved up next to him.

'They want her to lead them,' whispered Marie. The man only nodded. If you looked closely, a slight grimace could be seen across his face. This didn't really interest Marie though. What interested her was his power. Ever since she had first gained hers, she had not felt anything in any other that compared. Now she did. Indeed, now that the three of them were standing in a line, she could sense how their powers were connecting and feeding off each other. She and the man were different, they could not compare themselves to her but they were all of a similar ilk. Marie felt a sense of belonging, the likes of which she had never, not even in her happiest moments, allowed herself to dream she would experience. It was wonderful.

'What's your name?' she asked the man.

'I'm Thon,' he replied simply. She didn't mind that he didn't ask hers in return.

'And who is she?' At first he didn't seem to hear her but then a glint flickered in his eyes. He moved so he was standing next to the woman, whose attempts not to look awkward were beginning to fail. He addressed the crowd with the same magically magnified voice that had become something of a hallmark of the day.

'All hail mayor Rachel!' he yelled and the chanting of 'You' instantaneously made the leap from pronoun to name. 'Rachel, Rachel, Rachel' it went.

Finally she was beginning to seem comfortable with the situation. Marie suspected that she had never wanted to be given a position of power. Her agenda must only have been to save Marie's life and then restore some kind of order to the city, but now they were calling for her and turning them down did not seem to be any kind of option. For the first time, Marie saw Rachel smile. Then she raised a hand and the city erupted in noise.

Word flew around the streets faster than news of a new batch of stonk in San Hoist. They had a new leader! Louie was gone! Magic was not only legalised but celebrated! And that wasn't the only celebrating to be done. It turned out that the mood of tension that had hung over Durpo was very easily transformed into a mood of merry inebriation. And while the city celebrated, those who had become the new council sat with the old council.

6.

The chambers had ordered themselves quite naturally. On the one side sat Rachel, Thon and Marie surrounded by the conspirators who had assisted with the former two's plan. On the other sat the existing council, or at least the remnants of it. Those who had publicly allied themselves with Louie over the issue of magic had the good sense not to be present. The conversation had been friendly and formal but then, the council were not trying anything. They knew their number was up and they were lucky still to be in good health. Rachel had in fact been very gracious, informing them that, pending a public vote, they would be allowed to stay in office. There were, however, going to be changes and not many of these appealed to the ears of the councillors. Men who had enjoyed the fruits of their esteemed positions for far too long. Worlds like 'equality' and 'fair distribution of wealth' were not concepts that had ever much been discussed in these chambers, at least not without an accompanying snigger. Yet here they were being banded around like it was the most normal thing in the world.

For someone who apparently had not wanted to take charge of the city, this Rachel clearly had a very specific vision of what she was going to achieve now she was in charge. It was going to be quite a different place. Servants and those with hard manual jobs were apparently going to be relieved of their duties. Those with great piles of wealth, present company included, were going to find that this wealth was no longer for the hoarding and was, instead, going to be used to help those less fortunate.

A few of the councillors made disgruntled noises at this, and Rachel stopped speaking as if politely waiting for their contribution which she would, as a matter of course, be willing to listen to. Oddly enough none of them volunteered any. Perhaps it was more the angry looking man sat to her left who put them off rather than the new mayor herself. For all the quiet power of Rachel, there was something dangerous about Thon. When Rachel had told them that they would be allowed, if the public deemed it right, to stay in office, Thon had been beaming daggers at them with his eyes, making it perfectly clear that this was not a conviction he shared.

This young man had, by all accounts, already killed today. The accounts differed as to whether it had been Louie who had fallen at his hand or another. But they were all absolutely convinced that it had been someone. None of the assembled councillors wanted to find out if he was capable of doing it again.

As the evening wore on and the sounds of celebration became even more jubilant from outside, the meeting eventually came to a close. The new ruling body of Durpo had been established and it was a magical one, one the likes of which the world had not seen in a long, long time. And as to whether that was a good thing or not, perhaps only a war can determine.

Chapter 3.

The Forest in Sight.

1.

It remembered the moment of its creation all too well. Most don't remember their birth and, for that, they are the lucky ones. Lucky not to remember the pain or the trauma. The strange sensation of coming into being was not one it cared to remember. It tried its very best not to think about it but often failed. The moment of its birth was the dark point but, soon after, it had come into such beautiful light. It had seen its master and the master had given it a name. The name was Morshev.

From that moment on, Morshev had known the big why. The why that haunts most for at least part of their lives. The why that drives people to religion, drink, drugs and all manner of other things: why am I here?

Morshev knew why. To love and to serve. Two words that can arguably never appear in the same sentence if one hopes to describe a relationship devoid of hierarchy. In the relationship between Lomwai and Morshev there had been an awful lot of hierarchy. Morshev had strained every fibre and sinew to serve the master and to make him happy. Living in the great black house, Morshev had cooked, cleaned and done anything master had asked and had done it joyously. In the few moments after her birth (for after a while, Morshev had begun to think of herself as a she), before that silky white light had washed over her, Morshev had been lost, a discarded foetus on a cold stone floor, waiting only for time or the elements to do her justice. But then the light had come and with it the purpose, and so much stronger than the purpose had come the love.

Her master had told her she was beautiful and the pleasure had been almost too much to bear. Then he had beaten her and the pain had taken her far away to the other end of the spectrum. She had cried and apologised and as each fist came down she loved him all the more. Not for a moment did she ever consider the vicious, selfish cruelty of the enchantment he'd placed on her. But then, she couldn't. Lomwai had become a master of design rather quickly and left no loopholes in his spells. Odd that he was undone in such a crude fashion really.

Morshev wasn't aware how long they'd lived as they had. Sometimes the days felt endless. Such is the way when you are so hopelessly and destructively consumed by love. Especially with one who hurts you. Often she blamed herself and tried to do better, but he only punished her more and this she could not understand. His cruelty looked to her like teaching and she tried to express her gratitude for every lesson. Though often he didn't want to hear it.

Then those other two had arrived in their world. Immediately she had noticed the change in her master. Normally he would be slow and measured in his movements, deliberating over every little thing. But once they'd arrived he had become anxious and frantic. Pacing around the room muttering to himself, sometimes breaking out of the pace he was setting to skip slightly. It upset her because it seemed to come with danger, and the thought of any danger coming towards her master... Yet she'd believed in his strength. Even when he'd seemed so irrational, she didn't really believe that there was a force on earth that could harm her beloved. She also knew that she herself would become a force to be reckoned with if anyone were to try.

The memory of that particular day was as fresh in her mind as if she were living it. It had not stopped turning over and over in her poor tattered mind...

He goes to the door and she knows why. He wants blood. A confrontation with two purposes and with two victims. She can see all of this but she isn't sure how. Normally her master is more difficult to read. Normally she is desperate to understand what is going on inside that head of his and normally she is left wanting. Now it is easy to see. Every thought he has is like a picture and what brutal pictures. If they were being painted by a real artist, he would soon run out of red.

He goes to the door, clearly the time has come. Suddenly she feels it...she must go with him. He cannot be left to march out there alone. All her belief that tidal waves and mountains could not harm her master evaporates. Her master is vulnerable, more than he knows, more than he can possibly imagine and he must not be allowed to walk out of that door without her. She scuttles across the floor, desperate to walk alongside him. He turns, seeing her rush towards him, and says something that hurts her. But, as ever, the little grain of hurt is engulfed by love and duty. She tries again and this time tastes his spitefully aimed boot. She must have gone to sleep after this because there is a time of black, and when the time of black is over, she has no sight of her master. All that exists of him are his noises, which are coming from the road outside the house. He is mocking, in the same way he mocks her, but he does not understand that not everybody is like her. Not everybody will treat him as he deserves and some may even bring harm. She runs at the door and just before she hits it she sees the shimmery film. He has cast a spell and the spell will not let her leave. She screams loudly, a scream of absolute agony, a scream of unwanted separation and inability to help a dearest love.

She screams because she knows what is happening. Lomwai is dying.

As his life force leaves the world, hopelessness and despair consume her, and again there is a black time. A time when emotion and loss weigh upon her like a stone and she cares not to try and get up.

Then the black ends and she hears them talking outside. Hears them congratulating and celebrating the one who killed him. It makes no sense to her. Why would anyone be happy? Why would one who has committed the

95

ultimate evil be lorded? None of this is comprehensible or palatable. Her rage comes out of her in the form of harsh dry retches that convulse through her. For the first time in her existence she has an emotion which challenges her love. It is the opposite and it is attaching itself to a name: Shabwan...to say it makes her very skin crawl, but say it she does. She repeats it over and over and over again as if chanting the name might break the seal on the door which has outlived its creator.

He is leaving. She senses it. Her chance is slipping and the thought of her revenge going untaken claws at her. She throws herself at the walls, willing them to break. But his wish was for her to stay inside and, even though he is gone, stay inside she must.

Then they start the fire.

It burns the black wood and the house fills with smoke. If it weren't for the fact that her enemy still lives and breathes then she would welcome death and hope it took her back to him. But she cannot give up, not when blood still pumps in her enemy's veins.

As the wood burns around the door, the magic struggles. She sees gaps in what was once impenetrable. She is on the edge of the black and she knows that this black will be her last but something keeps her awake, something gives her the strength to push herself forwards. As she tries to leave the door, the magic grabs at her. Like a million little hands it tries to pull her back in. She screams and does not recognise her own voice. The house begins to collapse and she is almost out, yet as the house falls the magic intensifies and grabs at her harder. The flames are all around her now. It is difficult to see through. As the house crumbles in on itself, she thinks only of revenge. Times like this are not for love or affection, they are for brutality.

As the house continues to fall, she snarls at the magic that binds her and thrusts forward one last time. The spell breaks.

For a second there is weightlessness, then a harsh landing, then black.

When she wakes she is under some smouldering wood, she is badly burnt but cares not. The wood must have stopped them finding her. Those who cheered and celebrated as Lomwai died would doubtless have made short work of her. She can hear them moving around very close to where she lies.

Morshev drags herself back into the wreckage where she is safer. There will be more black soon and she must get safe before...

That was how she remembered it all, and that was how it had played over and over again in her mind. She had lived in that wreckage until the others had come through, too weak to pursue. But once she'd heard that name again, she had found the strength. Now she was following these four, these four who knew where *he* was.

Sometimes she felt torn in two. Part of her desired to attack, to rip these four to shreds until they told her where he was. Then the other half would say the opposite: *wait!* For they would lead her to *him*. Why strike now and risk losing the fight or perhaps not getting the necessary information? If she acted rashly, she could end up either killing or being killed by her only lead to her ultimate prize.

It was easier said than done, though. Sometimes the war cry within her was so strong that she had to lie on the ground with her head in her hands to stop herself charging at them while they made their nightly camps. How she loathed hearing their happiness as they cooked and ate. The affectionate tones with which they mentioned *his* name, the bonds they shared, the connections...

With infinite struggle Morshev watched and Morshev waited.

2.

The sight of the forest hugging the mountains came sharply, and it was an odd effect. Such things should build gradually, starting as a thin line and becoming bigger. These didn't. It was probably due to the heat haze which gave such a blurry look to the horizon. Indeed, they actually saw the peaks of the mountains before anything else. Coki had been studying the horizon for some time, trying to work out why there was such definition to the point where the haze met the sky. It was difficult to focus while on horseback, and it had been a while before he was sure of what he was seeing.

'Look!' he shouted over the noise of galloping hooves. 'The mountains!' There were whoops and cheers from all sides and clearly the discovery was a joyous one. They rode extra hard that day and did not stop until the sun had completely set.

'We'll have to let the horses go I guess,' said Lewhay through a hearty mouthful of rabbit. 'They won't be able to manage the mountains.' They all nodded, somewhat solemnly. It wasn't something they'd considered and, despite all the pain and discomfort, they were becoming rather close to their mounts. It was a strangely unsettling thought that they would reach a stage of their journey when they would no longer wake up to see the four steeds relaxing together.

'I reckon one more days ride will get us there,' said Leeham, and Coki nodded in agreement.

'Mountain time,' he said rather absent-mindedly. It was another strange thought. As bizarre as their journey had been thus far, it had settled into a pattern, and the sense of familiarity had become something of a blanket, quite a necessity for people so far from both home and comfort zone. Routine, however strange, serves as an anchor in times when we are floating lost in the storm. The forests, and the mountains beyond, represented the last known barrier between them and Shabwan. Doubtless there would be more, but when they thought of the words of Morldron's flaming corpse, they could not help but feel that, wherever Shabwan was, it wasn't far beyond those grey triangles. Yet, for all the pride they felt at reaching them and the hope that Shabwan was just beyond them, the green and the grey represented a new challenge and it was difficult not to see it as an ominous one.

They would never have thought that riding all day and sleeping in the dirt by night would come to feel like this, but it had. In some ways they would be sorry to see it go.

'Wish we'd brought some stonk to give him when we find him,' said Leeham, who had clearly decided that the mood had become much too serious for his liking. They all burst out laughing. The idea of celebrating their reunion in this way in some place they'd never dreamed they would end up in was too ridiculous to comprehend, and it brought a welcome relief from the mood that the evening had been falling into.

A noise cut through the dark.

It sounded like an animal but seemed laced with the kind of spite and anger that you could only associate with something of intelligence. It was half way between a snarl and a word. The horses did not like it one bit and Lewhay and Leeham jumped up to calm them. Kayleigh and Coki also jumped to their feet.

'What the hell was that?' asked Lewhay, struggling with Kayleigh's horse.

'I don't know,' yelled Coki over the braying and clopping, 'but it sounded close.'

They had, hitherto, not spared a moments thought for the fact that they didn't have any weapons. Suddenly it seemed like the most relevant thing in the world. Coki knelt down in the road and picked up a rock. Kayleigh took hold of his arm. He wasn't sure if she was clinging on for fear or trying to stay his hand. He wasn't even sure that he had any idea what he was planning to do.

Slowly the situation calmed, but none of them truly relaxed. There is no greater discomfort than a fear of something you know is out there but cannot see. They were four swimmers in the open sea, and just beyond their field of vision was some kind of unimaginable horror. As the night went on, their treacherous imaginations painted worse and worse pictures of what had made that hideous sound. Some of them would have made a shark seem like a perfectly pleasant encounter.

They did not sleep, despite much arguing and claiming that watches would be taken. Lewhay and Leeham both seemed so determined to martyr themselves that Kayleigh eventually insisted that it would be she that do it, at which point Coki claimed that if anyone was staying awake on watch, it would be him. Eventually they decided that no one would be on watch. They would all stay awake together. If something was going to attack them, it would be much better to have four alert fighters to contend with it, rather than one awake and three all groggy and disorientated.

It seemed a long time ago that they had felt the elation of seeing the mountains, or even the sadness of the impending goodbye with their horses. For that noise had told them only one thing, and it was awfully difficult to try and put any other spin on it with the deep black of night all around you. There was something out there. Something which sounded both hungry and angry in the worst possible ways.

They all tried not to but couldn't help themselves, couldn't help but stare intently at the black around them. Once you focused on it, it seemed that, rather than being one colour, it was in fact many different shades, and, like wax balls in oil, these shades were lazily drifting around. When you are looking for something, you almost inevitably see it (although not when its something you've lost) and they were seeing a lot. Every time a slightly deeper shade of black touched a lighter one, they saw a monster. Every time their pupils refocused as they strained them even harder, they saw a claw or a talon. Every snort from the restless horses nostrils had them jumping out of their skin. Their heartbeats did not settle into a steady rhythm for the rest of that evening.

None of them would have said it at the time for fear of bringing down the morale of the others or losing face, but that night was one of the worst they had ever experienced. It was the same kind of mortal dread that a real bad trip can bring on, only this time there was no telling yourself that it was all in your head. Whatever was out there was most certainly real...and it was hunting them.

Chapter 4.

The hunt.

1.

Following Eree was like following a dandelion seed in a hurricane. She was clearly trying to cover her tracks and therefore must not want to be found. This gave Veo hope, as it suggested that things between her and Gask were well and truly finished. But it made his job of finding her much harder.

The Gods all shared a connection and could send messages to each other across vast incomprehensible distances. They could also, to a degree, sense where other Gods were. But if someone did not want to be found, they could close off these connections.

Not completely though.

If Eree had not been in hiding, her location would have been instantly knowable to Veo, especially with how he felt about her. As it was, there was only the faintest of traces in the air. The last little bit of energy that Eree had not been able to completely keep within herself as she'd travelled. As Veo followed it around suns and through meteor storms, he tried not to let himself get too excited. Was it possible that she'd left this little channel ever so slightly open for his benefit?

Mind you, if that had been her intention, she could have made it slightly easier for him. The trail was leading him to endlessly diverse and unlikely places. Ice worlds, whose only inhabitants were small lizards, resting peacefully beneath the surface. Planets completely covered in water, whose residents would one minute be walking upon the surface like it was stone and then dive in and swim like dolphins the next. Even planets with no life seemed to have been visited by the wandering Goddess. What *was* she looking for?

Every time Veo arrived somewhere new, he got the same sensation. She had been there alright but she certainly wasn't there now. It was almost impossible to tell if he was getting any closer to her or not. Perhaps he was doomed to follow her for all eternity, never getting any closer or any further away. He would not entertain these thoughts for long. Veo was not a God who ever doubted his own abilities. Gask was more powerful than him, it was true, but better? A ridiculous notion.

He did not know whether it came from her relaxing, or perhaps becoming exhausted, or whether she deliberately allowed a bit more of herself to escape, but something changed. And it was in this change that he saw his opportunity.

Suddenly he knew where she was.

The little ghost of a light which had been dancing around his mind, pulling him to and fro, to places beautiful and places hideous, suddenly glowed just that little bit brighter. He no longer needed to take the route she had been spinning him, like a spider whose attic corner was the whole universe. He could now go direct. And she was not far away.

Veo flew like a comet. The space around him, no stranger to sudden and invasive forces that shatter its typical calm, was blown apart. The speed at which Veo moved almost transcended the laws they had created. It was as if the universe itself had to change to accommodate the burning arrow that was tearing through it. He closed himself off to the other Gods, for if he didn't, then they would sense his activity. But he did not close himself off to her. It was, in a way, a strange decision. It was completely contradictory to what he was trying to do. A hunter who has been stalking a deer will not, once he gets close enough for the kill, run screaming towards it, he will remain hidden until the fatal moment. Veo had burst out of the undergrowth and given the deer every possible warning that he was coming.

But perhaps it was not so strange at all. By giving her the opportunity of escaping once more, Veo would learn that which he desired to know beyond all else; did she really want to escape from him?

For one of the few times in his life he felt genuinely nervous. As he slowed and breached the atmosphere of the world of Svin, he felt his gut clench. His normal cold reserve seemed lost to him. The green world raced up to greet him, and he felt like he knew as little about himself as this hitherto unvisited place.

He landed and caught his breath. It had been quite a distance he'd just covered. Possibly an unprecedented amount in one journey, especially in such a tiny span of time. It had taken a lot out of him. He looked down at his hands and was more than a little shocked to see that they had holes in them. He could see the fresh green of the grass in his palm, though there was no grass in his hand. He looked at his arms and saw the same problem; parts of his body seemed to have disappeared as he'd travelled. Not a nice thing to find out at the end of a long journey, and certainly an issue which must be dealt with in the immediacy.

Veo knelt down and focused his energy on healing. It was only then that he realised what danger he was in. He'd been injured before, sometimes badly so, but healing had always come easily. The damage he'd now inflicted upon himself was clearly of a different nature to anything he'd previously experienced. As he watched in horror, the holes in his body began to increase in size, the edges burning like waxy paper. Veo grabbed hold of his knees and pulled himself into a ball, as if by making himself as small as possible he could hold onto his rapidly disappearing life force. He strained with all his might to stop it, but it seemed like the holes were not only appearing in his body but also in his mind.

Veo was dying.

It had all happened so quickly and soon there would be no more. Where did Gods go when they died? It was not something he'd ever considered. As his body burned and his mind began to break, Veo thought only of Eree. He raised his eyes and tried to picture her. There was a line of trees ahead of him, the beginnings of a forest, and behind them great, grey mountains. He focused all his energy into visualisation. She wore a white dress and stood just in front of the trees, like, well…a Goddess he supposed. He was glad that, in his last ever moments, he'd conjured such a realistic image of her. It genuinely felt like she was there, and there was no one else he'd rather have with him…

Images flashed in front of his mind, little gleams of silver, and he wondered if this was part of the dying process or whether he'd begun his journey into the place beyond, if indeed there was such a thing. He just hoped he wouldn't end up in the red place. He'd seen it once and that was more than enough. The silver streaks were playing with each other, like two strands of silk, completely dexterous and forming all sorts of things that he could not quite give a name to. It was peaceful to watch them, but he supposed that there must be more. It didn't seem possible that he would just stay here watching this odd little show for the rest of eternity. Nice as it was, it would probably get boring after a while and eternities are full of whiles.

It was an odd feeling having no body, as well you might expect. It reminded Veo of when they'd first become and when he'd helped Gask overcome Rez. Eree had been there then and she'd fought magnificently. He tried to gauge more of what was around him but could not. Whatever this place was, it was constricting him. He had no movement and no power, he was only a spectator.

Then the world rushed back towards him. The two silver strands grew fatter, like pythons digesting prey much bigger than themselves. Through these gaps, reality, if that was what it was, came charging back. Veo felt like he landed hard on the earth, but... surely he had been there the whole time. The world trembled around him with the force of it. Birds, none too pleased with it all, came pouring upwards out of the forest. Veo blinked a couple of times and then his eyes focused. Sure enough he was alive and, quite literally, in one piece. He looked around trying to find the reason for his inexplicable salvation.

That was when he saw *her*.

His heart stuttered. It had been so long since he'd actually seen her and now to be somewhere removed from the kingdom, removed from the place which had always suppressed the possibility of their love blossoming. It was one of the best moments of his life, and there had been a few.

'You were dying,' she said. It was strange, but it almost sounded like a question. Almost like she was accusing him of trying to do it.

'And you saved me,' he said. She nodded. There was a strange tension in the air between them. Was she happy to see him, or nervous? It was impossible to tell. Her body language did not read well. It seemed that, although she had indeed just saved him, she was now braced for conflict. He was struggling to think clearly, struggling to form the right words in his mind to put her at her ease. Looking back, the ones he did utter were an awful choice, 'Gask sent me,' he said. Her expression changed instantly. No longer was there the hint of happiness which had so excited Veo. As quickly as he'd arrived, he'd made an enemy of his love.

Wordlessly she turned and began to walk away towards the forest. Veo rose clumsily to his feet and staggered. He needed more time to recover from his ordeal but he could not let her get away, not after everything. The thought of losing her again…

'Eree!' he shouted and it reverberated around the mountains returning to him although she did not. 'Eree!' he yelled again and the braver birds who had remained in the forest now took their leave. He ran after her, his vision blurry but she a white, crystalline beacon ahead of him. As he neared her she did not turn, and he put his hand on her shoulder…at least, that was what he'd intended to do. The process of almost dying and then the subsequent recovery had left him in a pretty bad way. Gods, as is well documented, have an awful lot of power and, like the sorcerers, a lot of their skill is in control and regulation, rather than just blasting things apart. In his delirious and confused state, Veo had lost all ability to regulate anything and thus his hand crashed down onto Eree's shoulder with the force of a glacier and a hundred thousand times the speed.

She wheeled around clutching the resulting wound, eyes wide with surprise. He tried to find words, tried to express the horror he felt at what he'd just done. He would never have wished to harm one jet-black hair on that beautiful head. For a moment there was nothing, and then she attacked.

Veo and Eree's relationship had gone through an awful lot in a very short time. Less than a minute ago she had saved his life and now she was trying to kill him. I think most of us have probably had experience of relationships like this one way or another. What we've had no experience of (in the vast majority of cases) is seeing two immensely powerful Gods fighting. Veo and Eree flew above the mountains locked in a death grip. It was taking all Veo's energy to stop her from killing him, so he had none to try to shout that this was a mistake, he wished her no harm…quite the opposite in fact. Eree was fighting viciously. She'd managed to get a strong hold of Veo and she was now flying at breakneck speed back down towards the mountains. She was going to smash him into the top of one of those mighty peaks and it wasn't going to be pleasant. His arms were locked behind her back and, even at a time like this, he couldn't help but notice how nice it felt. He tried to wriggle one hand free and punch with it. He had to loosen her grip. As the mountains accelerated towards them, he realised he wasn't going to manage it.

He was going to have to think bigger.

Drawing on all his creative abilities, he clove a hole between the mountains. Eree braced for impact but there was none, instead they were flying through a tunnel which exploded ahead of them as they flew. Veo was literally cutting a hole through the earth. Finally he got enough of his arm free to push her away. She hit the wall of the tunnel hard, as did he, and they bounced back at each other. This time she sought not to grab him but to smash. Her small fists flew at him with power enough to lift whole castles from their foundations. He blocked what he could but took a fair few hits. He did not want to reply in turn, but he would not survive long like this. So he too began to hit, and it hurt him a great deal more than it hurt her. And still they fell, plummeting deeper and deeper into the tunnel yet staying only ten feet above its bottom. Veo was struggling to maintain the concentration needed to both build the tunnel and stop her blows but he had to do both, for if he stopped building now, she might not be able to stop herself ploughing into the bottom. It was too risky.

Just as he was having these thoughts, she caught him right in the jaw and he smashed harder than ever into the wall of the tunnel. Then, as the next punch came in, light exploded in front of his eyes. He thought it was perhaps a result of the blow but he was so wrong. Their tunnel had reached its natural ending…well, more like half of it really.

Veo and Eree tumbled into the very centre of Svin.

There seemed to be some issues with gravity in this place as they were no longer falling, they were now floating. Not that flying would have been a problem. It was just that they weren't. For a moment they rested, floating not far from the great molten ball which stretched out as far as the eye could see. Great dollops of lava were flung out in all directions and fiery explosions erupted beneath them. It was a mini sun within a huge stone catacomb. Quite a sight to behold, although less impressive if you were involved in its creation. Again, Veo tried to form words. If he could just reach out to her and let her know that they could stop this fight. He was not Gask's assassin or his kidnapper. He was, indeed, nothing to Gask and everything to Eree. If only she knew.

Again she crashed into him. This time she grabbed his arms, swung him round and then flung him towards the inferno below. For a terrible moment he thought he wouldn't be able to stop himself. The lava reached out as if wanting to grab him and pull him in. Would this planet survive, Veo wondered, if he were to explode in its very core. It certainly wouldn't be pretty. He turned and saw Eree floating by the mouth of his tunnel. She was charging up a ball of energy in her hand, seemingly completely unaware of the danger they were in even by being in this place. They would not survive long down here, certainly not both of them. Veo supposed that it was now or never, he had but one chance to make this right and it meant putting his beloved in a whole lot of danger. But choices were for those not locked into a divine battle next to a planet's worth of lava. Veo flew straight and true, harnessing not only the last of his own energy but that of the great ball behind him. He saw Eree's eyes widen for the a split of a second, she had clearly not been ready for his pace.

Then, with all his might, he hit her.

It pained him to do it more than anything he'd ever done, and all he could do, as he watched her unconscious body flying back up the tunnel, was pray he had not done too much. He joined her on her upwards trajectory. The oxygen from the world above was pouring into the chamber and the fire was more than a little pleased to see it. Just as the ball threatened to swell up out of its chamber, Veo's tunnel began rebuilding itself. The rock fell back in and took the pressure of the force below. Veo, having used so much his remaining strength on his last vicious and mutually painful attack, was losing consciousness. His flight became slower and slower yet he still caught up with Eree. Taking her in his arms, he drove with everything towards the tiniest pinprick of light which he hoped against hope he wasn't imagining. The reality of his world mirrored that of the effects of losing consciousness. He was at the end of a long dark tunnel trying to reach the light at the end both metaphorically and physically. The tunnel was within another, and both threatened to defeat him.

Yet the warm body in his arms, still prickling with the after effects of battle, gave him strength. The tunnel was now sealing itself of its own accord, he had lost control of it and, if he could not keep ahead of it, both he and his love would be forever buried here. But while he had the Goddess in his arms, he would not be defeated. Rocks clipped at his heals as the tunnel's point of resealing came up ever closer. He closed his eyes and willed his heart to take whatever it could from the unconscious Goddess and…yes! There was something there to take, perhaps she was coming to. Anyway, there was no time for such speculating. Harnessing the little bit of extra power that they now shared, Veo drove on. The mouth of the tunnel grew bigger, the sun above it offering the most welcoming of lights. Once again locked in each other's arms, Veo and Eree flew out of the tunnel which, with one final crunch, sealed itself forever. The mountains, obliging sorts that they are, slid without fuss back into their previous positions.

The two Gods, finally both unconscious, fell into the forest. They lay there in a clearing sleeping as peacefully as children. To look at them you wouldn't suspect that they had almost destroyed a world. They had also, completely unwittingly, created something.

A group of little cave dwelling creatures in the mountains had just inherited a hell of a lot of power and seen a display that they could not have possibly imagined, and their tiny, exceptionally well-organised society had just changed forever. Veo wasn't to know this then, but one day these little creatures would have the biggest of influences on what happened to the God.

2.

Shabwan the fool watched on in amazement. When the Gods had fought, he'd felt such a sense of recognition but he could not tell where it came from.

Had he himself experienced a similar situation? It seemed hugely unlikely, but then...he was interrupted from this train of thought as the story was clearly about to continue. The two Gods, who'd been sleeping in that familiar little clearing in the woods, were coming to. Shabwan the fool flapped at the flying fish who were attempting to take his attention, and gave his mind back to Veo's story.

3.

Rather predictably Veo and Eree woke up at the same time. Even in the realms of the Gods it's difficult to escape clichés. For a moment they looked at one another and Veo wondered if she would attack again. So exhausted was he that he would probably just let her kill him. But she did not attack.

'Why did you want to hurt me?' she asked and he was amazed to see tears in her eyes. He had barely ever seen her show any emotion, despite all the time he'd spent with her. He opened his mouth hoping against all hope that words would come and, finally, they did.

'I didn't mean to...I came here to tell you...' he faltered. Was this the right thing to do? He was Gask's lieutenant, his trusted right hand man, perhaps even his friend. Then he looked up and met her eyes and such thoughts evaporated as quickly as morning dew in the desert (which wouldn't have had much business being there, to be perfectly honest).

'I love you.'

Then they were in each other's arms. As they made love, the forest swayed to and fro around them. Just as the world had been conspirator in their fight, it was now in their lovemaking. The exhaustion they'd both been suffering with after the battle, which had almost claimed both of their lives and perhaps a planet to boot, was gone. Euphoria took over the work that was normally done by other parts. When you are truly in love, one smile and a wink is enough to make you feel like you can run up a mountain. So when you're making love for the first time on the forest floor, the energy required kind of takes care of itself.

With the union of their bodies complete, they slept for what could have been months. It certainly seemed to be a different season when they awoke. Once more they made love and all was right with the universe.

4.

The fool didn't understand why he was being shown such intimate things but then, he was a fool. But perhaps he had a good point. Veo, watching on from afar, felt no shame or embarrassment that the young man was currently feeling confused by the most tender and personal moments of his life. He was far past that point now. There was benefit indeed and much to be learned from the way this young stranger was reacting to the things he saw. He wasn't exactly endeavouring to hide his emotions. Indeed often he cried out, adding his own dialogue and music to the story. Perhaps under different circumstances it would have been funny.

5.

Like so many love stories, and as I'm sure you've guessed by now, the story of Veo and Eree did not have a happy ending. And so as we rejoin the two lovers in the forest that has become their home, we must perhaps be a little bit sensitive that we are joining them at one of the worst moments in their lives. It feels wrong to intrude, but sometimes you must. As I said, Veo is now long past caring...

'Why would we go back there?' said Veo and later it seemed strange to him that he hadn't sensed the danger immediately. 'Do you want to fight him?' Eree only shook her head. Veo's mind clawed around for other possible alternatives, while resolutely ignoring the big one that could not in a million universes be the one he was looking for. She was staring at him now in a way he did not like. It was as if she was willing him to understand without her speaking. He couldn't understand why. Conversation had been flowing so freely and easily between the two of them.

'If we go back and tell Gask what has happened he will try to kill us both. Now this is absolutely fine by me, but such a conflict needs to be prepared for and I really don't see what the rush could possibly be...' There was something sneaking around the outskirts of Veo's mind. A bit like the creature that stalks Shabwan's four travelling friends and just as dangerous. They have their little circle of firelight and beyond it lies something horrible. Likewise, just outside the discernible parts of Veo's psyche there was something that he had no desire to entertain. A thought he would happily destroy with all the might that was his.

'We cannot live like this,' she said. The tears were streaming but her voice did not crack. He would have preferred it if it had.

The argument raged through days and nights, and once again the world around them became representative of what passed between them. The branches of the trees hung sadly down and no bird sang as the sun made its traditional morning appearance. Veo screamed that he did not care about Gask or any of them, all he wanted was her. He would live a life of exile, happy to be hunted by Gask for all eternity, happy even to fight him, despite standing so little chance of victory. There was no reason in all the universe why a love such as theirs should not be allowed. She wept and wept and said that she loved him. But love apparently was not enough on its own. He begged to differ and beg he did. Without her there was nothing. The life he'd had before and his dreams of taking control of the kingdom of the Gods felt as meaningless as the grass beneath his feet. As the reality of the situation closed in on him, he remembered the great fiery ball and the tunnel which he'd somehow saved them both from. Would now that either had claimed them. Perhaps there was a place beyond this one. A place where nothing prevented them from being together. Or even if there was nothing, just a blank abyss, then that would be preferable to what she was proposing.

Argue as he might it came to no avail.

'We must go back to him and we must pretend none of this ever happened,' she said. 'Our duty is to this universe and its protection. We have forgotten that and put ourselves first. Gask will by now have selfishly created these beings to do his work for him and we cannot allow more of this to happen. Don't you see where it could lead?' Veo couldn't have given a stuff (or any number of less polite vernaculars) about where it could lead. Gask and his damn guardians, or any other inhabitant of the universe, concerned him not. For Veo, it was only he and her. For her it was apparently not the same. Then she said the thing which he never quite forgave her for, much as he always loved her.

'If you love me, you will do this.'

She probably didn't mean it, but in saying these eight words she had condemned him to the life of a prisoner. Act and you hurt me, do nothing and you love me. It was worse than a death sentence. Before she'd said these words, Veo would have done anything to prove to her both what he felt and what they could have. He would have marched up to Gask in front of all the Gods, told him what had happened and then fought him to the death. He would have flown into the heart of a sun just to get her to see what she meant to him. But once she had spoken those words…there was nothing for him now.

Together they travelled back, barely speaking or looking at one another. Every second brought them closer to home, although that word now seemed as inaccurate as it were possible for a word to be. As they neared the kingdom, they shared one last kiss and Veo always remembered that particular moment as being the most painful.

Gask greeted Eree with a surprising show of emotion. Holding her tightly to his chest and whispering his apologies into her ear. He didn't even mind that every God present had come out to cheer and applaud. They had their queen back; Veo, on the other hand, had lost his forever.

Gask looked at him with tears in his eyes and mouthed his thanks. Veo had never received any token of gratitude from him before, he bowed his head in respect. As his heart broke in two, he took on his new mantle. He took on the character he must now live as in order to protect her. And thus Veo tricked the king of the Gods. not an easy thing to do by any means, and the chamber treated him accordingly.

Chapter 5.

Flow.

1.

The being that was Rez sensed the opportunity. His agent on the other side was nearing the point of success. Finally he was going to get another shot, and this time there would be no failure. The Gods, and the laughable parody of a universe they'd created, would all burn. As his desire grew so did the flow. He did not try to stop it. Let his energy pour forth. Once his agent had opened the smallest of channels, then all would come through anyway. Why not let them have just a little bit more in the meantime.

Around him winged demons, excited by the increase, flapped and screeched, occasionally lashing out and biting at one another. Rez's dimension was a fluid place where energy, rather than substance, made up all that there was. Soon he would crash through into the other dimension where the physical would be his to manipulate and then what a universe he'd build. But first he'd have to destroy every last living thing. He had no interest in what Gask had made beyond the destruction of it.

2.

There was more energy than ever and it tore at Lubwan. The spell whipped and lacerated his old skin. Blood flowed from several small wounds, which were fast becoming bigger. Yet still he focussed everything on that one point in the barrier. A stream of savage, jagged light flowed from his hands up into the twisted purple and red sky, where the barrier was beginning to buckle. Around the zenith of Lubwan's spell, the opaque barrier was twisting and looked like it was beginning to melt. Indeed, great lumps of it were starting to fall, like enormous blobs of candle wax, onto the hideous landscape around.

A landscape which was getting awfully busy.

For beings of every shape and form, great deformed monstrosities, were bearing down on Lubwan. He was stood on a ledge of a small cliff overlooking a vast flat plain, and over this plain all sorts of things were coming. Things that he had no desire at all to get better acquainted with. Leading the charge were the heinous four legged beasts, some with snakes for tails, some with great, elongated heads and hungry jaws. Behind them, coming at a much slower but equally inevitable pace, were the larger ones. Roaring they were, excited at the prospect of a feast. Magic like this had not been used here for a long time and they could not wait to devour the one who was bringing it.

Lubwan tried not to look at them. He kept his focus upon that little point in the sky. The barrier was almost broken; you could see around the spell a little circle of gorgeous blue daylight that looked nothing like the supposed 'sky' of this place. It gave Lubwan hope and brought memories flooding back. He batted them away. This was absolutely no time for nostalgia. Some of the sprightlier beasts were now climbing his cliff. They would be upon him very soon. Thankfully, as well as being determined to get to him, they were also determined that no other was going to, so fights were breaking out fairly regularly. It would only be so long though until he saw a great purple claw heaving its owner up onto his little podium. Then the following seconds would be both his last and also deeply unpleasant.

3.

'What the hell is going on!' screamed Kayleigh and she was right to ask. Around them the world was going mad. The forest ahead of them was thrashing about as if every last tree were alive and as light as a blade of grass, the noise it made was deafening. Above them the sky was thick with birds seemingly in a blind panic, flying in every direction. They had to cling onto their horses with all their might as they bucked and kicked.

Coki looked on in amazement as a thin crack appeared at the top of one of the mountains and then split it like a block of wood straight down the middle. The grass beneath their feet leapt into the air as if ripped and was then dispersed by the wind that had sprung up. Although, it was not like any wind they had ever experienced. It seemed not to be made of air but of something more…tingly, and instead of bouncing off their bodies it was going straight through them, as it did so they felt its power. Every last particle of their bodies seemed to shake and vibrate in time with the world around them.

'What the hell is that?!' yelled Lewhay. Coki tried to follow the direction of his finger, which was fairly difficult in itself, but then once you looked up it was not difficult to see what he was pointing at…

4.

Durpo was shaking.

People ran in a manner which they always seem to at times like this. Which, when you think about it, is a bit strange. How can you run from something which is everywhere? In the mayor's office, Rachel was trying not to explode. The flow was coming from everywhere and it was too much to control. Even those who had little or no skill could feel the magic flowing through them; imagine what it was like for one such as her. It felt like her body was disintegrating, as if only her will power was stopping her from becoming a human hourglass.

Eventually she fell and came to rest with her head below the window of her office. That was when she saw the sky.

Out in the streets others had also looked up, and once you did it was hard to look down again.

For the sky was on fire.

Up in the clouds, a section of the sky was twisting as if at the top of a great tornado, but there was none to be seen. The surrounding clouds were being sucked in to this burning plughole and beyond it there was...well it looked like more sky but what kind of sky would look so terrible as this?

'It's another world,' screamed someone in Durpo's main square and those around felt inclined to agree. There was clearly some world beyond this one and whatever, wherever it was, it was breaking through.

5.

The chamber was also shaking. Inside it Vericoos was thrown from wall to wall like a rag doll. He tried to get a hold of something, to wedge himself in somehow but could not. The red angry cracks in the walls were getting a hell of a lot redder and a heck of a lot angrier (hell of course being worse than heck as we're all well aware). The chamber would not hold out much longer and the doors were showing no signs of opening...

6.

Lubwan had dropped to one knee and was in danger of dropping to another. He was dying. The spell was quite literally tearing him apart and if he continued much longer there would be nothing left for the fast climbing beasties.

No sooner had this thought articulated itself in his exhausted mind than a hairy, clawed leg appeared over the lip of the cliff and was soon followed by another. The creature then heaved itself up and Lubwan saw its terrible jaws, salivating madly. It stood up on its hind legs and roared ferociously, extending one hideous claw skywards ready to slash it down upon the old sorcerer. On the foul things chest, a line of central mouths chattered and clicked horribly. Doesn't the damn thing have enough teeth? thought Lubwan as he prepared for the worst. The arm began to descend and everything went slow. The last thing Lubwan thought of was Vericoos, the grinning face of his nemesis was not an image that he was particularly happy to be going out with, but it didn't seem to be up to him anymore.

Then, like a snake recoiling, the beam of light that had been flowing between his hands and the sky shot upwards pulling Lubwan with it. As he flew he felt the air swish past his face and a clawed hand ever so close but not quite close enough. The last thing he heard as he exited that hated dimension was a thousand roars of anger from the plain miles below.

7.

Just as quickly as it had begun it was over. The great spinning ball of light in the sky, which was seemingly sucking the rest of the air into it, closed with a faint popping sound. All that had been utter madness was calm. The sky was as blue as it had ever been and the foundations of Durpo felt solid once more. In her office Rachel opened her eyes, she was alive.

8.

Many, many miles away the four friends looked at one another, too shocked to speak. The crack in the mountain was still evident but the forest now seemed to be behaving itself. The birds, although somewhat disgruntled, were going back to their normal business, whatever that is.

111

Only Lewhay had been looking up at the sky at the moment when the hole had closed and…well, he wasn't sure of much anymore. But if you'd asked him about it as, unfortunately, no one did, he would have said that he fancied he'd seen something ever so small come through the gap in the sky just before it had closed. Something that had then flown straight and true in the exact direction they were going.

He thought about telling the others but then thought better of it. There was enough going on right now without adding another mystery.

9.

The chamber was still in one piece although that was more than could be said for Vericoos. The old man had taken quite a battering. He put his hand up to his head and felt blood. Still, nothing that wouldn't heal. He wasn't sure what could have caused such a surge in the flow, but he doubted whether the chamber or he would survive another assault. The important thing was that it *had* survived and the confrontations were, as far as he could presume, still going on. It took him a few seconds to notice the slight but ever so significant change in the room and when he did he howled with animalistic rage. For, on one of the three silver plaques, something had been added. Something which could only mean one thing. It read: *The Fool, the Trickster and the Other*

Chapter 6.

Asylum.

1.

Durpo, the great city by the sea, was as calm as anyone could ever remember. Granted it had just been rocked, quite literally, to its very foundations but that was yesterday. And in times of progression and excitement, yesterday's mistakes and fears hurtle off into the horizon of history and few people even watch them go. Magic was now being openly used everywhere you looked. Houses were cleaner than they'd ever been. Stalls were erecting themselves and fish were being plucked out of the waters with no need for net or rod. Ironically enough, this meant that more were being caught than ever, not news that would have excited environmental activists, so keen to see the demise of the fishing net.

People greeted each other merrily and hearty laughter was heard anywhere you cared to listen. No one was in a hurry.

In the times of old, which were in fact only two days ago, the lives of so many in the city had been an eternal rush. There was so much to do and so little time to do it. Now there was so *much* time to do it, for the work of an hour had become the work of the moment and backs, which had once been almost broken by toil, were now straight and proud. Muscles, which had been twisted into impossible shapes, were loose as if they'd been massaged for hours.

Mayor Louie's legacy, a lifetime in the making, had been forgotten in the space of twenty four hours. For this was new Durpo and had there ever been a better time to be alive anywhere?

There were, however, those who were not happy. And they were the ones who had previously had the lion's share of the happiness. Those who had lorded their way around Durpo no longer felt secure in their great piles of wealth. Word travelled fast of what the young woman who now held the reins intended for their city. And to have an elite clique at the top of a pile it most certainly wasn't. When money is the currency to which all are slave then those who have it needn't worry about being in the minority. Quite the opposite. Their finances mean that they can live sheltered existences, protected from normal life and from contact with the have-nots by a barrier of coins. The fact that for every one of you there are ten thousand of them is not worth thinking about, because those ten thousand others are kept well in check by a system of beliefs and authority which owes an awful lot to you. The guard, or police or whatever they happen to be called in your universe, are not a state body, designed to keep the peace and ensure justice, they are your personal security firm, willing to do your bidding at a moment's notice. The laws, that you insist are upheld so brutally amongst the proletariat, are more like guidelines for you and yours. Nice ideas which, of course, you will follow the *majority* of time, but if it becomes in your best interests to cast a blind eye over one of those little rules then…why the hell shouldn't you?

Unfortunately, most of the people who aspire to these beliefs continue to do so throughout their lives, generally speaking, without negative consequence. You only have to look into our own government to see this brutal hypocrisy in action. Rioting and smashing the streets up is the gravest of offences and the offenders should be hung out to dry, whereas fleecing tax money from those who have such great need of it to further subsidise your own luxurious lifestyle…well, these things happen. I'm not claiming to be in support of the destruction and terror caused by riots, but I am saying that you don't have to be a genius to point out the flagrant disregard and hypocrisy which is rife among the ruling classes in all worlds.

The former rulers of Durpo, those who'd been ever so tight in Mayor Louie's little circle (and in his pocket), were quaking in their boots and I, for one, couldn't be happier.

For money, the building blocks of life, was suddenly not quite so important after all, and the traditional concepts of having and not were being ever so severely challenged. Rachel had apparently promised that no harm would come to anyone under her watch. But, as the rich looked out of the windows in their ivory towers and saw the party that was in full swing below, this offered them little comfort. Those they'd been so busy oppressing for all these years might not be quite so forgiving as the woman in the mayor's office.

As the majority of Durpo embraced the glorious new era, there were a select few who would have given anything to turn back time. Little did they know that circumstances were about to conspire in their favour. And I, for one, couldn't be unhappier about it.

2.

Thon came charging into Rachel's office. As usual knocking proved to be a bridge too far in the courtesy stakes. Rachel was sat at her desk and looked like she'd been deep in thought. Thon was exhilarated. He'd been spending a lot of time out in the streets, celebrating in public with his adoring fans, and then celebrating in a much more private fashion with smaller, select groups of them. Life had never been so sweet.

'The city is alive,' said Thon. 'It's amazing out there.' Rachel smiled at him. It was a warm smile but also a reserved one. There was something lacking in it.

'I trust you've been enjoying yourself?' Thon's only answer was to laugh and take a clumsy seat in the corner. He looked like he had not been to bed. After a while he clearly felt slightly awkward. He had, after all, charged into the office, boasted a little and then sat down without saying anything or asking Rachel a single question. Even an ego such as his would struggle to justify such behaviour as polite.

'So, how are you?' he asked.

'I'm fine,' she said, as ever giving little away. Thon suddenly felt frustrated. The lack of sleep and increased levels of blood in his alcohol stream were doing nothing to bring out his best side.

'And that's all you have to say to me is it?' he spat rather nastily. This time she did not smile and he felt her ever-potent threat. He may have gained something on gallows day, but he was still no match for her...not yet.

'What would you have me say Thon?' she asked and it was a genuine question. He faltered, he hadn't actually thought this far ahead.

'I just...I want to know what the plan is...we did this together, this is our city.' As he said this she stood up and slammed her hand down on the table. It crackled a little.

'This is not *our* city Thon,' she said, anger lighting her eyes. 'This city belongs to the people. The people have asked us to take care of it for them, not to own it. As happy as those people are out there, it will not last forever. New problems will arise and it will be our job to deal with them and help people.' He felt his own anger levels rising, much as he feared her.

'Then what was all that with the council about redistribution of wealth and whatnot? Is that not owning the city?'

'That was me trying to do what is best for now. I've spent my whole life watching people starve and suffer. I was given a chance to do something which I saw as good and I took it.' She sounded slightly defensive in spite of her conviction.

'And how exactly are you going to go about doing it?' asked Thon nastily. His cynical nature was giving him the upper hand in this little spat.

Rachel looked down. Perhaps she too was experiencing life a little further into the future than she'd actually planned.

'I don't have all the answers, Thon, but I intend to do my best and I'd much rather do it with you at my side than have to fight you every step of the way.' Her words cooled the superficial side of the argument but they stoked the coals in his heart. It was an odd dynamic. Initially, when power had been all that mattered, she was the one. She was the one people spoke of and the one they admired beyond all else. Now the coup was complete and they had entered into the world of politics, Thon need not fear her quite so much. For she was going to have to present herself in a different way now. The running of Durpo had been forced upon her and now she was finding, as all leaders do, that the ideals are the easy bit. If you are unwilling to resort to the ways of tyranny, then getting them into practice is what takes all your damn time and energy.

Thon could see cracks appearing in that which had seemed so unbreakable.

It was at that point that Marie entered the room. She looked worried.

'What is it?' asked Rachel. Marie took a second to catch her breath. Then she spoke.

'People have been arriving in the city from Hardram,' she said. 'Lots and lots of them.'

'From Hardram?' put in Thon, confused. He didn't have celebrity status in Hardram. Marie only nodded. Then continued, 'they say the chamber is breaking.'

3.

Rachel was sat in a very busy room. The remains of the council were all there, as were the conspirators who had helped them stage the coup, as were seemingly hundreds of other people, the identities of whom remained a mystery.

They had listened to the stories of the refugees. Stories of how the red lines had first appeared as thin as thread, but were widening and widening. The chamber, which contained something terrible, was breaking.

Common opinion differed slightly on what was contained in that odd floating room but it was united on the fact that it was something that was much better contained than loose. Most agreed, however, that it was a God that had once plagued the people of Svin and had conquered the city of Hardram ,while Durpo remained evasive. It was something of an issue of pride amongst the people of the city, in fact.

This point was now being made by some old idiot,

'Well, we held him off before and I'm sure we can manage it again!' This was greeted with a mix of cheers and utter outrage, which, while conveying the mood of the room well, also made it difficult to concentrate.

'You're saying we stay here and fortify?' asked Rachel and, as per usual, the room fell quiet as she spoke.

'Yes,' said the man. 'A little less confidently now he was communicating directly with Rachel. 'Why should we mobilize an army, when we don't even know for certain if anything's going to come out of it. Why not prepare here and then if something does happen, we'll be ready and if it doesn't then nothing has been lost.'

Rachel looked at the old man, some elder statesman of the old city no doubt, still determined that his way was the right way.

'What do you think?' she was now addressing the group of high-ranking Hardramians who had been established as envoy by the arriving refugees.

'There is a feeling in the air,' said a woman, and Rachel could tell from the way the others reacted to her speaking that she clearly held a lot of respect. 'A feeling that has been around ever since it started breaking…a kind of malice. Whatever is in there will come out hard and will come out fighting. If we are to fight back then I would prefer to have the element of surprise on our side.'

'You mean, better to be there waiting for it than to let it compose itself and then come for us?'

'Exactly,' the woman nodded. Rachel looked at Marie, the young girl looked quiet and thoughtful, the polar opposite of Thon who was clearly unhappy with his current lack of contribution to events.

'Hang on a minute,' he started springing to his feet. 'This woman comes to our city and starts telling us what we should and shouldn't do. Sorry but, who actually are you?' The woman did not look put off or intimidated. She's been dealing with Thons her whole life, thought Rachel.

'I am Calandra,' she said. 'Leader of Hardram.' She said nothing more, clearly not feeling the need to justify herself to Thon's outburst. The effect was a good one, Thon was unsettled. The woman had responded politely to his question but given him no more. In doing so she'd taken all the momentum out of his anger. He now looked vulnerable, like a man who wished he hadn't jumped to his feet quite so enthusiastically.

Marie smiled inwardly. It was nice to see Thon's bullying nature cut down so quickly and efficiently. The room had fallen silent and very quickly become a bit of an embarrassing arena for old Thon. He tried to slink back a bit, but it's not easy when you've made yourself the centre of attention.

'I agree with Calandra,' said Rachel. 'If we have to fight I'd rather it be on our terms.' Thon looked daggers at her.

'You want us to leave the city!?'

'No one will be obliged to join the fight,' said Rachel, though she said it to the room at large, not to Thon.

'We will mobilise anyone who is willing and who has sufficient magical powers to march to Hardram. There we will wait and see what comes out of this chamber, if indeed anything comes out at all.'

The room seemed to murmur in agreement. Rachel looked at Losh, 'Will any of your guardsmen be willing to join the fight?' Losh nodded, I will spare anyone I can, he said.

'But of course it must be their choice,' added Rachel. Losh looked surprised at this. Giving his guardsmen a choice in matters had not been a huge part of his career.

'I will put the word out,' he said.

The atmosphere in the room was a resolute one. Much as Thon was standing there with his mouth wide open, the rest of the room seemed decided. The young woman had been sure footed in her decision making and it was a decision they were willing to follow. It was odd that a few weeks ago no one had known who she was. Now she was their leader and she was leading them to battle.

'The word must be put out in the city also,' said Rachel. 'We are going to need help from those with power. Losh, I am assuming that as we travel you will be able to provide some basic training.' The captain of the guard nodded. 'Then we shall recruit as quickly as we can and leave. You all felt what shook our city yesterday and it seems to me no coincidence that we are now confronted with this news. We do not want to be caught out by this.'

'And what of the city while you are gone?' The question came from somewhere, but no speaker became obvious. It didn't really matter all that much, Rachel supposed. The question was what mattered, not who was interested in the answer. The truth was that she had none. So much had happened so very, very fast and now they were being called upon to make yet another difficult decision. She knew nothing of the city really or how it should be run, she knew noting of politics beyond her own ideas of what was right and wrong. And, as we all know, the unfortunate truth is that such simple, sensible thinking does not tend to get an awful lot done. The camel is the horse designed by a committee and all that. Rachel trusted the word of these new strangers, especially those of their leader who, she was pleased to see, was a woman. Clearly Hardram was more forward thinking than the old Durpo had been. And if she trusted them, then there really was only one call to make. Thon could come or not come but she hoped against hope that he would. She did not want Durpo left under his care.

'Losh,' she said turning again to the captain of the guard. 'You know this place better than I do. You have served it for a long time. Who would you see left in charge while we are away?'

Losh was quickly becoming aware of what his new role entailed under the new mayor. Louie had always treated Losh as a dispensable commodity. Someone whose value was next to nothing despite the fact that the city would have fallen apart without him. There wasn't one occasion where he could remember Louie asking for his advice in anything beyond the absolute superficial. Now he was being asked to select a caretaker leader for the city as they departed for a battle against an unknowable foe.

'There is someone,' he said.

4.

James Walshoon had been a good servant of the city, but never an ambitious man. He had always done his best for his ward but had struggled under Mayor Louie. Never had much time been given to those whose ambitions stopped at improving the lives of those who'd elected them. What kind of work was that? Hence James' long and largely unnoticed life of servitude. He'd been popular in his area amongst those who he'd managed to help and was generally regarded as a good man. But once he'd stepped into the offices of the council, he'd been something of a figure of fun. A nobody whose ideas, once plentiful had become fewer and fewer with every harsh laugh he received.

Over the years he had become more and more invisible. Still he would attend the council's meetings and still he would try to argue his point and defend what he saw as right, but rarely was his voice heard. Or so he'd thought. Clearly someone had noticed because Losh, the captain of the guard was now suggesting that he take over the running of the city.

It was the most shocking moment of his life, as you might well expect.

Suddenly all eyes were on him, most notably the beautiful young woman who had graciously accepted the monumental task that she was now willing to bestow onto him. Losh was smiling at him encouragingly, it was strange. He felt like they'd always shared a mutually respectful relationship, Losh being the conscientious fellow that he was. But they had rarely spoken and certainly were not friends. Apparently Losh had taken a keener interest in James than anyone else at the council.

He was dimly aware that a decision was required of him. The small matter of whether or not he was willing to become caretaker ruler of the city while it went to war. James thought of his wife, she'd always believed he was capable of so much more than he himself had. She would be surprised by all this but would not doubt, for a second, that her husband was capable of whatever was asked of him. He was a man of duty and duty was calling in a voice louder than he could have ever imagined. As he opened his mouth he wondered, for a second, if words would come. They did.

'For as long as you want me to do it, I will take care of the city.' And just like that it was done. Thon was looking like someone had kicked him hard in the ambitions. But he said nothing. Losh was smiling broadly at James.

'This is excellent news,' said Rachel.

'I will leave my second in command and a large enough guard to run the city at your disposal,' said Losh. 'Beyond that, we will start recruiting and look to march on Hardram as soon as possible.'

You had to feel for the city in some respects. It had been through so much and now it was to go through some more. The new order was less than two days old, and now it was mobilised for war. Rachel had taken on the responsibility of mayor and, for all her doubts, she had done a damn fine job. The public and the council alike were happy for her to make the big decisions and to build the new Durpo. It was not something she herself had wanted but she'd been willing to do it nonetheless. Now, just as she was beginning to get her head around that first challenge, she was now to become a leader of an army. Not a trained army, at least not for the most part, more a gaggle of willing volunteers all trying to master new found abilities. It was certainly not something she'd ever asked for but she, like Marie, understood that a gift had been given to her. Her power was vast and such a thing could only have happened for a reason. It would have been churlish beyond belief for her to turn her back on the city...or the world. And it seemed that it was, indeed, the world that was under threat. She had known yesterday, when that terrible force had almost ripped her to shreds, that the world was under threat. The rest of the city's inhabitants had forgotten about it so quickly but she had not. But then, they had not felt it like she had. Then these newcomers had arrived and brought with them this news of a terrible evil poised to escape. It could not be coincidence. She knew not why the power had been bestowed to her but she knew, beyond anything else, that she must use it to help. Initially, she had believed that her responsibility would be to the city alone, but now she saw that it was much greater than that. If the evil burst forth then the world

119

would burn and she would not be the woman who stood by and let that happen. She trusted Losh, having seen how bravely he'd fought on gallows day and how quickly he'd reacted in an attempt to save Marie. It was a strange contradiction but one she liked, a man who was willing to fight even against his better instinct and yet was still able to realise, once the crucial moment came, the difference between right and wrong. He had sought her out as quickly as he could after the initial affray and explained to her that he had been no supporter of Louie. He had only led his men on gallows day in the hope of preventing a full-scale riot. She sympathised with this and accepted his apologies wholeheartedly. She also sensed how well he knew his way around the politics of the city, despite having never been directly involved in them.

That was why the decision had been his and she sensed he had chosen well. They had no choice but to put their faith in this James and hope all would be well on their return. She felt some confidence that it would be. There was something you could trust about the small unassuming man. A kind of anti-Thon-ness which comforted her.

Three days later the volunteers were amassed, about two hundred in all. Many more had wanted to come but Rachel had imposed tests to check that their magical abilities were up to scratch. She did not want people coming who would not be able to defend themselves. They were joined by about a hundred of Losh's watch and the man himself. Losh had left his second in command, Hani, in charge and told him to work closely with James. For Losh suspected that, in the wake of Rachel leaving, those who were none too pleased with her appearance may take the opportunity to stir up some trouble. Hani was not a man to be messed with and was wily enough to deal with the worst that the sly old foxes of Durpo could throw at him. With any luck they would return to find the city much as they had left it.

That was, of course, if they did return.

Chapter 7.

Three's a crowd.

1.

Shabwan was weeping, but he was also laughing. The two conflicting emotions pulled him in all directions. Part of him felt the heartache of the whole thing but to another part it all seemed entertainingly bizarre. Why had they all let it get so serious, he'd enjoyed the parts of the story when they'd fought and blown the world apart. It seemed annoying that they'd finished it with such a serious and upsetting conclusion. It had made him cry and he didn't want to cry. It made his eyes feel funny.

As he wiped the tears away, he became aware that he was no longer alone. A figure, not the one who had asked him for his trust, a new one, was advancing on him. For a second he did not know who he was looking at, but then he recognised the gait of his walk and the way he held himself. It was the God from the story. It was a strange sensation to see him as it seemed to Shabwan that this was the first time he'd encountered anything truly real. The figure who'd tested him had existed, it was true, but he had not been *real* in the way that Shabwan and Veo were.

There was also something real in the God's hand and it wasn't something Shabwan liked the look of. It was long, thin and shiny and, more importantly, very sharp. Shabwan tried to back away but the God was advancing fast. He seemed to have lost the face he'd boasted in the retelling of the story and replaced it with a horrible wooden mask. The expression chiselled across it was conveying all the malicious intent that must accompany the silver dagger he was holding.

The same part of Shabwan that had laughed at the funny images of the story was trying to get a foothold, but the impending mortal dread was keeping it at bay. Now was no time to laugh, much as he wanted to.

The God placed a heavy hand on Shabwan's shoulder and, once the fingers had closed, he knew there was no escape for him. The grip was so much more than physical. It rooted him to the spot, frozen still as a statue. All he could move were his eyes and these were glued to the silver blade that had now been drawn back and was pointing directly at his chest. Bizarre images popped in front of his mind, a burning house, a rock and a grinning bottle. Then the sky cracked.

It was a complex idea but one which manifested itself simply enough. It began at one horizon and went all the way to the other; suddenly giving Shabwan a sense of the space above him, there was an end to it! The God was also looking up and his grip on the shoulder lessened slightly. Shabwan was suddenly able to move again. He hit the arm hard but to no avail.

Indeed, the God didn't even seem to notice.

Shabwan, as he still wasn't able to escape, thought he might as well have a look at whatever was transfixing his mortal enemy. There it was, although *what* it was…

A light was flying down towards them, like a flaming arrow. Or perhaps, more accurately, a burning log from a great fire in the sky. Perhaps that was what there was beyond that thin crack. But then it couldn't be a bit of wood, or if it was, it was making an awfully human noise.

'Aaaaaaaaaargh' it seemed to be saying. Then it was upon them, a flash of light and then an impact. The link between Shabwan and his would be assassin was finally broken and he was able to roll away. When he got to his feet and rubbed his eyes clear, he was more than a little surprised to see that someone had joined them in this odd place. It was an old man and he did not look in a good way. A tattered old cloak, ripped in some places, completely absent in others, seemed only to be held to his body by the matted blood that was coming from endless wounds in the old man. His head was cracked across the top, in what looked like the nastiest of the injuries, and his eyes were bulging, almost completely red.

He and the God were looking at each other, seemingly in a state of equal surprise about this latest turn of events.

'You!!' yelled the God finally with the air of someone who was having to take in an awful lot of information very quickly.

'Me,' spat the other and then, quite literally, spat. 'It's been a while.'

2.

Recollection washed over Veo the trickster. Finally the dots were joined.

He'd decided, while watching the boy giggling and spitting at his life story, that he was going to kill him. It had been his suspicion from the start that this would end up being the function of his guest. He wasn't sure how he knew but he knew. Kill the boy and then see what came later, he could always bring him back to life if it turned out he'd made some…ahem…fatal error. But then just as the opportune moment had arrived so had the old sorcerer, and his memories had come flooding back. If the boy was his key, he was now looking at his prison warden. The one who had put him here, and he wasn't even *him*…he was part of *him*. To get back to wholeness and to freedom he was going to have to kill both of them.

3.

Lubwan lunged and smashed the God in his breastplate, the impact was sharp but Veo took the sting out of it with a downward block. As Lubwan swung in a hook, bearing with it a fistful of glistening magic, Veo ducked and the old sorcerer spun a full circle like an old drunk. As he completed the rotation he was greeted with a crashing elbow to his face and hit the ground hard. Veo jumped in the air and, as he began to descend, lined up his knee with the sorcerer's bleeding head. The impact would be more than enough to squash it flat. Shabwan didn't know who this stranger was, but in the wake of

122

recent events he had to conclude that he was a friend. Or if not a friend then preferable to the fellow who'd been about to stab him. It stood to reason. And if he didn't have reason, then what the hell did he have. Throwing his arms out in front of him he yelled a war cry, though it came out more like a burp. From his hands, instead of the white-hot energy he'd envisaged, a stream of madness came forth. Multi-coloured ribbons, fish, lumps of wood and what looked like pastry along with a great load of fruit flew outwards, and, ridiculous as his attack was, it was enough to force Veo back. For a moment the three of them stood there. Shabwan didn't know whether to laugh or not. Then a large fish landed on Veo's head and laugh he did.

The God, apparently, did not find it quite as funny and roared. The knife in his hand broke out of its original dimensions and became a great golden sword. He swung it at Shabwan and, this time, it was the sorcerer's turn to step in. He leapt up and, throwing up a sleeve of his cloak, which suddenly became as solid as a rock, he diverted the swipe. Shabwan threw up his arms, hoping something a bit more battle wise than fish and confectionary would flow forth. It did not. Indeed, it seemed Shabwan's contribution to this battle wasn't going to feature in any top ten lists. I'm not sure who would be keeping one anyway.

The sword was on its way back round and Shabwan had no cloak, especially not one he could make into a shield. The old sorcerer had made it look so easy. As the blade cut ever so slowly through the air Shabwan saw his own demise come with it. Soon his head would be spinning like a top, no longer the property of his body.

Then he was airborne. It took him a few seconds to adjust, and when he did he was laughing ecstatically. He didn't really know why, but it was probably something to do with the fact that he was now lying in the sorcerer's arms as they flew at breakneck speeds over the kingdom of the Gods. He craned his head up to see the God flying after them in hot pursuit. They were going to have a hell of a job getting away from him.

Chapter 8.

In the Forest.

1.

A stage of their journey was complete, meaning they had to say goodbye to their equine buddies. The final days ride to the woods had not been a pleasant one. Where there had been shouting and goading of whoever was bringing up the rear, there were now nervous shoulder checks. Even though they all knew that they were riding towards something, it felt awfully like they were running away from something.

The forest rose up to greet them and brought with it another uncomfortable memory. It was difficult to relax when the image of the seemingly placid trees thrashing about like tentacles was so fresh in the mind. The large crack separating one mountain into two served to remind them further. Without it, they might just have been able to convince themselves that what they'd seen the other day had been some bizarre figment of their collective imaginations. As it was, there was no such convincing. The world they were about to enter had temporarily become a hostile and dangerous place. Mind you, it was probably still preferable to what was out here. Would it follow them into the forests? There was perhaps only one way to find out, but they hoped they never would. They were deliriously tired after their sleepless night and following days ride but the idea of sleep brought no warmth or security. Indeed, it brought quite the opposite. While they slept they would be vulnerable.

The goodbye with the horses was emotional, as they had well suspected. It was heartbreaking to see the confusion in the beast's eyes. Why were they not continuing? Hadn't they been good mounts? they seemed to say. None of them said it, but all held the same suspicion that whatever had made that sound and then spent the night stalking around the outskirts of their camp may well nourish itself on the poor unsuspecting horses before continuing its pursuit of them.

Once in the woods, they began searching for a good spot to sleep. The trees indifferently watched them pass as they had watched many before. Soon the four friends found a small clearing which, coincidently enough, was where Vericoos and Shabwan had camped together before Shabwan had been taken by the Oo-jas and Vericoos had finally replenished his talent. This time they did agree on a watch rota. Sleep, as undesirable as it was, had become a matter that they didn't have a great deal of choice in.

Coki took first watch. It was terrifying. Whether it was because it was the first time he'd been alone with himself since they'd heard the noise, or whether the forests offered infinitely more scope for their fire to cast terrifying shapes, he wasn't sure. But he was seeing a lot of stuff. Still, none of it seemed to be attacking him and the two pans he clutched in his hands, as if his life depended on it, would make fine weapons if it came to that. He just hoped he got a chance to get a good swing before it was too late.

After a long time had passed and his eyes had begun to close, he woke Lewhay. His initial intention had been to take watch for the whole night, but once he'd begun to fall asleep he knew that his selfless act had slipped well into the realm of the opposite. If their watchman fell asleep, they were as good as dead. For there was no denying that something was out there. He could feel it.

2.

Upon being awoken, Lewhay's first instinct was to strike. You would have struck too if you'd been having Lewhay's dreams. Luckily, despite his massive levels of tiredness, Coki's reactions were still enough to ward off most of the blow. Lewhay grunted apologetically and stood up. There was little need for communication, and they didn't want to wake the other two. Lewhay took up a his new position, disorientated and bleary, but it wasn't long before the uncomfortable sharpness of anxiety set in. And soon he too was falling victim to the paranoia that had kept Coki awake for much longer than he ever should have been. As he stared out into the darkness, he tried not to let the little flashes of what could have been movement distract him too much. The fire was playing tricks on him. He sat with his back against a tree and tried just to concentrate on what was really there. It felt nice to have something solid behind him. The bark was smooth and seemed to welcome the curve at the base of his back. Soon enough his anxiety began to lift and his mind felt more focused.

He wasn't sure how long had passed but it had been a while. His back was beginning to get stiff so he stood up. It was probably time to wake Leeham for his shift. It wouldn't be a long one. The darkness had taken on that quality that it does just before dawn.

Lewhay put his hand on Leeham's shoulder and began to gently shake. Then something hit him hard and he went down.

3.

Morshev had been trying her best to hold off. She had come close when they were out in the open that night, the night when her snarl had betrayed her existence. But she had controlled herself. *They will lead you to him,* this was the mantra she chanted again and again in her head as every instinct screamed at her to rip and tear. They were in allegiance with her master's killer and they must be punished, but their time was not yet.

The next day they had rode fast and she had fallen behind. It did not trouble her as there was only one road that they could follow and their heavily eavesdropped conversation had made it perfectly clear that they were heading to the forest. She would catch up with them when they next stopped.

It came as somewhat of a surprise when she came across their four horses, wandering about aimlessly a short distance from where the forests began. There was no sign of the four and she guessed that they must have got their use out of the four creatures in front of her. As she neared them, they looked up and panic was plain to see in their eyes. They bolted together. Whether they stayed together by accident or not she didn't know but she had no trouble leaping onto the hind of the weakest. Her sharp claws tore through its flesh and its back legs buckled. The other three were soon gone; any camaraderie they had shared was not enough to keep them around. She feasted and her strength grew.

It did not take her long to find them in the forest. Theirs was the only fire and, as she got near, she felt the same overpowering wave of hate begin to cloud her judgment. The four of them shared such a bond, she could see it in the way the watchman was staying up for as long as he could. He desired to give comfort to the others, to let them sleep. She had known a love like that; a love stronger than that, and the one they would do anything for had taken it from her.

She wondered how far away their friend was and the thought of it troubled her. It was not something she had thought of until now. How long would she have to live like this? So close to the feast and not allowed to touch a morsel. It didn't bear thinking about so she tried not to. She settled down to rest but it did not come easy. The boy watching for her was not twenty feet away. She could be upon him in seconds and the desire to do so denied her a moment of true blackness. Instead, she stared into that offered by the wood and tried not to think of...well, anything.

Then a rustling stirred her attention. The boy had risen and was waking another. His tiredness must finally have defeated him. *Coward,* she inwardly sneered. If it had been her master in that position, she would never have slept. She would have died first. As he woke the other, the sleeper clumsily threw his fist out. They were edgy indeed. The boy had gone to sleep at last and found there only violence. Then he seemed to realise what was going on and he calmed. There was a moment between them and it was this that finally broke her resolve. The look in their eyes of such unspoken understanding, of such equality was too much to bear. All they had to do was look at each other and so much was expressed, gratitude, responsibility, affection. They could convey it to one another as easily as if it were nothing. *How dare they?* The right was not theirs. Feeling what was about to happen, she dropped silently to the ground and began chanting her mantra.

She tried to concentrate on the words, tried to think about what they meant. But with each chant the significance of each syllable seemed to drop away and replacing it was a wave of malice that eclipsed all that had gone before. The chant began to fade out and she stuttered and stumbled in her own head...*They will leee...They will...They'll...*soon, she could not remember where to begin or what any of it was supposed to mean. Like sexual desire, anger was consuming all parts of her and taking the reins. The time for thinking was at an end; indeed, she resented every wasted second that had led up to this moment. She was on her feet and moving fast. The boy was ahead of her, and red, which was nothing to do with the firelight, tinted the blackness.

<h2 style="text-align:center">4.</h2>

Kayleigh awoke to noise and Shabwan's face evaporated. It felt like an age before she truly understood what she was seeing. Her eyes seemed to have been naturally drawn to where the noise had come from and there she saw it. A slender black figure with its back to her. The back was covered in sharp white spikes, kind of like a hedgehog, she thought. Either side of the long thin spines, two muscular arms were raised in the air, small powerful fists sat atop them. The creature then pounded its arms downward into what it was kneeling on. It was kneeling on Lewhay.

It felt like a force beyond her own body propelled her forward, like when you are running and a sudden strong gust helps you along the way. Things seemed to be drawn towards her rather than she run towards them. She hoped against hope it wasn't too late, the arms had come down with such devastating force and now they were beating repeatedly on what must be Lewhay's head. As they came up again she reached the attacker and grabbed at its arms. They felt like metal rods. Then Kayleigh was airborne and, just before she hit a tree, she got a glimpse of Leeham.

<h2 style="text-align:center">5.</h2>

In many ways Leeham was still asleep but in others he'd never been so awake. There was no linguistic thought in his head, no inner monologue as there usually was. In its place was simplicity. Fear had become rage in the shortest of milliseconds once he realised what was happening to his friend. In violent situations you never behave how you think you'll behave. Fight or flight is all there is. Few people have the ability to muster cool one-liners or bellow war cries. In fact most true conflicts, the kind where life is in danger, carry little noise with them; everybody involved is concentrating too hard.

Leeham saw Kayleigh, approaching from the other side, grab hold of the arms which were raining down repeatedly on his friend. The next thing he knew, he only narrowly missed being knocked unconscious by her flying form. This thing is strong he thought, as he balled his fist. He swung his arm, desperately trying to harness as much of his forward motion into the punch as possible and it connected with a dull and satisfying click into the things jaw.

There was a moment of stillness. Then Leeham's initial satisfaction with his handy work dissolved. The thing was looking at him. It was jet black and completely naked. It seemed to have the body of a woman but lines of sharp spikes hung down where the ribs should be and also around the knees and the ankles. Its hair was also made up of these ivory needles. They reminded him of pari teeth. The face was that of a human, the features almost petite and pretty. Then she bared her hideous teeth and drool flew into Leeham's face. He panicked and threw another desperate punch, although the dim realisation that he had a better chance against one of the trees was slowly dawning on him. A hand, much blacker than the darkest night, was coming his way. He ducked and probably avoided decapitation in the process, but he did still take quite a clip. It spun him round and he found out much more about the taste of grass than he'd ever planned, he didn't like it.

Turning over, he found himself staring up at the creature that would kill him. The spikes, which had hung down before, now stood erect. Any one of them would be enough to finish him off. The hand which had previously been sleek and black was now spouting the same teeth like shards, and it would be these that ended it all, he supposed.

There was a flash of orange accompanied by a screech and, two seconds later, Leeham, much to his own surprise and delight, was still breathing.

6.

Oh no you don't, thought Coki. His only weapon may have been a cooking utensil, but it was a damn fine cooking utensil and not one that he would wield lightly. Seeing Kayleigh fly into a tree, he knew immediate action was required. Then he saw Leeham throw one of the softest punches he'd ever witnessed, and the imperative became much more so. His first thought was just to whack the beast as hard as he could around the temple. Simple, direct approach. Then the fire caught his eye. In one smooth movement he scooped up the majority of the burning logs into his vessel and deposited them with some force into the face of the creature. It shrieked in a satisfying way and clutched at itself. Adrenaline fuelled rage now replaced Coki's cold calculation. Screaming, and contradicting everything I said earlier about real fights being quiet, he hit out again and again. He felt fire in his arm. Not like the fire he'd just thrown, but fire in the blood. Fire that would allow him to continue hitting for all eternity if that were necessary.

The beast was covering its head and, try as he might, Coki could not find the killer blow. The frequency of his attacks was enough to keep it sheltered behind its hands, and he was sure he was hurting it, but he needed to get right in there. Throwing his arm to the full extent of its reach, he brought the pan up and over. Things went into slow motion and he saw the thing's eyes for the first time. It had sensed the changing tempo of the attacks and was ready to counter. As the pan came down the claws shot out. Coki suddenly sensed the vulnerability of his own skin. Could it be possible that he was about to become no more than a skewered piece of meat? Just as the white spines neared his chest, the pan found its target. The crack he heard and the shock wave Coki felt through his wrist were immense. The advancing death needles stopped. They eyes, which had lit up so brightly upon sensing their chance, were rolling.

The beast fell.

7.

With the smashing impact of the pan, Morshev felt black, deep, deep black racing in on her. For the first time since she'd attacked she was aware

128

of where she was and what she was doing. She was also aware that she'd lost. Blood lust had led her to her destruction and with her death Shabwan would be granted life.

As she fell her hand came to rest against a thin vine that was spiralling a tree. It looked like any normal vine but, as Morshev's fingers touched it, she felt something that she had not felt since her master had died. She felt magic.

8.

Coki was ready to finish the job. He yearned to check that his friends were ok but, unlike so many hapless sorts who have demised towards the end of a horror movie, he was going to make sure the job was finished first. He placed his feet either side of the beast's spiky head and clutched the pan's handle firmly. The first blow had cracked the skull, but he wanted to be sure. He raised the pan up as high as he could and then, with another contradictory cry, brought it down. As it reached the place where the beast's head should have been, there was an almighty...no, wait, there was nothing. Instead, the pan continued until it made a soft wet thwack, dispersing the grass' morning dew every which way. The creature was gone.

9.

They rested. They had to. The fight had taken it out of them but, thankfully, they were all in one piece. Coki more so than the other three. Lewhay's face was already coming up in a spectacular array of deep purples and blues, Kayleigh had been knocked out cold and was still shaking severely and Leeham had a nasty gash on the side of his head. But, despite their various wounds, the euphoria of being alive, and having won, was rife.

Whether or not they'd successfully killed the thing, it was gone. And if it *was* still alive then it was severely wounded. Coki swore he'd heard and felt the skull crack. Perhaps it just disappeared when it died, he'd suggested. They hoped like hell that this was true, but it didn't seem that likely. For better or worse they felt safe and soon they would be ready to continue. It was almost a relief to have got it out of the way. Ever since they'd left San Hoist, they'd all suspected that, at some point in their quest to find their friend, they were going to be forced into conflict. The thought that their first test had been against some unimaginable demon, and that they'd passed with flying colours, was a happy one.

Once they felt ready they continued on their way. There was a path of sorts leading through the forest and, although it was difficult to follow at times, its direction seemed to be true. They all felt that it must be leading them to the mountains and, indeed, within a few days it had.

10.

Morshev was transported to a world where everything was not. She existed but not as herself. She had borrowed, and as a borrower she was now at the mercy of the magic. She swam, feeling the crack in her head and feeling her life force ebbing out into the waters around her. It was as if it nourished them and they were hungry for more. Desperately she clung on. No longer motivated by hate and destruction, but love. Love not for her master but for herself. When suddenly confronted with the reality of not being, Morshev found that she cared much more for her existence than she ever could have imagined.

As she swam she came to two openings in the impossible sea. They looked almost identical but they were not. She knew that, and she knew she had to choose. Something had to be sacrificed. As the waters began to rush and pull her forwards, she knew she would not be granted the luxury of time. This choice was designed to be taken on an impulse and impulsive feelings, while not without merit, can do funny things. As she rushed forward, Morshev's eyes began to flit back and forth. If she'd had a concept of Wimbledon's centre court, then she might have likened it to that, then again, maybe not. It's bad to put words in people's mouths. As she bore down on the two holes, she did not feel ready to choose and thus her decision probably could have gone the other way. But it didn't, and as she left the waters of the magic to return to this world, all the feelings that had put her there in the first place settled deeply back into her mind. It was like putting on an old, malicious and unforgiving jacket.

11.

Once you got a bit of the way up the mountains you could see back over the entire forests and onto the flat plain beyond. The past of their journey was laid out before them and it was a beautiful sight. The four friends took a moment to look, just as they had on the hill that overlooks the Hoist. Below them lay the place where they had faced their biggest danger and, while they knew there would be more, they had survived. And now here they were, the four of them, together, climbing the mountains. For all they knew, Shabwan was just on the other side of these great grey lumps. They looked back for a long time but eventually they had to go on. It was a strange feeling, looking down over the edge of Corne and wandering if they'd see it again.

As they turned and continued their slow ascent, they could not have known that not one, but two beings were following them out of the forest.

Chapter 9.

The Fool and the Trickster.

1.

It reminded Shabwan of something he'd seen during the telling of that bizarre story. When the two Gods had plummeted into the centre of the earth together, it had seemed like the tunnel was building ahead of them. Areas which had been solid rock had been cloven apart as the Gods fell. Their ability was both creation and destruction. Shabwan suspected that a similar thing was happening to them now. Only instead of altering what was already there, they were flying into nothing. And, as they flew into the colourless void, something became.

It was not much to look at and, indeed, it was very hard to look at. They were travelling at such a speed that the world which formed around them celebrated the moments after its inception by becoming a blur. There was a lot of colour though. The world which had not been moving so quickly was all white marble, save for the oddly beautiful flashes of nature. The world that was forming now seemed to be mostly natural. Yet it was as if the three of them were in some kind of cocoon that passed through it all. One minute they were racing across an open desert plain, then the next they would be under the sea but, despite all this, the space immediately around them seemed to stay them same. A whole spectrum of random creation, born of the equal creative powers of a trickster, a fool and a sorcerer was spilling out into nothing. And the three who created cared not one iota. Indeed, Shabwan was the only one who'd noticed. But then, he was also the only one who wasn't concentrating on flying.

Veo was getting closer. The energy which had formed the seal around the three was getting smaller too. Try to imagine, if you will, a little ball of white light flying at the speed of a bullet across absolutely nothing and leaving in its wake the parody of a world; great warped landscapes, some upside down or on their side. It was a scene which would have given Escher a headache. Veo's pride would have taken quite a knock if he'd seen it. He'd always considered himself one of the best creators, perhaps second only to Eree. But, of course, this was not his work alone. In the universes the chamber had created, all had the power.

'Shabwan,' screamed the man who was holding him. 'You have to stop him!!' In the time it took him to say this they had left a mountain range, greater than the Alps and coiled like a spring, in their wake. Moments later the whole thing was consumed by a great fish wearing a top hat (this was probably Shabwan's contribution).

Veo's fingers were close to Lubwan's ankles. A few more inches and the

131

God would be upon them. How to stop such a one, thought Shabwan. He peered out of their glowing sphere and found little there for inspiration.

Then he noticed that there was something hard pressing against his leg. He looked down and, resisting the temptation for crude jokes, saw that no part of the old man who was carrying him could be responsible for such a feeling. It must be something in his pocket. He slipped his hand inside and found a knife. It was strange that he should have one and it was such a small thing that he wondered what possible use it could be in this place of infinite possibility. Especially against the terrifyingly powerful entity that was fast closing on them. Yet it did have *something.* It wasn't immediately obvious; you had to hold it in your hand for a moment or two before you noticed that the little knife, while not capable of spewing fiery deserts into the abyss, did have some power. There was a tangible quality of realness to it. And, while this may seem like tautology, it was, in fact, not (so there!). Much was real in this world but not in the way the knife was. The paving stones his feet had called home as he'd watched the story of Eree and Veo play out had been real, he'd stood on them. But they were not believable in the same way that knife was believable…no, believable was the wrong word, *unchangeable*…that was it. For, as solid as the paving slabs and everything else here was, they were not permanent. Veo, Shabwan and the old man, they could all make and they could all destroy. And nothing that they made would necessarily last more than a moment. Not so this knife. For all its lack of size and apparently unassuming nature, it had something that nothing else in this place had.

Without knowing what would happen or why he was doing it, Shabwan waved the knife. If you'd blinked you would have missed it, but it happened alright. No one could have known this more than Veo. One second he was hurtling along in this strange cocoon of light that they shared, every fibre off his being straining to grab the sorcerer's ankles, the next it felt like he hit a brick wall. One where every brick was made of an entire mountain compacted into the traditional breeze block shape. The impact almost killed him…with his last conscious thought, he noticed that the young boy and the sorcerer were already almost at the edge of his vision. Had there been a horizon, that's where they would have been. He was going to struggle to catch them now.

2.

Shabwan and Lubwan landed and the old sorcerer immediately collapsed. His eyes were rolling back in his head. He did not look good. Shabwan tried to get him off the floor but could not. His weight was that of the dead. Around them, the smallest of little worlds had formed, it was round like a planet but smaller than a house, it had but one tree. Under this Lubwan lay and tried not to die. Around them, as far as the eye could see, there was nothing. They were alone. Shabwan the fool laughed, though he didn't really feel like laughing. Something important was happening and he was missing

132

it. A tiny raincloud appeared and began dispensing its load onto his head. A micro fork of lightning lapped the tree. Shabwan shooed the petulant cloud away and tried to concentrate. This man had saved him, there was no doubt about that, and what was more, he had a nagging feeling of recognition. Who was his saviour? He stared hard at the man's unconscious face trying to focus the image. His unhelpful mind was painting stupid things onto it. One minute all would be normal, then a ridiculously oversized moustache would pop into existence and wave at Shabwan. It was hard to know where the face ended and the ridiculousness began.

Still, it was safe to suspect that this fellow had never been much of a looker. He had a huge forehead and a strange kinked nose. His mouth was too small and his eyes beady. Plus he looked like he'd been beaten around a fair bit. Perhaps by a small army all toting wooden sticks. So much damage could not be the work of one man alone.

Then the memories came. Though they came not as clear images but more like a code. Had Shabwan passed his test then perhaps he would have seen it all more clearly. We can only speculate. As it was, he was given little snatches that needed piecing together. Little nibbles of sound and light arrived in his brain in no particular order. In another world he'd had similar experiences trying to piece his memories together after a heavy night.

He saw the room where they had fought but he was not seeing it through his own eyes. There was another...one who had told him of this. But why was he seeing it? There was a fight between two men, while another...no. Not one other but three. They writhed and they shouted and the other two battled fiercely. He knew both the men. One of them he was looking at now...the other...

'Vericoos,' said Shabwan. It sounded odd on his tongue. Yet it was the right word.

'That's right,' said the old man weakly. Shabwan had not realised that he'd regained consciousness. 'He's the reason you are here.'

'Where is here?' asked Shabwan.

'That is not so important,' came the reply. 'What is important is that Veo is coming. You did not kill him and he will find us. When he returns you must be ready to kill him.' Shabwan nodded. It all seemed logical enough to him.

'Who is Vericoos?' asked Shabwan and couldn't help but notice the lines of anger that appeared all over the battered old face as he said the name.

'He is a very tricky man and it is his trickery that led to you being as you are now.' Shabwan didn't understand. How was he now? 'But you are not the first to fall victim to his trickery, trust me, I should know.' Shabwan was intrigued. And seeing as they had some time on this strange little planet they'd made, possibly the smallest in history, I'd have to check, it seemed like as good an idea as any to find out what this old man was talking about.

'Tell me about it,' said Shabwan the fool and in the vast nothing around them a story was told...

3.

Together they commanded the army of the sorcerers. For if they did not then the God would be victorious. It was too much work for one man alone, but together it was possible. The names of Vericoos and Lubwan were of the highest order. Everybody in Durpo and beyond knew who they were and knew they could trust them. The God was vicious and terrifying in equal measure. They all knew this. But with two such men at the helm, they did not worry. For there was nothing that Vericoos and Lubwan could not achieve, not when they were united.

Together they were sat, in the same room that Mayor Louie would one day occupy. They were discussing the same thing they always discussed these days. Veo.

'That last attack was touch and go,' said Lubwan. 'I wasn't sure we were going to be able to repel him.'

'Agreed,' said Vericoos. 'He is learning.'

It was troubling news indeed.

With each new attack on the city, Veo had some new ideas, and these ideas were becoming better and better. This latest time, he had driven the very earth that surrounded the city up against the defending walls. The sorcerers had run to the battlements and fought hard to drive the ground back. But Veo had created a ramp with his earthy surge and his beasts; cows, horses and even hares, all crazed and sporting bloodshot eyes, driven wild by possession, had charged upwards. The combined strains of both repelling the deranged beasts and forcing back the earth had been difficult and a few sorcerers had paid with their lives. Veo himself had hung back, no doubt waiting for the perfect moment to take to the walls himself, and once the animals had begun taking the majority of the sorcerer's attentions, that moment had come.

And he had damn well nearly succeeded.

Vericoos and Lubwan had fought together as they always did. Side by side they battled the God, holding him at the base of the slope, which now provided a direct route into the city. Veo raged and roared, driving himself forward against their spells. With each step he took the beam of magic holding him back intensified. It was dangerous. Both Vericoos and Lubwan could feel the potential of what they were holding. If the God had got much closer then the beam could have become much more than a beam and the city could have become so much less than a city.

The other sorcerers kept out of the way. Their power, impressive as it was, was nothing compared to that of these two. Without them, Veo would have broken the city walls long ago.

As the God screamed and took laborious step after laborious step, the two sorcerers held him and began to scream themselves (I'm really starting to

134

regret all that stuff about the silence of true conflict earlier). The colour of the beam changed from bright white to deep, bloody red. Veo was disintegrating, much like he had after his pursuit of Eree. He could not hold on like this for long. The two sorcerers locked their arms out ahead of them and put absolutely everything into the beam. Veo, by way of contrast, threw his apart so as to take their attack full in his chest. He launched himself forward, breaking out of his lumbering gait into a run that was...well, lumbering. But a run none the less.

They could see the whites of his eyes. He was as close as he'd ever been to the city. Despite all the chaos around them, as the other sorcerers did their level best to drive back the very peculiar and agitated barrage of wildlife, there seemed to be no noise. Other than their voices that was. It was as if they were screaming into an abyss but one with no echo.

As Veo stumbled almost within grasping reach of the two sorcerers, his wooden mask a perfect portrait of malice, the beam threatened to buckle. So much energy was now contained in such a small amount of space. It seemed to have sucked all the surrounding air into it. The two sorcerers were no longer breathing. Veo raised an arm to strike. If he were to succeed then the beam would be broken. Its existence relied on the complete focus of its two creators. Even a scuff round the side of the head could be enough to shatter its parameters and then...well, the best case scenario would be having to fight Veo hand to hand. The worst and much more likely case would be that there was no need to fight anymore. There would be nothing to fight for.

The hand did not strike, however, and the subsequent few seconds of Veo's life were not the most pleasant. They were spent in the air and ended with a crashing introduction to the dry earth. The God rolled some distance before he eventually stopped. Then he lay for a while. Spitting dirt out of his mouth and massaging his vision back into focus Veo the God had failed again.

But he had come damn close, and so we return to the point at which we originally joined the two sorcerers.

'It was more by luck than anything else that we survived,' said Lubwan. 'If we have to face him again like that, then I'm not feeling at all confident.' Lubwan looked at his best friend as he said this. It was a fairly big moment. It was the first time either of them had spoken of defeat. They had, of course, thought about it. And, as with almost everything that they thought, they'd thought about it together. All was shared on some level and fear broadcast pertinently. But there is always something about verbalisation which tends to spark a new level of intensity.

At that moment another man entered the room. He looked like he'd been through the mill. To look at Vericoos and Lubwan, you'd never suspect that they'd been in such a fight so recently. They looked well kept and unruffled. Indeed, if you didn't know better, you might be foolish enough to accuse them of being types who didn't like to get their hands dirty. Fortunately, everyone did know better. No such allegation could be levelled at the young man who had just entered the room. Matthias looked like he'd been dragged through a series of spiky, unforgiving hedges backwards and then flung through them again in the other direction, perhaps two or three times. Their old academy friend was nowhere near as talented as Vericoos or Lubwan, but you could not fault him for trying.

'How are you feeling, Matthias?' asked Vericoos, though he did not seem interested in the reply. His mind was very much elsewhere.

'Yeah I'm alright,' said Matthias. 'Those beasties tore into me yesterday though.' He tried to grin but didn't quite manage it. He was a perceptive lad and couldn't have helped noticing how, despite being victorious, this had almost been their worst, and therefore last, battle.

Lubwan looked at his friend. It was such a strange dynamic, the three of them. Two of them so infinitely powerful and the other so...normal. It was a harsh description and one that Matthias would have hated. Being called normal is much worse than being called a complete...you know what. Complete 'you-know-whats' have something about them, they threaten or they contradict or they have something that another wants. Normals do not. Normals are liked by all, because no one has a reason not to like them. And by the Gods do they wish people had a reason not to like them. Lots of people suffer from Matthias' affliction, but then perhaps they are blessed not to be affiliated with the two most powerful men on the face of the earth. It was true that young Matthias had enjoyed a lot of privileges during peacetime, had benefited from the status and respect which was a natural trickle down effect of having friends in high places. But that was Matthias' life: trickle down. Anything he had, he had because of them and, behind his back (sometimes more obviously than others), people sneered. To them he was an errand boy, a sorcerer of little quality who held his position in Durpo not through merit but through fortunate living arrangements as a student.

Matthias hated it.

It was not that he was jealous of his two friends. Such feelings were not part of his makeup. Indeed, in many ways he was the superior of both of them but perhaps not in the ways that 'mattered'. Matthias loved his friends as a friend should, and really didn't care how much more *talented* they were than him. But he did care that other people cared so much. He hated being judged in any way, but he especially hated being judged as a comparison. It was dehumanising and what was worse was that he'd never asked for it. It wasn't as if he lorded it around, boasting and bellowing about how he was best friends with the best of the best. It wasn't like he even mentioned them if it wasn't relevant (which, unfortunately, it was a lot of the time). But yet still people spoke about him in that same way: the lap dog, the servant, the brown nose. As time wore on, Matthias found himself spending more and more time with his two friends, soon they were the only people he felt comfortable around.

Then the God had come.

Since then everything had changed. Wars change the way people are with each other. And much as they didn't wish it to happen, Vericoos and Lubwan began pushing him away. It was just difficult to concentrate on anything other than that which was imperative, and when Matthias was hanging around...well, they were discussing how to defeat a God; the single biggest threat the world had ever known. What help could Matthias be? These words were harsh and they weren't said. But there are many ways to convey an idea, wittingly or unwittingly.

'We need to be ready for a swift reprisal,' said Vericoos. 'You know how quickly he heals.' Lubwan grunted his agreement. It was true. The God could heal and be back upon them much quicker than they could reorganise the city.

'Speaking of which, why the hell haven't you sorted yourself out Matthias?' Lubwan regretted the question the moment it left his lips. Healing was a matter of consummate ease for Vericoos and he, as well as many others. For Matthias it was harder work and work that would take a bit of time. Especially after the kicking he had quite clearly taken. Matthias looked embarrassed.

'I just haven't had time...A lot of the others...I've been helping.'

He trailed away. Lubwan would never have wanted to hurt his friend but he had done just that. And, in their current environment, there wasn't a great deal of time to be worrying about whose feeling you'd hurt.

'Go and sort yourself out,' said Vericoos. 'We don't need anything at the moment.' Matthias took his leave, nodding to them both as he left. He felt miserable as he headed down the stone corridor that lead to the office. He'd only wanted a bit of company. Still, he understood how busy they were and how desperate times were getting. Indeed, as he walked a wave of embarrassment began to set in. Why was he so concerned about his own feelings at a time like this? Especially when his two friends were working tirelessly to save humanity. He was being selfish by needing anything from them at a time like this. Feeling as lonely as he'd ever felt, Matthias went home.

4.

Vericoos was lying in bed but he knew sleep would not come. Yet, although his mind would not rest, he still diligently assumed the position each night even if it was only for an hour or so. It made him feel like a human. This was a feeling he'd once taken for granted, but the more exhausted he got as they moved further and further into this conflict, the less he felt it.

Lubwan had been right. They had come about as close as it was possible to come to failure without actually failing. If the God had not buckled when he had and his mighty hand had connected with either of them, then he would not now be in his bed. He would probably be in the ground, as would they all.

137

Their world was one where margins were fine and meant absolutely everything. While the other sorcerers could battle with what Veo threw at them as a unit and compensate for each other's mistakes, help each other in times of peril, he and Lubwan enjoyed no such luxury. The others took part in a great team sport where chaos reined and lives were sometimes lost. And he was so grateful to them for it, without their efforts they would have failed long before. But what they did, brilliant as it was, could not be compared to what he and Lubwan must undertake.

Their battle with Veo was a game of chess. A fight which would go down to the smallest of tactical decisions. It took so much from him, having to use every last molecule of his power while his brain was almost ripped apart. The beam that had held Veo back was not something anyone else could have created, and no other would have understood the complexity of keeping it together while one such as Veo raged against it. Could he do it again? The disturbing truth was that he did not know.

He also did not know what the little fleck of purple light dancing above his head was. It was beautiful. Something of magic no doubt, but...perhaps of a magic he had not yet encountered...was it possible? He, the most powerful sorcerer on the planet (a title both he and Lubwan gave themselves), encountering something new in his field. The purple gleam enticed him, whispered to him, promised him things; and as it did, his inhibitions wandered.

Before he knew what he was doing, he was moving. Following the little purple creature through the streets like a drunk chasing a dream. He had the presence of mind to raise his hood for he did not want to be seen. Whatever this thing was, it was for him alone. Soon it had led him out of the city. He was wandering over the same grass that had oh so recently risen up and tried to allow their enemies into the city. Enemy, he corrected himself. Veo fought alone, that which accompanied him did so unwillingly.

The night was a bright one. Almost like the moon was trying to tell him something. Although it could promise nothing so exciting as this little thing. Vericoos had never felt like this before. He had always been a man who understood what being in the public eye meant. And thus was always the picture of dignity whenever he might be seen. The people of the city relied on him for protection and morale. What would they have thought if they'd seen him stumbling along outside of the city walls as if completely intoxicated?

As the city became smaller, almost to the point where its walls could fit within your field of vision, he heard a voice and it was a voice he knew.

He was going to die.

'Vericoos.' It was only his name, a single word comprised of a few sounds, yet it could not be happening. They had fought so hard, been so organised, defied all the odds and now here he was. About to be struck down in a field like a common cow. Lubwan could not hold out alone, the city would crumble and soon after the world. And there would be only one person to blame. One person responsible for the enslavement of the world. And that person was he.

Veo had not yet struck but Vericoos was tensed for the blow. Tensed for the strike that would end his life and open all the doors. It didn't come. Instead came more words.

'We should speak.'

Vericoos couldn't understand what was happening. Last time he'd seen this individual he had been ripping himself literally to shreds just to get close enough to kill him. Now he had him in his sights, as vulnerable as a rabbit, and he had done nothing. He couldn't have changed his mind so quickly.

'There is something that I have become aware of, something that I think will also be of interest to you. Perhaps we have both been fighting the wrong battle.'

Vericoos' head still felt a little fuzzy. Whatever that little purple thing was, it had had a strange effect on him, one that was not easily brushed aside.

'The magic is not as stable as I believed and if you and I do not act soon, then this world that we are fighting over will be worth fighting over no more.' Vericoos still couldn't find any words to say to the God. Here was his mortal enemy, the being he spent every waking moment (so every moment) plotting the demise of. He had assumed that these feelings were more than mutual, yet here was Veo talking about how they might have a shared interest. And he couldn't help but be intrigued by what the God was saying, for it was something he himself had long suspected.

'You know of what I speak,' said Veo. Not as a question. 'Perhaps I can show you something that will help you.' Veo waved an arm and all changed. Vericoos was no longer stood on the fields outside of Durpo, he was stood on a grassy plain between two forests in another time, and he was about to watch the demise of Krunk.

As he watched, all his worst fears became true in front of his very eyes. The magic, that which he loved the dearest of all, was as fragile as he'd always suspected. No, it was worse than that. Vericoos had sensed it during the casting of their most vicious spells. He'd sensed the angry nature of what they were trying to hold onto. He'd sensed the potential for it to explode outwards consuming all. But he had never, nor could he have ever, imagined how...*alive* it was. Their greatest love had the potential to turn on them and wreak havoc and the only solution, he thought as the spell that cleansed the earth ripped outwards consuming him and Veo, was to lose everything.

They landed back in the fields of Durpo. Two who had just witnessed something of massive significance.

Yet, much as they thought that they'd reached a point of new enlightenment, and in many ways they had, they had not grasped the true significance of what they'd seen. For, while they both now understood what the magic was now capable of, they did not realise that they'd just seen the inception of an instrument which would one day ruin everything for them.

Life's funny like that.

'Can it be stopped?' he asked the God. He could never have imagined being so interested in what Veo had to say. His reply came in the form of a nod and a single word. The simplicity of the word did not convey the horror of what it entailed. But then, they often don't.

'Unification,' said Veo.

5.

Vericoos was back in his bed. He had lain here originally with the hope of getting some rest. Even though he had known that to be impossible. Then the word impossible had become something of a theme of the evening. He held his mind firmly shut. For the first time in his life, it was absolutely imperative that his best friend remain unaware of what was going through his mind. It was a strange feeling.

Vericoos had never felt so alone. He was grappling with the most difficult decision of his life. Earlier that evening it had all been so simple. They against he, good against evil, freedom against tyranny. Now he wished for that simplicity, yet knew it was gone forever. Now his choice was of the kind that we all hope we'll never have to make. The kind of choice that puts *what* we want against *those* we want.

Anyway, as you well know dear reader, Vericoos chose Veo and the horror of requiring the death of those he had loved to achieve his aim. But why he did this is going to have to wait until another day. Because old Veo, with a flagrant disregard for narrative, has just smashed into the little world where we left Shabwan and Lubwan, and the time for storytelling has very much passed.

6.

The planet buckled but did not break as Veo landed. Lubwan and Shabwan were thrown into the air. Shabwan had felt calm as the old man's story played out around him. He had felt close to sanity, whatever the hell that was. As the God landed he was propelled back into madness. Not a place you want to be when you're fighting for your life. Which is most certainly what Lubwan was now doing and he was in no fit state.

Lubwan raised his hands and formed a shield, but even as he formed it he knew he might as well not have bothered. Veo's blows rained down upon him and, while the shield did do something, it did not do enough. The fists were coming through and they were coming through fast. Veo was not going for any form of subtlety in his combat. He was going to plough Lubwan into the ground. There was only one thing for it. Abandoning his shield, Lubwan swung an arm upwards. Clenched within it was all he had left, his very life force in his hand. Enough, if not to kill Veo (if he even could be killed in this place), then to send him spiralling off into the abyss and perhaps buy the boy a chance. Trust his luck that he'd fallen into a universe with such a weak division of the boy. It seemed an awful long time since something had gone Lubwan's way.

As his fist came round so did Veo's and one was moving so much faster than the other. As the impact shook his head, almost removing it clean from his body, Lubwan's consciousness extinguished like a candle under a lake's worth of water. Milliseconds later his form was spinning through the abyss, no longer creating only falling...

Shabwan stood but couldn't focus. The world around him swam and tried to make him laugh while the advancing God wanted to kill him. It was no time to laugh but he did anyway. Yet, part of him was working as it should. Some distant, almost incoherent voice within the maelstrom told him to reach for the knife. And while the rest of the world obeyed it not, his hand did.

His fingers, seemingly now operating exclusively of the rest of him, perhaps annoyed with being attached to such uselessness, had clutched the hilt. The God was almost upon him, but the fingers had time. They knew what to do. As Shabwan stabbed upwards he smelt victory. It smelled like...stonk, bitter and gritty, not the way victory should smell at all. The knife was still down by Shabwan's side, barely a quarter of the way through its intended upward trajectory, when Veo's mighty, clenched fist smashed into his head. The impact snapped his neck.

In the vast nothingness that contained them, all that was Shabwan's popped out of existence.

Moments later, all that was Veo's did the same. The God stood victorious in nothing. And, just as he was wondering what would happen next, his question was answered. For in front of him there was a door and on it there was a handle. Veo the trickster put his hand on it and pushed it down. The door opened and through he stepped. He left behind nothing apart from a motionless old sorcerer drifting further away into the nothingness.

Book 3

The Reluctant Hero vs. The Conquerer.

Chapter 1.

Welcome.

1.

Shabwan landed, already prepared for a fight. The world he landed in did not confuse him. He knew where he was and what he was doing. Vericoos had clearly done a good job of holding this particular part of him together. Ahead of him lay a God, a God who must be destroyed for Kayleigh and for the entire world.

There was not much to this place. Around him there was nothing, although it was obligingly becoming something in order to give him something to walk on. Ahead of him, however, there was a castle. Shabwan felt his nerves flutter as he looked at it. He certainly had a fight on his hands. The castle was not so much a place to live as a great vehicle of war. Indeed, it seemed almost human in its shape. The central turret rose up to a great viewing platform that had an almost head like quality to it, and the great walls seemed more like folded arms than anything. Smoke was rising from what would have been its nostrils and there was a glowing red light atop the viewing platform that only added to the impression that this building could rise up out of its foundations and crush him like an ant.

Shabwan swallowed and steadied himself. There was no good in letting the place get to him. No doubt that was exactly what the castle's creator had planned. For the person who had built the monstrosity could only have done so with a fight in mind. The thought of Shabwan, small as he was, going up against the castle seemed ridiculous, but he knew that this was not how it would be. In this place he was more than just one man. He could do things. He wasn't quite sure how he knew this. Had Vericoos said something? He wasn't sure, but what he was sure of was the fact that his immediate surrounds were shaping themselves to his preferences. The nothing around him had become a path, not unlike the one he had once walked upon when he'd wanted to speak to his mother. Back when he'd been in the other place. The path thinly spiralled off toward the castle and Shabwan had no doubt that it would lead him up to the very gates. But he knew this was not all that he was capable of, not by a long shot. He felt the potential in the emptiness, a potential that was his to shape. The castle did not look so daunting when you knew that the space around you was a potential weapon waiting to be born. All of it! Well, all of it apart from that which was Veo's. But Shabwan wasn't going to let that worry him. If his foe was spending his time hiding in a castle, then he would just have to break it apart until he could drag the God out of it.

But, unbeknown to the confident division, he wasn't going to be allowed to do any such thing until he had been tested.

2.

It was finally time. The conqueror had waited and waited and then waited some more for this day. He had never lost hope that at some point in his future, even if there was no time in this place, he was going to get his opportunity. Something would come along that would allow him to smash his way out of this prison. For a prison it must be. Then he would retain his rightful place in the world of the real and continue his great mission. The universe would not be in the hands of his enemy forever. He had a new master; one who would deliver on what he promised and the legacy of the old Gods would be forever lost. Veo and Rez would be the new kings and the universe would be just how they wanted it to be.

But he was getting ahead of himself. There was business to be taken care of right here and right now. And it had appeared in the form of a tiny human being. Veo's first reaction was of the aggressive variety. The castle stirred around him, wanting to rise up, wanting to reach out one of its great stone limbs and crush this human like the nothing that it was. Then he calmed himself. He'd always known that a conflict would hold the key to his escape from this place. He'd know this ever since he'd passed his test, and he'd always held onto the belief that his friend on the outside would send him someone. Now it had happened, but the thought of terminating this human in such a crude fashion did not seem like it would offer him escape. There was more to this situation than that. Sure as he was that he was looking at a key, he was not yet sure that he was seeing the keyhole. A fight there must be, but it seemed to Veo that winning the fight was, perhaps ironically, only half the battle. His path to freedom truly lay in gauging the manner in which he must defeat this newcomer. And what better way to gauge than to watch a test. Especially one created by the subconscious of the one who was about to face it. For that was what this place asked of you, he'd realised.

As he'd smashed apart the parody of the city of Durpo, thus passing his test and winning back his powers and memories, he had sensed that the city was not the creation of the nothing around him. It was his creation. The new world that contained him had demanded a test, but what that test was lay in the hands of the candidate. He often wondered what the other two slices had come up with, he also wondered if they'd passed. He hoped so. He wanted to leave this place very much in *one* piece. Being carved up as he had was something he wanted to put long behind him.

Veo leant over the rail of his platform, a platform that made up the bottom jaw of the great stone giant in which he resided, and watched. How would the newcomer fair in his test, and what was he about to learn about him? Veo could already sense that, small and seemingly insignificant as the young man was, there was something completely unique about him. Something that separated him from other human beings. And in this lay the reason it was he who must be fought.

3.

There was someone coming towards Shabwan and it certainly was no God. It was a man and one Shabwan had seen before. One he had killed. It did not make sense that Lomwai could be in this place. Shabwan had banished him from the earth, but had he sent him here? It seemed almost impossible. But then, here he was, looking none too pleased.

Shabwan tensed himself as the magician approached, ready for a fight. Confidence exploded within him along with a boost of adrenaline. He'd already killed this git once. How difficult could the second time be? Then he realised how big the cape was that Lomwai was wearing. There was a great deal of space around his body, as if he were wearing a great wicker cage and the cloak was merely a decorative cloth. Lomwai was grinning horribly at him, Shabwan saw long thin teeth barely contained by those nasty lips. He yearned to reach out and smash them. The magician was standing in the way of his quest, potentially destroying the whole world in the process. What right did he have? Hadn't he done enough damage already? Shabwan broke into a run along the narrow little coastal path that led first to his test and then to his confrontation. As he neared the magician, he balled his fists. He'd done it pretty manually the first time round and wasn't afraid of doing the same thing here. His other divisions would probably have been pretty shocked and outraged at such thinking...what had he become? Still, the reluctant hero had no such worries. That was until he'd almost reached Lomwai, and the nasty grin took on an extra look of malice as the magician flung his cloak open.

Beneath it was not a wicker frame but instead four more people. They did not look anything like he remembered them. Battered, bruised and skinny they were now, their hair lank and clotted with dirt and blood. Indeed, it took him a few seconds to recognise his four friends. When he did, he could only stand there, mouth wide open, eyes wide. If it had made no sense that Lomwai was here, it made even littler sense that he could have taken his four friends with him.

Had they been killed too?

He tried not to think it, but could not stop himself. The thought of it almost dragged him to the floor. Indeed, it felt like great hands were now clawing at him, trying to drag him off the edge of his little coast path. He yelled out, reaching a hand towards his friends and Lomwai sneered. The magician, who seemed to have no body of his own, just that leering face and his cloak, drifted backwards out of reach. The four people trapped beneath the cloak were jerked backwards as if bound by invisible ropes. They cried out in pain and clung together. Shabwan burned to reach them and release them from whatever dark enchantment was keeping them there. He looked up at Lomwai, wishing death upon him with more fire than he would ever have thought possible.

As if taunting him, the magician, or at least his disembodied head, began drifting faster. Shabwan's four friends stumbled and fell. They could not stay on their feet and were dragged along by their invisible bonds. Shabwan stopped running. The more he ran the more his friends would suffer. He was going to have to be more intelligent about this.

He stopped moving and looked not at his friends but at Lomwai. The magician had been laughing uproariously as he watched Shabwan chase after him. Now he stopped. He met the young mans eye. There was competition here. Lomwai did not just want to kill him, he wanted a lot more.

'What do you want with them?' Shabwan yelled, his voice sounded deeper than he remembered it being. 'Why don't you let them go and come and lose like you did last time?' This certainly seemed to rile old Lomwai. He snarled at Shabwan and, for a moment, his face took on the characteristics of another. He seemed undecided about what to do. One moment he would glance at his captives, then at his enemy, then back again.

'Come on then!' yelled Shabwan.

Lomwai seemed to have heard enough. He snarled and dropped his cloak; it hung for a moment and then became a jet-black cage which dropped over Shabwan's four friends. They screamed but were not hurt. For a moment Lomwai's head hung there; a ridiculous specimen, floating like a balloon in the middle of nothing. Then his body began to form. Streaks of power, jet black and deadly, raced out of their surrounds at great speeds. As they reached the head they slowed, with a noise like sharp steel through air, and bound a body for the head. Within a few seconds, enough of these things had sped in and Lomwai stood, fully formed, several feet above Shabwan's path. His body was now featureless, more like a silhouette than anything, but a three dimensional one. And it was big. Much bigger than Shabwan's.

Something caught Shabwan's eye. Something below him. Before, the path he'd made had been floating amidst the nothing. It wasn't like there was anything there but neither was there an absence. Now there was most certainly something lacking. Below his path a great canyon had opened up, so deep he couldn't make out the bottom. Either side of his little walkway there was now certain death, not only for him but for his friends. He tried to change it, although he didn't really know how, he tried to bring the ground back up, tried to widen the path, but nothing happened. The creative abilities, in which he'd previously felt so much confidence, seemed to have deserted him. The world, at least while Lomwai was around, had become fixed and Shabwan had made his coliseum without granting himself much of an advantage. Indeed, he was now perilously perched on what looked more like a tightrope than a trail and was facing an enemy to whom the laws of gravity were much more like recommendations.

As if sensing his enemy's discomfort, Lomwai kicked the cage that held the four friends. It was already precariously balanced, its edges sticking well out over the side of the path, and under the might of the kick it swayed dangerously, like a seesaw. Shabwan saw Kayleigh fly dangerously into the side of the cage. Her weight began to pull it downwards but then one of the

146

others grabbed her and pulled her back into the centre. Lomwai laughed greedily.

'It's not about them,' Shabwan roared. 'Fight me damn you! Try to win the fight you couldn't before.' Lomwai snarled and floated forward. He now hung directly above Shabwan. The cage, for the moment at least, was safe. Lomwai was breathing heavily but had still not spoken. Instead he just looked at Shabwan who, having secured the safety of his friends, was not up for waiting any longer. 'Come down here and fight me!!' he screamed, his voice reverberating around the canyon that threatened to become his tomb.

The next second Lomwai was upon him. He dove downwards, forcing Shabwan head first into the hard earth. Shabwan brought his knees up as he fell and used the magician's momentum to propel him over in a clumsy flip. As they rose to their feet again, Shabwan was ever so slightly quicker. He used this extra second to smash the magician hard in the side of the head. It wasn't hard enough though, for as soon as he'd landed the blow a bolt of energy crashed into his stomach. For a moment he was airborne, then his back found the hard, smooth metal of the cage. The impact sent it rolling backwards like a great dice. Shabwan turned and, as if in slow motion, saw the cage up on one of its corners turning ever so slowly, but unmistakably, towards the edge. He leapt forward, propelled by so much more than his body alone. Then, at the last possible moment, he managed to get a hand around a bar.

As he heaved the cage back onto the path, his eyes met hers and for a second everything stood still. He did not want to fight anymore. He didn't want to save the world. Someone else could deal with Veo and he could just rest here in this moment. Then her eyes widened and he knew what was coming. A blow, almost powerful enough to send his eyeballs running free, like absurd tadpoles, smashed into the back of his head. There was blur and little else.

Something dragged him back and, whether by cat like instinct or sloth like fortune, he evaded Lomwai's follow up. The consequences of the missed strike provided him with the opportunity he needed, and the decision that followed was certainly not made by the part of him that had just melted into Kayleigh's eyes.

Lomwai's arm was now trapped in the cage and, as he tried to free it, there was little he could do to defend himself. Shabwan took hold of his great chest and heaved. A moment later, the magician, the reluctant hero and the cage containing his four friends tumbled off the side of the little footpath as one. The air rushed by although it was not really air and it was also not the only thing rushing. The walls of the canyon were also in an awful hurry and Shabwan didn't doubt that their friend and eternal ally, the ground, would not want to miss out on all of this. He had to strike now for all of their sakes (well, except Lomwai's). Using the cage to gain the maximum leverage he brought his arm crashing down again and again into the magician's head, but it did not yield. Lomwai laughed at his efforts but could not free his arm to deliver anything meaningful of his own. As they fell, the cage spun between them. Shabwan's four friends were having the worst time, banging from one side to the other. Their screams tore at Shabwan but he had to ignore them. If he couldn't take the magicians magic before they hit the floor, then all was over.

Perhaps you see the consummate ease with which the reluctant hero could admit this to himself in a way that the romantic would never have been able to. It was the secret that Vericoos had stopped himself revealing as they'd left Payinzee and that only Thon was aware of in the infant magical empire of Durpo. Killing a person of magic takes what they have and gives it to you. This is why it has always been considered the gravest of crimes in all of the empires of history. If one person were to take another's power and go unpunished, then where would it end? Could someone kill every last sorcerer in the world? Could one person hold all the power? Could it be unified? These were questions that no one had ever wanted to know the answer to. That was until Veo had come along. Veo, who had led Vericoos to believe that the world's only salvation lay in unification, and Vericoos had believed him...and now, here they were. And if Shabwan didn't sort himself out soon, he might as well not have bothered coming.

He was now situated on the other side of the cage to Lomwai, and the magician was growing. As he grew, he lashed out with his now more dangerous arm, forcing Shabwan to use the cage for defence. He needed a weapon and he needed it fast. Swinging himself down, he came face to face with Kayleigh once more. She looked at him, eyes wide and pleading, but he had no time. What use was emotion when soon they would have none? He grabbed her hand and prised her fingers open, she was holding something. It was a rock. But she did not want to give it to him.

What madness was this? Could she not see that he was trying to save them? He tried with all his might to wrestle the rock from her grasp but she clung onto it. He looked into her eyes and saw fear there, mistrust even. What was he possibly going to do with the rock apart from save her and everybody else's lives? Or perhaps she'd prefer it if they and everyone else died, he thought savagely.

This thought gave him the little extra burst of strength that he needed and, ignoring her cry of protest, a sound that would normally have stayed his hand more than all else, he took the stone and swung himself up over the lip of the cage.

The world went slow. One great arm lashed out towards him, and he was forced to throw himself flat in the air to avoid it. He rolled along the top of the cage and rose up onto his knee. The arm was coming round again. It was no longer sleek and polished but veiny and bulbous. Grabbing the cage with both hands he tweaked it slightly. The effect was just enough. Lomwai's hand still being trapped within the bars meant that as the cage moved he did too. The slight movement was enough to send his arm flying harmlessly over Shabwan's head.

Lomwai was now wide open and Shabwan knew exactly what to do. He'd done it before, after all. Three hits was all it took with his little rock and the magician's head, preposterously small against the great ebony body, broke. As it did he felt the same feeling he had in Payinzee that day, although at the time he had not been equipped to understand it. He felt the magical force within Lomwai transfer into him, and with it a world of potential opened up. Gravity need no longer be obeyed quite so obediently. Shabwan, the reluctant hero, stopped falling and was now floating. Floating in the vast space of the canyon. Above him lay Veo's castle and he was now well equipped to storm it. The God better be scared, or if he wasn't, then he sure as hell soon would be. Shabwan began to fly upwards, elation exploded within him. He had passed his test and gained power immeasurable. The air was rushing again, as were the walls, but this time they were going to a place that need not interest him. A place which, it now seemed laughable, had once threatened him but now offered nothing.

Below Shabwan, the now magical being, the representations of the four he held most dear crashed into the bottom of the canyon. What little life they had was instantly lost.

Shabwan didn't even glance back.

4.

Unlike Shabwan, the conqueror's confidence was ebbing by the second. Veo now had some idea of why this young man had been sent to him. But then…so much more didn't make sense. He was not a sorcerer, but it was feasible that a normal human could kill a magical being and take their…but it was *hugely* unlikely. You rarely heard stories of normal people overpowering sorcerer's for good reason; it didn't happen. And if he was no sorcerer, yet he had taken this power…then how…there must be something more to him. There was certainly more to this boy than met the eye. He was not strictly speaking a human but then…not quite a sorcerer. But to say he was somewhere between the two didn't do him any justice.

When Shabwan had first arrived, Veo had laughed at how easily his great fortress could have lunged out and crushed the boy like the lowliest of insects. Now he felt glad it was there. Now it offered him security. And where before he had not even considered the possibility that this fight would be in any way taxing. Now he was not so sure. He was still the conqueror. He was going to win. But it might not come as easily as he'd first suspected.

The boy now landed on the path he had created. How flimsy it looked there; like a sheath of wheat waiting to be bent or pulled apart. But, before this thought had even finished forming, the nothing around the path began to become something. It filled, very quickly, with matter that was most certainly not Veo's. He felt its malice towards him. So this was how it would be then.

The castle against the world. He had defeated much longer odds in the past, though the stakes had perhaps never been so great.

The boy looked up at him. While he could not yet see Veo, the God being concealed from view on his platform, he could clearly sense where he was. This thought unnerved him. He'd had enough of doing nothing, but was not quite ready for the fight just yet. There was more to learn about this boy and he was going to learn it.

Veo leant over the balcony and fixed his enemy in his sights. He opened his mind and a great beam of red light flew out straighter than any arrow. Shabwan couldn't have lifted so much as a finger to react, it was so quick. His head was now connected to Veo's by this thin but brilliant beam. Through it, the contents of Shabwan's head would be Veo's to digest and he had as much time as he liked to do so. The force would hold Shabwan in place for as long as was necessary. At least he hoped it would.

So Veo stood there, poised in the mouth of his beast. And all that he asked Shabwan yielded. He had no choice. But Veo made once crucial mistake. He didn't realise that the channel he'd opened was no one way street and thus, while Veo found out exactly what it was that had made the chamber choose the reluctant hero, Shabwan found out exactly why it had selected the conqueror. And soon we will join him.

Chapter 2.

March.

1.

Both literally and figuratively, the people of Durpo were having trouble catching their breath. Revolution had come like a speeding arrow, severing the old from the new. Louie was already fading into the collective memory, which, considering the time he spent at the helm, was quite exceptional. Rachel had taken charge at the behest of the people and a new era had been set to begin. As a newcomer to politics, you could easily have forgiven her for hoping for a period of calm. A time in which to settle into things. There was much for her to learn, and she would have learned it willingly, but she would have had no desire to rush.

Instead, she had been forced to mobilise an army and was now leading it to war. A war against an invisible foe. One they knew next to nothing about but one who must be feared all the same.

With her were perhaps three hundred. The guard made up at least half of this number and she was immensely soothed by their presence. Losh was the perfect second in command. He never did anything to challenge Rachel's position, while constantly doing all the things that she could not or did not know how to. She could not have been more grateful to him.

The other half was made up of their handpicked volunteers and some of the higher-ranking refugees from Hardram. They'd been very strict when it came to choosing who could go with them. Only those with the highest command had passed the test. Many, many more had wanted to join, but they had been uncompromising. Rachel was not ready to be responsible for anybody's death and, if people weren't up to defending themselves, then that may well be what they were leading them towards.

'The march of the new empire of Durpo towards an invisible and perhaps non-existent enemy' didn't have a great ring to it. The poets of tomorrow might have a hard time getting that into a verse. But that wasn't why they were doing it.

Marie and Rachel were becoming closer by the day, and Thon did not like this one bit. It jeopardised everything that he was planning. The two of them could almost always be seen together at the head of the column. Sometimes talking seriously, other times laughing. Thon mistrusted both modes and often found excuses to interrupt when things looked like they were getting a bit too cosy. He felt like he was being edged further and further out of the group and, what was more, these newcomers, Calandra from Hardram and Losh in particular, now seemed to have more of a stake in things than he did. It was infuriating. Had he not played just as big a part in the revolution as any of them? Had he not been plotting the downfall of Louie and risking his life in secluded chambers long before Rachel had appeared on the scene? Why did all eyes always flick in her direction when decisions needed to be made or authority needed to be stamped?

Yes, she had so much power, more than anybody else. He was well aware of this fact, but...

Thon had learned a lot recently. And one of the things he'd learned, he was almost certain, had not been realised by any other. Rachel was more powerful than him, that was plain for all to see. But it needn't always be that way. The girl Marie had a great deal of power too, but she was by no means on a par with Rachel. Thon would not shy away from conflict with Marie. Indeed, he would be fairly confident of victory. And with that victory would come something extra special. Something which might mean that he needn't live in Rachel's shadow anymore.

Still, he had to be careful. He needed allies and he needed not to be seen as dangerous. The whole city and, more importantly, the army were happily unified under Rachel's banner. Morale in the camp was good to say the least. People laughed and joked by night and basked in the new confidence they had in their identities. Under Louie they had been nothing. Pawns in a great game, which they stood no chance of winning. Now, under Rachel, every man woman and child in the city felt like a stakeholder. Durpo was no longer only something they lived in, something that happened around them. It was something that was theirs to share, theirs to build together. It was a feeling that built love and camaraderie and, whatever he did, Thon could not be seen as anything that threatened this.

If he was, he would not last five minutes, and thus the new plan forming in his mind was going to have to be executed with the utmost skill and discretion. Some people, I suppose, are just never happy. Thon had already been part of one coup and now he was chomping at the bit for his second.

2.

That night they set up camp as usual. The mood was a good one. Songs were sung and liquor was consumed. You would not think that they were marching to war. But then, perhaps they weren't.

Thon had been sitting with some of the guard, trading stories. Some of his had been true, but they were not in the majority. Now he was making his drunken and increasingly clumsy way over to the tent where, once again, some kind of meeting which he was not part of was taking place. As he entered the tent, almost tripping on a guy rope as he did so, he was greeted with a warm blast of laughter. Clearly Losh had just said something amusing.

The atmosphere changed when Thon entered the room. He felt it happen and he was sure as hell that they all did too. He did not quite belong in this little group. But that didn't mean that he wasn't going to make his presence felt. The eyes that now watched him with a mixture of suspicion and resentment (at least, that was how he saw it) would have to shape up if they didn't want to be put out. As he spoke, it was difficult to keep this murderous anger out of his voice, 'So…what's been going on this evening?' he said, and took a seat at their table. As he sat, he put his hand down on the table a little too hard and everything jumped. Losh and Rachel were looking straight at him. Marie and Callandra shared a glance. It was only the liquor in his blood that allowed him to keep his nerve. Unfortunately, it didn't come with charm included.

'I've just been out spending time with some of the people.' As he said this he looked hard at Rachel. She didn't intimidate him as she normally did. He left his words hanging in the air as if they were the most profound of statements. The corners of Marie's mouth turned up slightly. Losh looked less impressed. Rachel was unmoved.

'And how are they doing?' she asked. Thon seemed taken aback by this. Clearly he had rehearsed all this, however briefly, and Rachel was not following her lines.

'They're fine,' he managed. Now he felt foolish and he was beyond the point of turning back. That bitch Calandra was giving him devil eyes. What right did she have? She'd turned up here asking for their help, and now felt she was *better* than him, was now sitting at the table where things got done and things got decided. A table which he should be at the head of.

'We were just discussing whether we're covering enough ground each day,' said Rachel. Her display of courtesy infuriated Thon more than the thinly veiled contempt of the others. 'What do you think?' All eyes were now most certainly on him. This was his chance to redeem himself slightly. He'd entered like a drunken bull in a china shop, a teenager crashing their parent's dinner party, but now Rachel had asked for his opinion and they were sitting quietly waiting for the response.

'Yeah…I think so,' he said, trying to muster as much sobriety and authority as he could into his voice.

'Actually, we were thinking that perhaps we could step it up a gear. You can clearly see that our people have not spent all their energy.' Thon was dimly aware that he might be under attack. Did Calandra mean what he thought she meant? A drunken roar that became a song of sorts arrived just in time to break the tension and confirm Calandra's point.

'But, of course, we don't want to tire them out to much,' put in Losh. 'He was not addressing Thon.

'No, of course not,' replied Rachel. 'And we want to do nothing to jeopardise their high spirits. But the sooner we reach Hardram, the sooner we can feel a bit more secure in what we're doing.'

Her point, like almost everything she said, was well conceived and clearly delivered. It was non-offensive and had everyone's best interests at its forefront. But this did not stop Thon from seething as she spoke every last syllable. Part of him yearned to flip over the table and go straight for her throat. Magic be damned, he would be more than happy to go old school.

Rachel sensed his feelings but it did not show on her face.

The rest of the evening passed uneventfully. They spoke as a group and Thon soon sobered up. As he calmed, hostility towards him lessened and by the end of the evening he was partaking equally in the discussion. You would have been forgiven for thinking that the tension had diffused. That Thon had transgressed, yes, but had not damaged relationships or left a lasting bad memory. Unfortunately, such forgiveness, however much it might have meant to you, would have little bearing on what was to come. For something was afoot in that little group. They, like their marching army, were so vulnerable, so new to what they were doing. And within them there was a poison. They might be able to patch things up temporarily with Thon. They might be able to smooth over the cracks in the frayed relationship and appease his ego, but they could not solve the ultimate problem. Thon was not happy, and men like him don't bear unhappiness well. In Thon's eyes, the world owes him something and anyone who is standing in the way of that delivery is in danger.

And right now, everyone in that tent is standing between Thon and what Thon wants.

3.

The next day, as they marched, they met some others coming in the opposite direction. They were the final refugees of Hardram. Those who had stayed the longest. Marie couldn't help but notice the affection they obviously held for Calandra. They were clearly not from the higher rungs of society but greeted their leader in a relaxed fashion. They were full of respect but also completely confident of their right to speak with her, and equally confident that she would listen. Their society was obviously organised a lot better than ours, said Marie to herself. She felt privileged to have Calandra walking with them. The former leader also had a solid command of magic. Not one that could rival hers, Thon's or, of course, Rachel's, but one that could hold its own amongst the guard and the volunteers they had brought.

The travelling people they met were made up of a few families. They said they had stayed in Hardram longer than all the rest because they couldn't bring themselves to leave the city. The eldest member of the group, a woman with fewer teeth than eyes, was doing most of the talking.

'We couldn't bear to leave the city all by itself,' she was saying. 'The more people that left, the more we thought that we too should leave. But the longer it went on, the harder it got.' Calandra nodded sympathetically and Marie suspected that she could detect a hint of guilt in her body language. Shouldn't the captain always be the last to abandon a sinking ship?

'Then, the other day, *it* happened and we knew we could stay no longer.'

'What happened the other day?' said Rachel, cutting into the conversation almost rudely. The old woman looked a little surprised to have been addressed so abruptly but soon gathered her composure.

'I'm not sure what it was,' she said. 'But it was damn dangerous, that's all

154

I know.' The rest of her group seemed to agree with this sentiment. They nodded enthusiastically, as if each lateral movement of the head was more likely to impress the seriousness of the situation.

'We thought the whole city was going down,' said the woman, now seemingly pleased that she had such a captivated audience. She had become like the narrator in some ancient tragedy, delivering the all-important monologue, while those behind her moved in unison, adding the necessary auditory punctuation. 'It was as if the sky was opening up and there was some world beyond it. Some terrible place, we could see bad things there…'

'What kind of bad things?' asked Calandra, concern etching itself deeper into her face as she listened.

'Unspeakable things,' said the woman before contradicting herself. 'Things with too many arms and too many teeth. Things that looked hungry. They were small it seemed, but I only reckon that's cos they were a long way away. It was as if whatever keeps the bad things out of our world was stretched to breaking point. It could not have held much longer. I screamed, "It's the end of all things" and we all thought the same, didn't we?' Again, the nodding chorus left not a shadow of doubt that the storyteller yielded truth and nothing more. 'Then, just as it was all about to break, it stopped…but that wasn't the end of it.' She paused thoughtfully as if deciding how to lay out the next sentence. 'For the chamber was affected by it too.'

'How so?' asked Rachel, glancing at Calandra.

'There's something going on up there,' said the old woman. 'Something the likes of which I've not seen before…I mean, we've all known for sometime, as I'm sure you are aware Calandra.' Calandra nodded at this. 'We've all seen how whatever's in there is not going to be contained for that much longer. But after that day when the sky opened up, well, you get the feeling that something's changed up there.'

She was getting tired from all the talking and she needed a moment to catch her breath. 'It's almost like there's a fight going on in there, not so much like something's trying to break out, although of course there is that as well, but it's also like there's something going on inside. Some kind of clash *in* the chamber. It's no longer straining just to get out, it's sort of…eating itself.'

The division between those from Hardram and those who were not became so evident. The Durpoians looked at each other, confused by what she was saying. Those from the city to which they now journeyed did not. There was a certain understanding, Marie half supposed and half read, that came from living under the chamber your whole life. It must be such a strange sensation, your city lying under this constant threat, this airborne prison. And they didn't even know what it contained. Marie was not at all surprised to see that they'd developed some kind of warped understanding of what was going on above them. Some kind of sense, she supposed, of what was happening, even though it could not be seen or understood. The little glances that passed between Calandra and the travelling families told Marie a lot about what living in Hardram must have been like. For all the equality that seemed to exist in their city, there must also have been great discomfort, and it was a weight that they'd all had to bear. A weight that had now driven them from their own homes and left them with nothing. And now it was a weight that they all had to stop, before it dragged everyone and everything under.

They bade a fond farewell to the travelling family and continued on their way. It had been an enlightening encounter in many ways, and it affected the march. When they stopped that night, after walking many more miles than on the previous days, the mood was not as raucous. And it was only partly down to being more tired. Somehow, hearing of what they were to face coming from the mouths of people who were fleeing from it had raised the tension in the camp. Minds that had previously wanted to unwind with song and ale after a hard day's walk now sat quietly. Thoughts had wandered onto what lay ahead and would not be returning until their creators had reached the same physical space. It was as if the army had slung their minds forward, like a fisherman casting a net, and that net was now hooked on the spires of Hardram. The intervening period was no longer to be enjoyed, and thoughts of the conflict were no longer to be ignored or pushed away. For something was coming their way, and the encounter with the refugee family had confirmed just how real it was. The fight was one from which they might not return.

4.

Lying in his bed, Thon was playing over the day's events in his head. He too had learned something that day. Like the others, he did not feel quite the same as he had done. He had seen something that he had, until now, not been sure existed.

He had seen fear in Rachel.

It had not been much, just a glimmer. But it had been there and it gave him all sorts of hope. The night before, as he'd sat at their table like some kind of obedient dog, he had begun to lose hope. Rage lived within him, desire to unseat Rachel and to take his rightful place was as strong as ever. But the reality of achieving it had never seemed so distant. The other four were now a unit, a well respected and increasingly well bonded collective. And while they were so, his opportunity to attack would never come. He'd hoped to isolate one of the others in secret, begin a slow campaign against their new leader. Perhaps Marie, if handled correctly, could slowly have been brought round to his way of thinking. But then last night he had decided no. Marie was Rachel's, as they all were, and Rachel was theirs. What a cosy little set up it had become and how could it possibly be disrupted with such a fearless, yet unassuming, champion of the people at the helm? Those had been the uncomfortable thoughts with which he'd eventually drifted off the night before. A sense of acceptance he would never have believed possible served as an even more uncomfortable duvet than the wiry rug he lay under.

But today he *had* seen it. He didn't completely understand it yet, but he'd seen enough to give himself hope. When the old woman had talked about the sky opening up and about the surge that they'd all felt (Gods, it now seemed like an age ago), there had been a deep fear within his mayor's eyes. There was something about this that affected her in a way it did not affect the rest of them. It carried a threat, they all knew that, but it did not seem to Thon that Rachel was merely acknowledging how bad it would be if the sky opened up and the dregs of another world came pouring in. She was worried about something more and, unless he was very much mistaken, it was something that affected her on a personal level. Very rarely, in the time he'd known her, had Thon seen selfish emotion in Rachel. The situation had dictated that she become the voice of the people and this had transcended into her personality. She did not make decisions for herself, she made them for the city. Even in her most relaxed moments she still wore this cap of diplomacy.

This was why Thon was so certain of what he'd seen. It was different to everything else. The look that had come into Rachel's eyes when the old woman had spoken had not been a fear for the army, for Durpo or even of the world beyond the sky. It was a fear for herself. A nice selfish fear that was so bitterly satisfying for Thon to behold. In one smooth moment, it showed him not only the humanity of his enemy but also the vulnerability. It showed him that which was so well hidden but was also there to be broken.

As sleep began to take him, a thin smile played with his lips. The ghost of a plan, so fragile he dared not think too hard on it, lest he scare it away, was drifting around in his mind. Like silk he would allow it to spin around, catching more and more of itself, until it became something to be reckoned with. That would be when Thon would strike and, even though the chamber was fit to burst, he had time.

Chapter 3.

Mountain.

1.

They were almost there. The yards of mountain disappeared easily under their feet. And, as tired as they felt, it only seemed to get easier. The air was thinning and the terrain was steepening. Indeed, sometimes they were forced to climb, nothing too challenging but climbing none the less. Yet none of this mattered to them. They could climb all day and all night if they had to.

The mood since the confrontation with the thing in the woods had been one that knew no bounds. They say that if two stand together, then even the Gods are powerless to stand against them, and here stood four together. Though they could not have known then that it was, indeed, a God that stood against them. They would not have held much interest at all in any of these ideas. Proving whether or not ancient wisdoms stood up to literal translations was not what had inspired them to set out on their quest, but perhaps it will prove an interesting side effect all the same.

As the sun set they decided to stop. The mountain was asking more and more of them and, determined as they were, they were not so delusional as to think that climbing in the dark was any kind of good idea. So instead they made a small fire on a ledge and moved in closer together. The difference in temperature was becoming increasingly noticeable. As they watched the great, all seeing orb sink below the horizon, back over from whence they'd come, tiredness began to suck them in.

'One of us should still keep watch,' said Kayleigh. Coki muttered in agreement. They had no idea what they were up against and, much as they'd given it a good going over, they had seen no evidence that it was dead, only that it was gone. It would have been stupid to assume that it could not return. There were no takers for the first watch. When the threat had been so evident, they'd been falling over each other to offer their services. Now that the watch had become more of a precaution, it wasn't getting volunteered for quite as competitively. Indeed, after a few minutes of no one saying anything, it seemed as if all four would fall asleep.

Kayleigh caught her head sinking onto Coki's shoulder, it felt warm and cosy. It fitted the contour of her head nicely, it reminded her of Shabwan. Perhaps it was the uncomfortable nature of this thought that jerked her into life, or perhaps it was the realisation that they'd all drifted into sleep and left themselves vulnerable.

'Someone needs to take watch,' she said, more testily than before.

'Not you though,' said Lewhay. She let it go. He was in one of his goading moods and had been all afternoon.

'Yeah I don't mind,' she said, sounding a lot like a person who did mind.

'Nah I'm up already,' lied Lewhay. He was sprawled out, his legs dangling over the edge of their little ledge. Unaware that he'd just made a rhyme, Lewhay turned his head away from Kayleigh and began snoring. She seethed inwardly. Might as well be her then, she supposed, although a fat lot of good it was likely to do anyway. These three weren't going to be up to fighting anything. They couldn't even keep their eyes open. Kayleigh hitched herself up onto a ledge that was slightly higher than where they were sleeping. As she rose up, her vision adjusted. She was now able to see beyond the blackness that made up the outside wall of their fire. Without that glow sucking everything in, you could make out the night-time silhouettes of what was around you. She could still make out, over on the horizon, a deep red glow. The last little bit that the sun hadn't bothered to take with it...

But it wasn't the only red in the sky.

For a moment she thought her eyes were playing tricks on her. Then she craned her head round, following the rival glow she had picked up.

There it was. There was no denying it. She almost screamed. For from behind the jagged peaks of the mountains, a deep red glow, far brighter than that of the fading sunset, was emanating. The peaks, rather than formidable obstacles still to be crossed, suddenly seemed more like they were protecting her. For that light behind them could mean nothing good. It was not like any light of this world, even the light of a fire ravaging through a city would have been preferable. It was almost an anti-light, Kayleigh thought, as rather than illuminating, it was encroaching into the space that should have belonged to other things. Imposing itself as an almost physical presence rather than touching what was already there.

Kayleigh, like most, had always seen illumination as her friend. The night was there to be feared but you could rest assured that the morning daylight would always chase it away. Night terrors can only exist temporarily, for their very existence relies both on your belief and the holes that you can paint them in. Light takes away these places and the belief, which to the childish mind can seem like the ultimate of truths, stands no hope of survival. That was how Kayleigh had always thought of light, a friend which could be relied upon, even when all else was failing. But now, staring upon this deep, red, bloody glow, she would have happily swapped it for the pitchiest of pitch blacks.

She thought about waking the others. They should see this. They should know. But she couldn't quite bring herself to do it. She wasn't sure she was ready to see the panicked looks on their faces. It was all she could do to hold herself together, and she had an uncomfortable feeling that one of the boys would probably raise the issue which she was trying so hard to ignore. The glow probably had something to do with Shabwan.

The beast in the woods had felt like their ultimate test, the passing of which had opened up the sprint finish to Shabwan. Now it felt like the

159

appetiser to the huge gourmet dinner that burned ahead of them. *What the hell was it?*

Kayleigh did not sleep that night. The tiredness that had tried to glue her head to Coki's shoulder had been replaced with a wave of the most uncomfortable nervousness. How could she possibly relax with that great ugly light looming over her? She felt tiny. The glow gave the mountains a strange effect, almost beyond three-dimensional. It was a bit like being on stonk, she thought, you were suddenly aware of space in a different way. And this awareness, rather than being a thing of beauty, made Kayleigh feel like a small fly. Perched in the wide open, just waiting for any of the incomprehensible things that had become her enemy to reach down and swat her.

As the daylight arrived, the red was still visible but not as noticeable. She did not point it out to the boys as they woke. They were too concerned with expressing their guilt that she'd taken a whole nights watch. Lewhay especially seemed eager to make it up to her and, as they continued on, her pack was much lighter than usual, whereas he was sweating like a hog, despite the cool mountain air.

It was later that day when they saw the oo-ja.

Chapter 4.

Mind swap.

1.

As Shabwan lay there unable to move, Veo's story was played out for him. The God did not know it was happening and would have done anything to stop it. But he was too concerned with doing exactly the same thing. As the story of the reluctant hero played out in the conqueror's mind, so the opposite happened. Shabwan saw everything that had led to the current predicament. Seeing, however, as we have already picked up a fair whack of this story during our travels with the other two thirds of Shabwan, we needn't concern ourselves with all of it. Instead, we shall enter at the point when Lubwan so rudely interrupted our last foray into Veo's past. We shall, therefore, join an awfully depressed God, living back in his kingdom, a place that couldn't have felt less like home. A place where he is forced, every day, to see the woman he loves, who he knows also loves him, in the arms of another. In the arms of one he must report to and serve.

Not a happy place, I'm sure you'll agree.

2.

Every day was the same. There was no purpose to anything.

Before, there had always been purpose. As a God, you were always doing something. If you weren't then why the hell not? There was a universe out there, containing, at any one time, several planets on the brink of exploding themselves and potentially letting through the horror that dwelt in other dimensions. If you couldn't busy yourself in such an environment, then you didn't really deserve a job.

The concept of time was, of course, also massively different to the Gods. There's no end to it. Simple as that. Humans, in my experience, love to think in chapters. It makes sense of life. It makes the incomprehensible slightly less so, and helps to organise the confusing filing cabinet that is memory. It also helps to define you as you grow. That was me back then, you might think, that was me in a different chapter, not the me of now.

The Gods don't think like this and it's for a simple reason: they're not building towards an end. For them, only a forced death offers an ending of sorts, and egos such as theirs don't conceive that such an end will ever come.

Thus, the life of a God is one of an eternal and unwavering purpose. The universe is their charge and will be so forever. There is no end in sight, save for that which they refuse to acknowledge.

None of this had ever seemed like a problem to Veo. Now it did. It felt like the biggest of problems, for it meant that his eternity was to be spent watching his love in his master's arms. The future was as bleak as could be

161

and the only thing that matched its bleakness was its longevity.

This particular day, Gask had sent for him as usual. Veo didn't care what it might be about. The only thing that concerned him was her being there. Which, of course, she would. She always was. He did not allow her far from his side these days. But this wasn't what hurt most. It was seeing her so content that ripped at him. Whether she was pretending or otherwise it was impossible to tell. And yet, he felt like he'd got to know her so well. The time they had spent together on Svin, no matter how much it hurt him now to think of it, he knew that they had shared something there. Their brief relationship had been far more than anything that she'd ever shared with Gask. Theirs had been a thing of reality, a thing of joy. When he saw her stood next to Gask, he saw none of that. But then, he didn't see any sadness either. She had resigned herself to a life and was now going to live it forever. She was going to stay by his side for as long as the Gods survived.

Veo was only mildly interested to notice that Gask was agitated as he entered his chamber. Such a sight would once have roused him. He would have wondered how it could feed into his plan. He would have watched and waited, seen exactly what Gask was up to and what armour chinks this was presenting him with. As it was, he took barely any notice. She was stood there as she always was and, as always, she greeted him with calm politeness. He in turn responded as he always did and a little more of him died inside.

There was no reason to listen to Gask, no reason to carry out any of the duties he might require. But he would continue to do so anyway. There was a pride within Veo and even though he'd lost everything, to let others know this would be a disgrace. Veo was a man broken but he would never be one who was seen as such. Instead, he would carry on as he always had, only now without ambition. He would not dream of Eree, he would not dream of the day he would rob Gask of his throne and finally take up his rightful place, he would not dream of anything. And not doing so gave him a kind of savage pleasure, a deep, bitter satisfaction. The universe had conspired to take anything he'd ever wanted, which was a cruel irony considering he was one of its creators, and now he would remove himself of the little he had left. Rock bottom was perversely preferable to hanging just above it.

'How can these damn fools still think like this?' came Gask's rhetorical question. 'They still think that waging war is some kind of answer!? They've all seen how perilous it is when we try. I've seen the barrier stretched about as thin as I care to and, if we go ploughing into these worlds, then they're only going to fight harder.'

Veo had been so absorbed in his own world that he only vaguely knew what Gask was talking about. He'd heard snippets of conversation about the kingdom. More and more magic was apparently flowing through. Gods had been killed, battles were flaring up. A lot of the kingdom Gods seemed to feel that a strong assault was needed. The humans, as was customary when the flow increased, were becoming too big for their boots and rough justice was a logical reprise. But it came, of course, with a huge level of risk. Huge dollops of crude magic coming together could create cracks and when enough magic together…they'd all seen the forms it took. It brought a chill to think what would happen if Rez could blast all his energy through at once.

'We needn't be reactionary,' said Eree, carefully. As she spoke, the intensity of feeling within Veo notched up a level. To see her was not to hear her voice. Both had to be dealt with as separate entities. 'We should give them a chance to voice their opinion in council. As has always been the way.' Gask turned and looked at her. You could not help but notice the difference. Before, he would have raged at such a comment. The rage was still there, the eyes betrayed that much, but it seemed the emotion was not to be granted an outward form. Eree had changed the dynamic between them. She had left, something he had not truly believed she was capable of, and now he missed the security he once had. In that moment, Gask had never looked more human to Veo. It was a thought that would once have excited him. Now it did little. But that wasn't to say it didn't do something…perhaps Veo was not quite as dead inside as he'd thought.

'The council meetings are always the same. They rant and rave and talk of all these hair-brained ideas and nothing ever comes of it.' Like a lot of rulers, Gask was always quick to gloss over the fact that the reason nothing ever came of these meetings was because he didn't allow it to. 'What do you think Veo?'

The question came as something of a shock. It showed another clear change in the king of the Gods. He now openly exhibited a lot more respect to his second in command. Ironic really that it had come at an unwanted time. Veo did not answer straight away and Gask took his silence for thought. In a way, it was.

'Perhaps the council meeting is a good idea,' said Veo. 'It is always preferable to give the others the illusion of involvement, even if nothing more.' He was on autopilot. No feeling backed up what he said, but this seemed like the kind of thing he would have said, had he cared.

Gask deliberated before speaking again, looking carefully from Eree to Veo. Seeing them both but seeing so little.

'Perhaps…you might want to have a bit more of a vocal role in this meeting Veo?' It seemed to pain Gask to ask this, but you could see his sharp old mind working away. 'You have, after all, been there and seen it…perhaps, if they heard it from you. Perhaps, if you told them the danger that we face…perhaps then they might not have such cavalier attitudes towards war.'

Gask was staring long and hard. Veo met his gaze. Could the God really not know how much he wanted to rip his throat out? Surely the message must burn out of him in some form or other. It was everything he could do to keep himself from lashing out. He did not understand how, when they were holding eye contact like this, Gask could not sense how things were.

Then he noticed Eree was looking at him and it all changed. Everything that had been ultimate truth now lay in the dust. This is the nature of such intensity of feeling. One minute you have confined yourself to a lifetime in the gutter, the next you're in heaven. Veo spoke to Gask. He spoke as he always had done. But he did not think in that way.

'Of course I will speak to them,' he replied.

3.

The chamber of the Gods was silent, which was far from a common occurrence. But this served only to highlight the seriousness of the issue. They had argued about this before, but not like this. You could feel the difference in the atmosphere, both literally and figuratively. The magic was flowing harder than it ever had.

In itself, this was not a huge problem. The universe they had created was strong. It would absorb huge amounts of the stuff before it buckled and broke. At least it would have done if it wasn't populated by such damn idiots. They had all seen it before; magical wars breaking out, either between warring human factions or aimed in their direction. The results were usually similar, devastation and death. Sometimes they had found themselves on the death side of things. Their consensus was, therefore, a fairly universal one. The magical empires of the universe were to be hit harder than they'd ever been hit before. Single Gods would not wage these wars. They would travel as an army and, together, they would visit such devastation on those who practiced magic that soon the universe would be a much calmer place. If the retribution was swift and violent enough, then the humans would not be able to rise up in number and they wouldn't find themselves confronted with potentially barrier-ripping levels of concentrate.

They could all see this was the way, so why couldn't Gask? Never had their leader been so isolated against a commonly held belief. To the other Gods, there could be no flaw in this plan. The flawed idea was to do nothing. Stand by while humans attacked each other and Gods alike. Allow them to bring such destruction on themselves. Perhaps they'd even open up a channel while they were all sat up here talking about it. Then whatever energy he so feared would come pouring through and they'd all be none the wiser until it was much too late. Perhaps their old leader had lost his nerve. Perhaps he was no longer fit for purpose...so who was going to challenge him then? These points in their little huddled conversations were the ones at which people suddenly became a bit less forthcoming. 'Well...' they would say, which, as we all know, is a word of little use to anyone, and then things would lose their momentum. Yes, they were angry and yes, this was about as important as it gets but no, they weren't really up for being the one to raise it at council. You should do that, they would helpfully suggest to one another.

Still, when the day came and they assembled as one, there was a certain bravery in the air and while no one wanted to be the one to start it, if the wheel of discontent began to roll somehow, there were more than enough of them to help it on its way. The air prickled with anticipation. Those who had never, in their wildest dreams, imagined challenging Gask began to think, why not? There was something different that day. Something that made you believe in yourself.

As Gask entered the room, however, flanked by Eree and Veo, fledgling courage faltered. The God's presence could not be ignored. As they'd spoken about him in corners and conspired in little circles, he'd become smaller in their minds. His natural authority and sheer power had diminished under the work of their minds' artist. Now here he was, in the flesh...and their minds' artist had been most unkind to him. Each footstep reverberated around the room, and it seemed an age before the three figures reached the podium at the far end. Finally, Gask, Veo and Eree took their seats for the meeting that would change everything.

4.

'I am aware of why you have come,' started Gask. He was not making eye contact with anyone in the room. His address was to all but to none individually. 'You all believe that you know better than me how we should handle this situation. You have come here today to tell me that we should wreak bloody mayhem on those we created. That we should give them a short and sharp reminder of who governs them and their worlds. Am I right?' There were murmurs of agreement through the room. Little ripples, as if Gask had dropped a stone into the water. 'I said, AM I RIGHT!?' This time his voice boomed out through the chamber and the ripples stopped. It was controlled rage but rage none the less, and it reminded the would-be-challengers just how much of the 'would be' made up their challenge. 'You call this meeting and, what? None of you are even willing to speak to me?'

He had a fair point.

Then someone spoke, a God named Varniss who sat near the back of the chamber. A God who had recently lost one of his closest friends to a gaggle of sorcerers. 'They must be stopped,' he said in a weak voice that became stronger as he continued. 'You must see this Gask. They are using magic so freely in some worlds. It is no longer just the sorcerers that can harness the flow and, more often than not, this leads to conflict. We've all seen what happens when they fight.'

'I must see this, must I?' Gask asked, his eyes boring through the room and locating Varniss. 'Do you honestly believe I don't know the dangers we face from magic?' His voice was calmer now and seemed all the worse for it. 'I know what could happen in any of these worlds, but I also know why I'm here.' The silence that followed this was not without a tinge of guilt. 'When we created this place, we created it for life to exist. We created it so that others, apart from us, would live and breathe upon it. Do any of you remember those days?'

The question was an uncomfortable one. It was true that their original objectives had been much nobler than they were now. Yes, they had always

165

intended to rule. But they had never been cruel about it. They had ruled well and only punished or demanded sacrifice when necessary (whenever that is). But over time things had changed. As the flow had increased, those who they'd given life to now fought against them, and not only against them but against each other. And as they did so, the wall, which held back an evil the humans were not even aware of, wore ever thinner.

And as the wall had worn away, so had the values of the Gods. Gask was now reminding them of that uncomfortable fact. The fact that they'd neglected their duty. The fact that they were putting personal safety ahead of obligation. None of them wanted to hear it, but all knew it was true. Gask sensed victory and continued, 'I am not so cowardly as to think killing endless humans is worth preventing what *might* happen. I'm not going to sanction that you all go out waging bloody war because you're so damn afraid that, *one day*, we may be called upon to face Rez again.'

If the floor had been sentient, it would not have felt the least bit comfortable with so many eyes upon it. Gask was good, that was why he'd lasted so long. But he was about to make a mistake, a mistake which would one day change everything.

He turned to Veo,

'Perhaps you'd prefer to hear from someone who, unlike you, has actually experienced something of which they speak. Perhaps, if my opinion is so redundant these days, you'd prefer to listen to Veo.'

The floor was finally left alone, for there was a new subject to be stared at. It was the first time all eyes had been on him and Veo remained unfazed. If anything, it filled him with confidence. He remembered what it had felt like to want this. Now was his moment. He remembered how Eree had looked at him yesterday. He remembered the hope that he had seen in her eyes and he remembered Svin. He hadn't really planned this, though he had known it was coming.

Veo took a couple of steps forward to ensure he was as central as possible. He hadn't planned what he was going to say, as indeed he hadn't really planned *to* say. But once it started, it came fast and easily.

'None of you have ever seen the place where Rez is now imprisoned,' he started. 'Or am I wrong?' Silence confirmed that he was not. 'None of you have seen what could burst forth from that place, and yet all of you have imagined it is something we will be unable to deal with.' Gask nodded. Veo was doing well, a natural politician. 'Your judgment has apparently spurred you on against your leader. A leader who would rather preserve humanity than selfishly destroy it to secure our own safety.' No one was challenging, even though Veo was leaving himself open. Their argument was not only based on self preservation. For if Rez burst through, they doubted that anyone or anything would be spared, divine or otherwise.

Gask looked at Eree, she was not looking at him. He looked back at Veo, preparing to savour the moment when his right hand man would destroy the pathetic aspirations of these hapless fools, who had, once again, unsuccessfully challenged his authority. It hadn't been an easy decision, whether to call on Veo or not. It suggested weakness, turning to another. But now he could see it had been the right decision. Veo was doing a great job.

'I stand before you now and tell you that your leader is completely and utterly *wrong*.'

5.

Second only to Eree leaving, it was the greatest shock of Gask's existence. Never before had Veo spoken a word against him. The God, who he trusted most of all, had always carried out orders without so much as flinching. He was dependable and trustworthy and had even retrieved Eree for him. A task he thought had been doomed to failure. Now this same individual was calling him out in front of the entire kingdom. He had been blindsided and was now facing a very vocal chamber. Rage and confusion tussled within him for superiority. The rage did not care why anything was happening, it just wanted to act. The confusion felt differently and, temporarily at least, it won. Gask stood there, mouth slightly open, listening to his judgment being called into question by a man who was not even looking at him. He was, instead, working the crowd, playing them better than Gask had ever managed. And the tide of public opinion was becoming a tsunami to Gask's small and very flat island.

'Gask says that you have never seen this place, well, I would remind him that neither has he. There is only one God who has been there and he stands right before you now. He stands before you and tells you that your convictions are right. We should not stand by while the humans wear away the barriers we created. We should not stand by and invite our greatest foe in. A foe who will wipe this universe clean and start again. Gask asks you to remember when we first created. Well I ask you to remember before that. I ask you to remember when we fought. For that is what it will be like again. And while we've been here getting fat and lazy, Rez has been preparing. Look at yourselves and ask, when was the last time you *really* fought?'

There were no mirrors so they couldn't follow this command directly, but all but the stupidest got the gist.

'You are not the Gods who originally defeated him and, having seen what is going on there, believe me when I tell you, you are not Gods who will beat him again.'

Even though they were essentially being insulted, several Gods had risen to their feet and were cheering. Veo was a master of the theatre, a puppeteer who was now holding all the strings. Gask's clenched fist had never looked so empty. To his left, Eree could not believe what she was seeing. She endeavoured to keep her expression neutral. Occasionally she felt Gask's eyes on her but she could not meet the gaze. To do so would be to give away everything.

6.

Veo knew that the time had come to look around, but he had no idea what he would see. He did not possess the capacity of imagination to comprehend the rage he had induced. He had, ever since he'd seen the look in Eree's eyes the previous day, known that a conflict between he and Gask was to come. She'd given him hope again, whether she'd meant to or not, and he'd seen the solution. He wondered how he hadn't seen it before. Although he supposed a lifetime of servitude hadn't helped. She had stated that she must go back to Gask and he, in his foolishness, had not seen that for what it was. He had assumed it had been a choice made out of love, but it had not...well, not in that way anyway. It had been a choice of fear. The love she'd felt had been towards Veo, but this love had manifested itself in his protection. If she were to return to Gask then her love would be safe. She had sacrificed their happiness so Veo could survive.

He had not seen it then, but he saw it now. And once, in that singular moment of eye contact, the realisation had come to him, he'd had but one path. Confrontation.

While Gask lived they could never be together, but with Gask gone there was nothing that stood in their way. Nothing that would prevent them from ruling together in a life of eternal happiness. Idealistic beliefs perhaps, and very human ones. It seemed a new Veo had been born in that moment.

A plan was what had been needed but plans need time, and when opportunity comes knocking, you have to work with what you've got and think on your feet. Especially when you're thrown, unexpectedly, into the perfect arena from which to stage your coup. Veo had barely even made the decision that he was going to take Gask down, thus liberating himself and Eree, and, as a pleasant side effect, taking his rightful place as king of the Gods, when he'd found himself presented with the most unimaginably perfect opportunity. Stood in a room full of Gods all hating their leader, all resenting his every word and, with the trust of that same individual at *his* disposal...plans could be damned.

As he'd spoken, he'd felt the will of the room rise up against Gask. He knew that the important thing was to keep prodding. Bait the bear, but make sure all present knew that, when the fight was initiated, it had been the bear who came first. A killer acting in self-defence can be comfortably elevated to the status of leader. A killer in cold blood might not have such an easy passage.

Thus, as he turned back to face Gask, he hoped that the king saw just what a gauntlet was being thrown down and would respond accordingly. Whether he could win or not didn't matter so much any more. For they had reached the end of the line, it was death or glory-beyond-glory time.

Gask's rage, struggling on against the dumbfounded confusion he had been smitten with, suddenly found a stranglehold. As Gask made eye contact with his betrayer, it launched itself at the reins.

'So...' began Gask, ugly red tingeing the edges of his vision. 'This is how you want it to be.' The shouting of the other Gods was becoming background, as hearing clouded over. Both Gods were preparing themselves for battle, knowing this was all that could lie before them now. Sensing this, the other Gods began clamouring backwards up the marble benches of the chamber. They did not want to be too close to the action. Eree was reeling with shock. She reached out her hands, clearly desiring to stop what was happening. But no sound came from her mouth. She seemed almost childlike, a distraught toddler not understanding why her parents would speak to each other so angrily.

Gask and Veo flew forward at the same moment, like great rocks released from catapults. They smashed together with such force that the chamber cracked from floor to ceiling. They fell apart and Veo was much slower climbing to his feet. He felt the full force of a lightning bolt to his chest and was flung almost the length of the hall. His fight was to be over before it had begun. He felt like every bone in his body had been broken. Gask leapt forward, remaining at the same height for the full length of the chamber, then, as he descended, he brought a great fist down upon Veo's chest with the power to knock a small moon out of orbit. He had not, however, gone for the kill.

Veo writhed on the floor and tried to speak, he wanted to shout out to Eree, make sure that before he died she knew how he felt. Gask moved above him again, but did not strike. Instead he addressed the rest of the chamber.

'You see what happens when you challenge me!?' he roared. 'Do you see!?' Another thunderous fist shattered Veo's ribs yet further. He was beginning to disintegrate.

Gask pulled him up into a sitting position, eyes blazing. 'Why would you betray me?' he shouted. 'Answer me!' Veo said nothing. He would die happily, knowing that he had tried to do all he could for he and Eree, but he would not grant Gask anything. His killer would remain unsatisfied, always wondering why he'd been forced to kill. Gask's brow furrowed, 'Very well then,' he said and all present sensed the change in his mood. Veo's time had come to an end. The fist went back and lighting crackled. This time it would not be so forgiving.

'Nooo!' screamed Eree as she flung herself at Gask. Small as she was, she knocked him off his feet and the bolt that would have killed Veo instead created a gaping hole in the chamber roof. Light flooded in.

Gask got to his feet, staring at Eree. You had to feel for him really. It had been a day of incomprehensibility and now more was being added.

'You would protect him?' he said, eyes wide and devoid of all understanding. Hers were just as wide but held fear rather than surprise.

'I created the guardians,' he bellowed. 'I've secured the magical safety of the worlds. I've handled this and now you would all turn against me...even you?' Eree looked at him defiantly as he said this.

'You created a slave race, you made a mistake! You overstepped what we are supposed to do.'

'What we're supposed to do?' Gask spluttered and laughed as he spoke. 'I'm the king of the Gods, I decide what we're supposed to do.'

As he said this he turned back to Veo and drew the same lethal energy into his hand. As he swung his arm, Eree attacked him again, this time with force of her own. Gask hit the ground hard but then picked himself to his feet. He rounded angrily on Eree, 'What is wrong with you!? You would harm me to protect *him*?' As Gask said this, comprehension began to dawn on his face. It was comprehension of the most unwelcome kind and he would have forced it away if he could. He looked from Eree to Veo and then back again. 'Ah...I see,' he said, and the sadness was terrible to behold.

'Gask...' Eree began but was stopped as his fist hit her in the side of the head. She flew across the chamber into the marble benches and lay there unmoving. Gask, slowly and deliberately advanced on Veo, who was trying in vain to drag himself to his feet. As Gask neared him, he picked up a lump of marble that had fallen as the roof split. He smashed it into Veo's face. The God would never look the same again; indeed, from that day forward he would wear a mask. Gask looked down upon the bloody ruined pulp that had been the God's face and said two words, 'my woman.' It was somehow half way between question and statement, but at the same time not really anything like either. Then he filled his hand with that same white energy that Veo knew would end him.

But it did not, for something helped Veo to escape that day. Something that Veo did not understand. All he knew was that one moment he was on the chamber floor, awaiting his fatal blow, the next he was lying on the forest floor of the world of Svin.

Eree came to him, but not for some time. He had feared more than anything that Gask had killed her. And were it not for his injuries, he would have returned to the chamber to try and save her. As it was, he had not been able to lift himself from the forest floor. He was healing but oh so slowly, it would be a long time before he could travel again.

And then she was there, beautiful Eree. She had come and healed him, but then once again she had broken his heart. If he'd known what she planned to tell him, then he would have requested that she did not heal him at all. He would have preferred the opposite.

For they could not be together now and they never would be. She would return to Gask and beg his forgiveness and she would report Veo's death. For if she didn't, then neither of them would ever be safe. He would tear the universe apart if he needed to, killing every man woman and beast within it, until he'd had their blood. They were no match for him and, while she loved and would always love Veo, they could never see each other again.

'Why didn't you just let me die?' he asked her, his voice hollow. She wept and told him that she could not have. It would have killed her to do so. She

170

said goodbye to him and he was still too weak to follow. Whether he would have done or not, he didn't know.

All she had said was true. There was no happy future for the two of them. Veo could not defeat Gask and while Gask was alive, Eree must stay with him, for her own safety more than anything else. He imagined that Gask, egotistical as he was, would forgive her. And if she was forgiven, then she was alive. This, while tearing his ruined heart in two, did at least offer a grain of comfort.

7.

He stayed on Svin for a long time, wandering in the forests like a hermit. He didn't care what happened to him now. Embarrassed by his ruined face, he forged a mask from one of the trees. He did not want to be reminded of his defeat every time he caught his reflection in a pool. For the longest time he had nothing, no future, no reason only the ability to wander. Then, one day, a thought came to him. He had lost Eree and his life as he'd known it. He could never see her again and, if he wanted to keep her safe, he needed to remain here pretending to be dead. But, despite all of this, there was perhaps still one person (well, not exactly) who could help him.

Veo needed to find Rez.

8.

He journeyed as he had before. He went the same way across that barren landscape. Trying his best not to alert those things that dwelt in this place. He was sufficiently recovered to travel, but he was by no means wholly recovered. If the great magical beasts that stalked the purple plains were to find him, then the feast would be theirs. He needed to travel unnoticed to the point where he could see into the dimension beyond.

The point was a vast mountain. Jutting up into the torrid sky to the extent where it looked more like it was pouring out of it than reaching up to it. Veo climbed it as he had all those thousands of years ago. He had never, for one second, imagined that he would return to this place.

As he climbed he did not once remove his mask. It had become a part of him now. It was a barrier that separated him from what had gone before and what he had lost. He would not remove it until he had been successful. The day that Gask was no more would be the day Veo exposed, once again, the damage he had done.

He still thought of Eree but the thoughts had no consistency. They deviated from one minute to the next. At times, she was the most beautiful and pure thing he had ever seen. At others, she had betrayed him, she had sold him down the river to return to a life of safety. He tried to fight the latter. He tried to banish these ideas and remind himself that the reason he was here, the reason he was climbing this seemingly infinite mountain, was to be with her again.

Sometimes he was more successful than others.

He was about two thirds of the way up the mountain when he realised he'd been sensed. He could see a long way from this elevated point. Below him sprawled the landscape, disgusting beyond reckoning, similar to nothing that they'd designed. And upon this landscape came that which he'd feared. The hungry, magical beasts were coming and they were coming en masse. They would not catch him on the way up, but the problem with going up is that there is only one logical next stage. And he doubted that patience was going to be much of a problem for the waiting jaws.

Still, at this stage, there was nothing he could do. For all he knew, Rez would kill him before he got the chance to try and descend. Considering all that had happened, there was little point in worrying about it. So he did not. And up he went. Up and up and up. But not away, I hasten to add.

As the journey went on, the sky seemed to darken. There was no day and night in this place. Nothing as beautiful as a sun existed. Although it's worth noting that obviously I'm biased in that respect. I've only ever seen one from a comfortable distance. Forced up close to one, I'd be having no fun...although I might be having slightly more fun than Veo.

He was dragging himself now. Heaving his bulk up every inch. The mountain had become thin, almost ladder-like. It was more like climbing a tree than anything. Just when Veo felt he could bear it no longer, just as he was welcoming the idea of a backwards fall to nothingness, his hand hit the flat. Excitement rose in him. In spite of everything he had reached the top. In spite of all that had sought to destroy him, here he was, facing the next impossible stage of his plan but yet still undefeated. He hauled himself up onto the flat, circular platform that made up the impossible mountain's top and rested. Soon sleep took him and when he awoke he was not alone.

For Rez was watching him.

'Why do you come, God?' said Rez. It was not so much a voice, as Rez had no mouth, but it seemed that his thoughts would take on linguistic form in this place. The sound echoed like thunder and Veo doubted that there was any part of this world that was not touched by it. 'Why should I not swat you from this mountaintop, and let you become food?' As he said this, excited screeching travelled up from below. Veo could only guess at the number of beasts needed to make such a noise. He certainly wouldn't be enough to feed all of them.

'Because I need your help.'

There was silence after this. The great force that was Rez, so near but still unable to reach into this dimension, at least anywhere beyond the mountain's top, was thinking.

'What makes you think I would help you?' The question sounded genuine, it was devoid of any mocking tone. Veo's confidence began to grow.

'Because I can help you,' said Veo.

The clichéd response would have been obvious (as most clichés are). 'You!? How could someone like you help me?' Followed by a substantial amount of guffawing. Rez did not respond like this, for he was clever. And he could see something in this God. There was hatred within him. Something that could perhaps be harvested.

'I'm listening' said Rez, and in the waiting dimension there was silence. So Veo explained and not a detail was spared, not even the story of Eree. This was no accident either, as Veo wanted to be absolutely clear on one particular point.

'If I help you break through, then no harm comes to Eree.'

Veo wasn't sure if Rez would be capable of understanding any of this but he could only hope. How could the great conscious force that so threatened their universe have any concept of love or relationship? But Rez agreed willingly enough.

'Of course she will be spared, but none of the other Gods, and as for your creations…I can promise nothing. The universe will need to be made afresh.'

Veo thought for a moment, thought about the countless lives he was now holding in the palm of his hand. He could still turn away. He could try his luck on the return journey and maybe, just maybe, make it back to Svin. Did so many need to die to achieve his aim? He thought of Eree, and then he thought of Gask. He reached up and touched the crude wood of his mask, feeling it press against his ruined face beneath.

'I care not for them.' he said, and you could feel Rez's happiness in the empty atmosphere. 'Tell me what I must do?'

'Aaaaah,' said Rez calmly and slowly. The space where the air should be suddenly felt much warmer. 'Unification.'

And so it was explained to Veo how he could allow Rez through into their universe. How if he were to kill all the sorcerers on one planet, he would unify their energy and, in taking all of it, he would have enough power to drive a wedge through the three dimensions. The task would not be an easy one. Gods who had gone up against armies of sorcerers rarely faired well, but perhaps if he were to choose his world wisely and plan his battle carefully, then success could be his.

'Make sure you take out the powerful ones,' said Rez. 'That way you will take the most power and make yourself a formidable enemy most quickly. 'Will you agree to this task Veo? For if you do, then I can promise you a new place, a place not like this one, but beautiful. A place where you and I will sit at the helm and, of course, your other will be there too.'

Veo had made his decision, he had made his decision long before scaling the mountain but now he knew exactly what it entailed. He had lost to Gask and Gask had won the prize Veo most desired. He had left Veo a broken, ugly freak. A freak forced to live out the life of a dead man, just to protect the one he loved. One who he would never see again. Now there was a chance. Now there was hope. A big, potentially unwinnable battle lay ahead of him. But he had faced terrible odds before and this time he was going in with backing. All he had to do was force the smallest of gaps and Rez would do the rest. The great magical force would come steaming on through and all would be new. He, Eree and Rez would rule over the new universe and everything Gask had done would be nothing but memory.

'All you must do is pick your world,' said Rez.

Veo smiled, rising to his feet, 'I think I know the perfect one,' he said.

9.

Shabwan could move again. The connection had been severed. He did not know what had happened to him, only that he now knew almost everything there was to know about his enemy. Some parts he had experienced through Veo, others he had seen as an onlooker and most of the dots had now been joined. He knew why Veo had come to Svin and he knew why he had attacked the sorcerers. The God had sought to destroy them all so as to take what was theirs...just as he himself had unwittingly done, once in the real world and once again as his test.

Magic could be taken and if you were to take it all, then this other force could come through. Veo was willing to let all that existed in every form (which was a lot more than Shabwan's poor mind could ever have conceived) be destroyed, just to be reunited with his love and exact his revenge. He now knew what he was up against. A force of pure evil. One that would stop at literally nothing to achieve a selfish aim. Never had he felt such rage, not in this place or in any other.

The realisation of how much was at stake was still hitting him. Shabwan had thought that he was fighting to save Svin. In reality, the whole universe was his to defend. He really didn't remember asking for any of this. Still, there was no time for such thinking now. The great castle lay ahead of him, looking more than ever like it was ready to rear up, but Shabwan would not be going in alone. He now understood not only what power he had but also how to use it. He drew his arms up and, as he did, the world drew up around him. The grey misty nothing became solid and within moments he was within his own huge fortress. Unlike Veo's, his was made of wood and natural rock, rather than the polished stone that sat facing him. As the great artificial beast, which responded to his every twitch, rose up around him, the castle opposite also unfurled.

The noise it made was terrible to hear, thousand-year-old stone splitting and grinding against itself. And when the beast had finally fully unfurled, the sight of it was more terrible than the sound could ever have been. Hundreds of feet high it stood, taking both human and animal form. It was top heavy, a great muscular frame atop skinny bent legs, like those of a goat. Skinny as they were, however, they seemed to be having no problem supporting their load. In the mouth of the creature, absolutely minuscule in comparison to it, stood Veo the conqueror. He felt calm. Having learned all there was to learn about his enemy, he now had everything he needed...well, almost everything. For as much as he'd seen *all* that had led Shabwan to be here, the most important question had still not been answered. Why? Why was it this boy who he must defeat? It was not difficult to see that the boy was special. He had something different from any human Veo had ever encountered. But nothing that he had seen from the boy's life, or from his journey here with Vericoos, had yielded what it might be.

He had kept watching with such eagerness, kept living the boys life, in the hope that the next piece of the puzzle would be the one to unlock everything. But this enlightenment had not come. He'd followed right up to the moment when the boy had plunged the dagger, and recalled at that moment his own experience of the same action. But there had been no more, and the conqueror still did not truly understand who he was facing...

But it matters not, thought Veo. He's mine to destroy and he's all that stands between me and freedom. And as we now know, freedom for Veo means the end for all others.

Stood within his behemoth, Shabwan waited the last few seconds. He wanted calm in his mind, but it was difficult with so much magic flowing through him. It was prickling in the air, willing him to take control of this great creation and fling himself at his foe. Would their fight be one of skill or of brute force? Perhaps it was better not to worry too much about such things. Some bridges are definitely made for crossing at a certain point.

At precisely the same point in time and, coincidentally enough, at the exact same moment that the two other confrontations were playing out in the other parts of the chamber, Shabwan the reluctant hero and Veo the conqueror charged forward. The three confrontations were underway.

Chapter 5.

A Discovery Made.

1.

It was the strangest thing they had ever seen. A hairy little creature with a bizarre beak-like nose and no discernible eyes. It's little feet seemed to be carrying it onwards, although it didn't seem to know where. There was a lost quality to it. A being without a home, lost in the most unwelcoming of environments.

'What on earth is it?' Kayleigh asked, though she doubted very much that any of the others knew the answer, and she was soon proved right.

'I don't know,' said Lewhay completely unnecessarily and then added, with even less purpose, 'It's not like anything I've ever seen.' They did not respond, instead they just watched it. A tiny little thing, almost completely unidentifiable as living. If it wasn't for the great nose and those little hands, it could have just been a ball of scraggly leaves, or perhaps the abandoned head of a mop. Yet something about it transfixed them none the less. It was somehow comforting to see another living being up here. It made them feel less like they were trespassing.

After a while they decided to move closer towards it. They should really continue on. But there was something about this creature that felt important. None of them shared this for fear of sounding stupid, but they all felt it. They moved in slowly, not wanting to startle the creature and, as they neared it, it turned its tiny head to look at them. Or perhaps just to smell them as they still couldn't see any eyes. Then it ran.

It moved depressingly slowly and, for the first time, they realised that it was wounded.

'We should follow it,' said Leeham and, again not really knowing why, they all agreed. It was as if this little creature was having an effect on them. Or perhaps it was the thinning mountain air. Either way, they temporarily abandoned the quest, for which they were risking life and limb, to chase a small hairy creature across the narrow mountaintops. Although perhaps chase was generous, it was more like keeping a respectful distance. Despite its obvious fear and distress, the creature was unable to make all but the slowest of progress.

After a few minutes of this slow motion pursuit, they realised where it was heading. It was going towards a fairly large, especially considering the size of the creature, opening in the mountainside.

'Wow,' murmured Kayleigh. It was almost impossible to conceive that such an ornate entrance could be found up here, but it was equally impossible to believe that the entrance had not been made by something. The crafting of the rock around the lip was beautiful. Clearly whatever or whoever had made it had taken great pride. The little thing they were following disappeared into the dark and they stopped following. They stood on the narrow ridge that led to the entrance and looked at one another.

'Do you think we should go in?' asked Leeham tentatively. The others did not have an answer. There seemed little reason to enter this place. It was hugely unlikely that Shabwan was in there, and hadn't they been told that he was through the forest and *over* the mountains. This place looked like it would lead them deep *into* the mountain…but then, he could well have come this way. If Shabwan had traversed the mountains, then wasn't it conceivable that he too had seen this place and perhaps entered it? Even if they were unlikely to find Shabwan, was there not a chance that they could find some clue as to where he'd gone? Was there even a tiny chance that he was still in there?

This last thought was particularly unlikely, given the head start their friend had. But perhaps this wasn't really why they wanted to go in at all. Perhaps something else was calling to them from within the cave, enticing them onwards. Without speaking another word to one another, they entered.

2.

That's it, thought Morshev, carry on in. The magic she was beaming toward them was clouding their judgment nicely. She had been stalking so much more patiently this time. She had controlled her urges and bided her time, and now she was about to get her reward. The mountains had offered little opportunity of a successful ambush thus far, but Morshev had never lost faith that they would yield one. She had not suspected that her chance would come in the form of that strange little being, but it had none the less.

Attaching her will to that of the scurrying creature, she lured them onwards. She gave the cave a beautiful and hypnotic appearance when, in truth, it had neither. And like lambs they followed in. Lambs that were being led not into the welcoming arms of their shepherd, but to the far more proverbially common slaughter.

Morshev licked her lips. Once they entered the chamber they would be hers. She would kill three, and then the remaining one would have no choice but either to lead her to Shabwan or to tell her what she needed.

As they disappeared into the blackness, she too advanced. Their natural curiosity would now lead them onwards. Her spikes extended as the thrill of the hunt kicked in. She growled softly and then began to run. Her mind was now facing in one direction only, as was that of the other who followed on behind her.

3.

They were in a city, an underground city. It made no sense but was here all the same. And as big as it was, it was also so small. The cavern was big enough to contain a human city, but the dwellings and streets it housed were designed for those much smaller. More like the size of the little thing they had followed in here. There was a larger road that clung to the edge of the circular chamber and from it ran many little roads and streets, disappearing back further into the mountain. The road that they were on lead downwards and they followed it. Their minds were no longer with Shabwan, or indeed anywhere outside of the mountain. They had discovered something here; something amazing, and they would not be able to leave until they knew more about this place.

Like children they walked on, gazing around at the wonder of this little world. They thought not of their safety or what was around them. They thought not to look behind them into the darkness they were leaving. The lights of the little torches led them on, but were so small that they did not illuminate much. Then, without warning, the bottom surged up into view. And with it came the most terrible of sights.

Sprawled across the bottom of the chamber, too numerous to comprehend, were the bodies. Tiny little bodies, all with a large nose and tiny little arms and feet. The creatures, to their eyes, all looked identical to the little fellow they had followed in here. And now they understood the sadness. Was he or she the only one who had survived this massacre?

The only part of the room not covered with death was the strange altar-like rock in the centre. It now stood like some strange beacon, protruding out of the little ocean of bodies. The whole scene was heartbreaking to behold. For all the wonderment they had felt minutes ago, they now felt guilty. They had been enjoying this place like visitors taking in the sights. They had not realised that they were in a tomb. A tomb of what seemed like an entire species.

4.

They had stopped and Morshev knew that the time was right. They were preoccupied with taking in the great scene of death ahead of them. Clearly someone had been busy down here but Morshev cared not for who or why. She was about to get busy herself. She charged silently, moving speedily but with footfall light as a feather. Then something made her stop. She skidded to a halt and slunk against the wall. Immediately her magic changed her colour and, like a chameleon, she took on the exact likeness of her surrounds. Had the four friends turned around, they would have seen nothing. But they were unlikely to turn around as, ahead of them, the little creature they had originally followed down here was now approaching them.

5.

They all stood transfixed as the being came nearer. It no longer seemed to want to escape. Neither did it threaten, although what threat it could have posed asked a lot of one's imagination. Instead it seemed to want to communicate.

'Shaaaaaa,' it said.

They looked at one another.

'ShAAAA,' it said again, somehow managing to alter its intonation of a one-syllable sound. Kayleigh knelt down so as to be at a closer level to the thing. It did not flinch, but instead looked defiantly up towards her. There was something so curious about the little thing. It was everything a human wasn't and yet somehow…

'Shaaaaaaaaaaaaaaaawun!'

Leeham felt like someone had punched him in the face. He too knelt down. He must be hearing things. There was no way that…

'Shaaaaaaabwoon,' clearly the effort of speaking this word was challenging the little thing to its very limits, but it was so determined to get it across. And there was now little doubting what the word was. How on earth could it know…?

'Shabwan,' said Kayleigh softly, tears streaming down her face and dropping to the polished rock of the road. Here they made little pools as the rock neglected to swallow them up. 'Is that what you're trying to say?'

The hairy creature jumped and clacked excitedly and clearly hurt itself in the process as it let out a shrill cry.

'Oh, what is it?' asked Kayleigh. She tried to reach out. She wanted to see if she could help it. The creature clacked more but seemed unable to move. As Kayleigh touched it the clacking became a shrill shriek and she pulled her hands back as if from a hot stove.

'He doesn't want to be touched,' she said. But this did not explain everything. For even though Kayleigh had moved back and given the little thing its space, it was still making a distressed noise and thrashing its little nose about. Every now and again it would hold it still and reach its little arms out, although they barely extended beyond the tip of it.

Leeham couldn't understand it. The thing knew the name of their lost friend. It also seemed to know who they were and was trying, as bizarrely as it seemed, to help them in someway. Yet it was injured, and now they were trying to help it, it was getting most upset with the whole arrangement. There was something strange about its movement as well. It wasn't like it was thrashing around wildly in pain, more like it was trying to tell them something more…but then why would it not…before Leeham could finish the thought, he realised what had been staring him in the face the whole time. The creature was not in pain at all. Its concern was not for itself, it was for them, and rather than writhing around in pain, it was actually trying to gesture.

There was something behind them.

This realisation, as they have an annoying tendency to do, came a moment too late, and before Leeham could turn his head, let alone cry out a warning, Morshev thrust one of her ebony spikes deep into his back.

6.

She did not know why she had delayed her attack. The sight of the strange little creature had had an unsettling effect on her. There was something deeply wrong about it being there, surrounded by the corpses of its fallen kind. She had settled in to watch for a moment, and had been just as surprised as the four friends to hear the sounds it was attempting to emit.

Then the damn thing had spotted her.

How it could see her was a complete mystery. She was as well camouflaged as it was possible to be, and yet it had still seen through. What in the names of all the Gods was this thing? Cursing herself for delaying, she lunged forward. The element of surprise was still hers if she were to take it. Launching forward she sunk one of her great spikes into the nearest boy. Feeling him instantly fall limp and drop away she rounded on the others.

7.

Coki was aware of a flurry of movement but no sound. By the time he turned, Leeham was already dropping to the floor, a vacant look in his eyes. Coki's brain registered the blood but his eyes saw none. The world rotated around him. His arms felt powerful, but he did not know what to do with them. His friend was dead, that was what his brain was screaming at him, and if he didn't act, then they would all soon follow suit. Kayleigh was by his side and it was her scream he heard next. He could not see what had attacked her, but he recognised the colour of the thing that now protruded from her chest. The thing from the woods, he thought, as Kayleigh's eyes rolled backwards and her blood splattered his face.

He wheeled around, still unable to see that which had attacked them.

'Lewhay!' he yelled but received no response. 'Lewhay!!' He grabbed his friend, who was stood, mouth open wide, unable to believe. 'Lets go.' He took the weight of his friend, who seemed unable to move, and hauled him forwards. Seconds later, however, a force so much greater than his ripped Lewhay out of his arms. Coki turned, knowing what he was going to see before he saw it. Lewhay was flung hard against the wall and then, as he began to slide to the floor, a white spike, seemingly disembodied, was thrust deep into his chest. His friend coughed and blood flowed freely from his mouth. Lewhay did not even open his eyes one last time.

Finally Morshev revealed herself. She was just as terrible as he'd remembered. Her glistening, black body reflected the weak firelight so vividly and she was covered in those razor sharp spikes that had just killed his three friends. Coki could not form a thought. They were in the realm of the primal now. Revenge is not often a linguistic function within the brain. So forward Coki went with a beast-like roar. He knew he could not win, but he wanted this cursed demon to know that he went without fear. He would die fighting it. As he lurched forward there was a flash of black and then something hit him on the side of the head, something sharp. He felt warmth and his vision became tunnelled. He lay on the narrow road, aware that these next few moments would be the last of his life.

But the great black demon did not attack again. She knew she had already done enough. Coki turned his head with his last bit of strength. Some part of him clearly thought it would be nice to get one last glimpse of daylight, however faint, before he passed. He strained his increasingly blurred vision, trying to catch the slightest bit of blue. But, rather than the dim glow of day he sought, he saw something much brighter, and something moving at speed.

Perhaps an angel, was his final thought.

Chapter 6.

Hardram in sight.

1.

Thon, Marie and Rachel, all marching at the head of the column, were the first to see the city, but it was not the city that caught the eye. Not by a long shot.

The relationships between the three had been so much better since that night in the tent. Thon seemed to have adjusted the spring in his neck and wound it back to where it should be. He seemed to have settled into his natural position. He was not the leader, how could he be with Rachel at the helm? But, to Marie, it now seemed that he was content in his role as general. The people respected him and surely that should be enough. Marie was not particularly interested in who respected her or otherwise and so she found such things difficult to comprehend. But the more time she spent with this newer and less passive-aggressive Thon, the more she felt like she understood what drove him, and the more she sympathised.

She had perhaps even begun to think of him as a friend. As she had the others from Hardram and, of course, Losh. The memory of his presence as she'd made her way towards the gallows now seemed distant and impossible.

The marching had become much more taxing as every day Rachel and Callandra had pushed them a little harder. Marie understood that, as a person of rank within the army, whether willingly or otherwise, she had no business showing any kind of weakness. Her life had been saved by this same movement. Many of those who marched with them were those who had put their lives on the line on the day that was supposed to be her last. She could not put into words the gratitude and camaraderie she felt. These people had been willing to put her safety ahead of their own without ever having laid eyes on her. In a way there was no greater thing you could do.

Putting the self behind the cause is something that brings out the bravest and the best of people. Marie hoped that, if the roles had been reversed, she would have done the same thing…this she hoped more than anything.

Then the city came into view and above it was the chamber.

How could they possibly have lived like this? With it hanging above them? She knew it had not always been as bad as this, but even so.

The chamber hung perilously, spinning and jolting. The cracks that crisscrossed its outer walls burned with a deep red light and the sounds of battle came from within. The old woman had been right, it certainly seemed like the thing was fighting internally rather than simply trying to burst forth. But what was even worse than the chamber was what was above it. The red light from the cracks seemed to be sucking the sky in towards the chamber, dragging in wisps of cloud which soon became no more. As they watched, birds too were pulled into the great red glow. Although glow was deceiving, it was more like a cloud itself. A dull throbbing cloud expanding outwards and clawing at all that around it with a hunger that could not be sated.

'It's breaking the sky,' said Marie. Thon only nodded. He too was thinking not only of what the chamber was doing to the sky but also of what they could see beyond. It was difficult to focus on any one thing, as everything was moving so fast. But there were definitely things beyond the thin film of air. Marie thought once again of the old woman's words. There was something out there, something which they would do very well to remain protected from. Rachel was staring at it intently, but as usual her face betrayed little of what she felt. Sometimes Marie wished she could tell more of what she was thinking. This was, most certainly, one of those times.

Rachel turned to address the army, 'we will take up our positions outside the city walls,' she said. 'And there we will make ourselves ready. Whatever comes out of the chamber, we must be ready for it.' There was no audible response from the crowd. 'I SAID!' roared Rachel. 'WE MUST BE READY FOR IT!! This time the crowd cheered and what a cheer it was. Before them lay the most terrifying sight they had ever seen, and its nature remained a complete mystery. But they had not come this far for nothing.

Chapter 7.

Explanations...Well, Almost.

1.

There was a lot of black. Black was everywhere, but black was also something. It seemed more logical that there would be nothing. And there was logic too. All of these things seemed to suggest being, and he was sure that this couldn't be right. What business did he have existing? He remembered all too clearly the moment he'd lost his life. The nothing that had swirled in over him had been dogmatic in its approach. It was going to leave nothing behind.

But then, there was something here. It was not consciousness as such, more like a vessel. And if he were a vessel then perhaps he wasn't gone. Perhaps he had not lost everything. As these thoughts became clearer, he sought to remember. What had happened before his death? Who had he been? Who, perhaps, was he?

There was a little glimmer now amongst all the presumptuous black. Nice it was. Dancing about like that. It made him feel peaceful, but then another part of him warned against this. Now was not a time to relax, now was a time to fight. But fight what? And fight how? He didn't have tools with which to fight. And yet the voice that called out to him to do so became ever stronger. It was like a strange song, simultaneously lulling and driving him. Then he realised he'd been wrong. There was not one thing here but two. Two things were calling to him and it was from them that the feelings of conflict stemmed.

The little light, which flickered so seductively, whispered of peace and happiness. It offered him rest that would last and never be challenged. It spoke of rolling fields and open sea...*the sea!* He remembered something about this. Maybe he had once lived in it, no, that didn't seem right. He hadn't lived *in* it. The other light interrupted these thoughts. It was strange to see how, even though its message conflicted with the other, they were not at war. They were, instead, two possibilities, floating in nothing but promising everything. But what different everythings they were. One lulled him into visions of perfect rest while the other spoke of duty and of fight. It should have been a no-brainer but it was not. For as unattractive as the idea of fighting seemed at a time like this, it was not something that could be ignored. He was not being asked to fight others. Nobody wanted him to hurt or kill, they wanted him to fight for himself.

As he thought this, images swam in with the two milky lights as if he were in some kind of deep-sea fish tank, populated by the kinds of fish whose bodies seem to be made only from light. The images stirred things in him;

feelings which, while not as warm and fuzzy as those offered by the light, were attractive in their own way. The other light promised him eternal gain, but to go towards it he would also have to lose something forever. He didn't want to lose it. The thought sparked fear within him, a new feeling in this place and, without another moment's hesitation, he reached for one of the lights.

Vision raced back to him, scattering the lights like a frightened shoal upon the arrival of a shark. Moments were needed for him to take it all in, for it was quite a sight. He was lying on rock, smooth rock, washed that way by some now absent water. He was not the only one lying. His three friends were also on the floor. As they'd fallen, they'd created a crude circle, not unlike the camp fire positions they'd taken up when alive. As this thought arrived it brought back memory, all of it, and a fresh wave of shock smashed into Coki like a falling boulder.

His friends were dead.

Then he realised they were not alone. How he hadn't realised this before was something of a mystery, as the woman who sat in the middle of them was the brightest thing in this murky place. Her naked, blue tinted body glowed, but that was not all that was glowing. As if this newcomer were some strange spider, blue tendrils, emitting the most beautiful of light, connected her to the four fallen friends. She sat in the centre, eyes closed, body quivering. At first sight she had appeared peaceful, but it was not so. Whatever she was pumping along these blue beams into their bodies was taking it out of her…she was healing them. Coki could feel it, and as he did his heart leapt. If he was alive then did it perhaps mean that the others…he wouldn't allow himself to think it. Not yet. For now he just had to work with her. For her magic was doing much, but his strength was required too. He closed his eyes and focussed. He tried to shut off his mind. He would not think of his three fallen friends or the other that they were missing. Instead he lay there, repeating the same simple mantra to himself again and again…*heal, heal, heal.*

It was working.

Soon he had the energy to raise his head and prop himself with his elbow. He tried to signal to their saviour, tried to get her attention. For, much as he didn't want to break her concentration, he did not need her anymore. He could take care of himself now, and wanted only that this blue woman heal his friends. Emotion washed over him again as he thought this, but he fought it back.

'Hey…' he croaked in a fashion that would have embarrassed even the smallest of frogs. 'Hey,' he tried again with a bit more conviction. This time her eyes flickered, but as they did so the beams weakened. Coki's heart almost undid all the guardian's good work by jumping out of his mouth. He didn't know what to do. To alert her would allow more energy for his friends, who clearly needed it more. But then, to alert her might also break the beams altogether, and he didn't know whether she would be able to re-establish the connections. You had to hand it to Coki. For a man returning from death he was good at gauging situations, thus making him a good friend of any narrator.

As his strength grew, so did his resolution. He could feel his body taking in more energy and, good as it was, he hadn't seen so much as a flicker from any of his three friends. Every ounce of this stuff he was taking was another ounce that might save his friends. He had to stop this.

'HEY!!' he roared and the guardian's eyes opened. For a second the beams became thin as reeds and Coki feared he'd made the wrong decision. But they did not break, and the surprise in the woman's eyes as she'd opened them soon became understanding. Coki felt the weight of his own survival drop onto his shoulders as his beam disconnected. Then the three remaining beams swelled up to a size greater than they'd ever been as four. It was at that moment that he saw the tiniest of flickers of movement. It was Leeham's fingers.

Staring at them all, not daring to move, breathe or hope, Coki simply waited. Having made his peace with his own death, he was now praying that his friends would be spared that fate. And, finally, after what seemed like an age to rival all others, the beams receded. In their wake they left three confused, dazed but very much alive people. They looked at each other trying to make sense of the impossible. Memories, impossible memories, flitted in and out of range. No one spoke for some time.

It was Sheeba the guardian who finally broke the silence. But she did it not by speaking, instead she collapsed. The four friends dragged themselves over to her with varying degrees of difficulty. Alive they were, but healed they weren't.

Coki looked down at the woman, if that was what she was, who had saved them. She was more physically beautiful than any he had ever seen. She was also in deep trouble. Her body was quivering and shaking, as if she were immersed in icy water, rather than the strange, balmy warmth of the chamber. Coki hugged her to himself. She had saved him and his friends at a huge personal sacrifice. As he held her he began to cry.

'You must go!' Her voice was high and failing fast. 'You must follow where they have gone. I made a terrible mistake…Vericoos… the sorcerer is not to be trusted.' They looked at one another. There was so much to ask her it was hard to formulate one question. She didn't seem to need them to. 'Your friend is beyond the mountains…Vericoos seeks to use him as his key…stop him.'

'Key?' said Coki. 'What do you mean key?' The woman's time was clearly running out fast. If they could not get her some help, then she was soon for the same fate from which she had rescued them. It was then that Coki saw the body of Morshev, laid out in eternal rest slightly further down the tiny road. In death she looked much more human. The white spines had all but retracted into her and her shape had become almost indistinguishable from theirs. It was strange that he felt no anger to look upon her. Perhaps he'd used up all his capacity for any new emotions. Relief and happiness were still flooding over him with such severity.

'Vericoos seeks to open the chamber,' continued Sheeba laboriously. 'And if he does, then our time, all of our time, is up.' It didn't make any sense to them, but all they could do was listen and hope. Hope that meaning would come together out of the mist. 'You must go over the mountains. You must reach your friend and you must stop the sorcerer...' as Sheeba said this, her head fell backwards and came to rest on the stone floor. She was gone.

The four friends looked at one another. They'd been spared death by one who had now died for them, one they'd never so much as laid eyes on. It was a strange feeling, one that cut into them like the spines of Morshev.

They left her body there. It hurt them to do so but there was no way they could give her any kind of burial. Even if they carried her up out of the chamber, there would be nothing they could do on the cold hard rock of the mountain.

'What did she mean, key?' asked Kayleigh, more to herself than any of the others.

'I don't have a clue,' said Leeham, tears rolling down his cheeks. 'But we were right about the old man.'

They were all thinking of him now. That strange old man they had beaten to a pulp in their hometown. A cunning old trickster who had somehow persuaded their friend to leave with him...to leave and become some sort of key. What could the old man have possibly needed Shabwan for? It made as little sense as anything else. All they now knew for certain was that Shabwan was in trouble and, by the sounds of it, if they didn't reach him in time, so was everybody else.

They found a narrow winding path that led them through the highest part of the mountains without taking them right up to the actual peaks and, on the evening of the next day, they found themselves looking upon the city of Hardram. That was when they understood.

2.

They say that what goes around comes around. But then, *they* say a lot of things and a great deal of them turn out not to be true. But sometimes, just sometimes, they do. Sheeba had given her life in an attempt to make up for what she'd done. She had allowed herself to be fooled by Vericoos. She had healed his talent and sent him on his merry way. She had allowed herself to be hoodwinked by the fact that he sought to destroy what was in the chamber. She had not immediately realised, however, that his plan had been to put this thing in it first.

After he had left her, after his healing, she had felt uneasy. She did not often doubt her judgment, but she had doubted it then. What was it about the things the old man had said...? There had been something wrong, but something that it was difficult to put your finger on. These thoughts had lingered, although while replaying the conversation in her head, she had never been able to decide if her fear was legitimate or some paranoia born of the changing times. Her wondering had been brought to an end as the chamber was opened.

She felt it rip through the skies. That which had lain dormant for so long was momentarily erupting, and then another entered. The young man with whom Vericoos had travelled, the one he'd been so keen to rush off and save, he was the key. The key to Veo's release. And if Veo were to escape and finish what he'd started, then everything would be over. It mattered not how few sorcerers there were in the world. The flow was increasing again and the God would harvest enough magic.

She had not known what to do. For the first time in her existence, she was lost. She could not approach the chamber herself. To do so would be suicide. There was already enough energy flowing from it to fry her as she approached, such was her sensitivity to magic. Then another opportunity had come. The four friends following in the wake of Vericoos, and the other. They had bravely come after their friend and perhaps offered salvation to so much more than they could comprehend. In the wake of their first battle with Morshev, she had found them all flushed with the joy of victory, invigorated by surviving a true attempt on their lives. She had felt such confidence within them.

She had followed them at a distance, not knowing when to approach. Would they trust her? Their trust was everything and, after all, they'd already been attacked by one strange being in the forest. Their trust would be at a low ebb.

Then she had seen the other return. At first she had not been sure if it was her or not. She felt different from when Sheeba had first sensed her. It was not until she'd laid eyes on her, near the entrance to the cave, that she'd been sure that the one who shared her path also posed a threat. On seeing the beast charge, she had followed but she had not been fast enough. By the time she'd reached the bottom of the oo-ja's chamber, three of them had been slain and the fourth was lying unconscious. But all had not been lost, not yet.

She fought the creature. They tore at each other, both things of magical power but one also posing a severe physical threat. Sheeba had gone at it with everything she had and it had been enough…just. As she'd sliced her suddenly razor sharp fingers across Morshev's throat, she too had fallen. The effort of the fight had depleted her almost to the point of death, but there was still so much to do.

Hauling herself into a sitting position, she had begun to heal and, well, you know the rest. Right up until the point where the four friends left her, rather ungratefully you might feel, and this is when we now join her.

She lay there peacefully, her life force was abandoning her slowly and oh so regretfully. She'd loved the world she'd been appointed to guard. Even if her creation had been cynical, she had made the best of it. She had turned her enforced addiction into a thing of love and beauty and it had been no small achievement. Now it had come to an end, and she would die not knowing if she had saved that which she so loved. But, as I said before, ever so often stuff going around and then coming likewise is not meant in a bad way. Sometimes it's not meant as a threat or a warning or a smug little I told you so. Sometimes it's deserved, and as Sheeba lay there, her heart not beating but her life not yet completely gone, tiny figures began to appear from the surrounding streets. Soon there were enough of them to lift her. After some clicking and grunting which could have sounded something like a discussion, they picked her up.

Chapter 8.

The Reluctant Hero and The conqueror.

There comes a time in most peoples' lives when they consider they have reached some kind of crunch. I believe crunch time is the common phrase, but I may be wrong. For most, it is perhaps the realisation that your life isn't turning out quite as you planned and it might be time to go for that job you've always thought was beyond you, or finally approach the girl or boy you've never quite had the courage to talk to. For Shabwan, it was when he found himself contained within a massive humanoid juggernaut, made by the creative abilities of a third of his whole in a micro-dimension where he was almost infinitely powerful (both creatively and magically), fighting against a God, hell bent on destroying the universe, who was also contained within a similarly gargantuan machine of war. Swings and roundabouts as they say. Anyway we're not here to observe my overly long sentence construction, we're here for the fight. They always draw a crowd, and this one is going to be special.

The force of the two creations was beyond anything. With each blow came the force of the dimension which contained them. As they punched and parried, cliffs jumped into existence and were then shattered. Lightning bolts, thicker than villages, smashed into their forms. Million-mile-an hour winds forced them away from each other and then the space left would allow them to crash together again, like sharp horned goats or those dinosaurs whose names escape me. Inside the heads of these two titans, Shabwan and Veo played out the dance themselves. Every movement of theirs was mirrored by the behemoth that contained them. And by all the Gods were they evenly matched.

Once more they thundered together and this time they grappled. With their mighty hands upon each other shoulders they tried to haul each other to the floor. As they did so, the two heads came close together and, for the first time, Shabwan and Veo got a good look at each other. They stood there on their respective platforms, frozen in a half squat with their hands outstretched, mere feet away from each other. Neither called out as to do so would have been to waste energy. This was not a fight for clichéd taunting of the other or boasting about the ease with which the fight was going to be won. This was a fight for winning.

Shabwan locked all his energy into his shoulders and allowed the magic within him to flow forth. The difference it made was instantaneous, both to his strength and to his mind. He felt a slight buckle in the air beneath his hands. He pumped more magic forward and Veo dropped to one knee. The force of his castle hitting the ground created vast shockwaves. Cracks appeared both in the castle and in Shab's monster. Shab tried to force his elbow over onto the others head, but could not quite do it. The arms of his beast were glowing with the magic he was forcing through. But it was not enough.

Out of nowhere, his opponent freed an arm and brought it smashing up into his platform. The force of it flung him from his feet and he landed hard. His behemoth stayed vertical, temporarily stunned. Then it began to fall. Shabwan clung on to the side of his little platform as it plummeted downwards, then came the impact. It would have killed him outright if it weren't for the magic hurriedly healing his wounds.

As his vision swam back into focus, he saw the great foot of what had once been Veo's castle about to stomp down on him. He kicked a leg out and caught the foot with his own. The magic that had been healing him began to flow fast and hard up his leg. Stepping back, you would have seen the great pillar of two legs separating two enormous man shaped things. One of them was powering a great blue steaming energy upward while the other was attempting to crush the first under the pure might of its bulk. They stayed like this for some moments, locked together and unmoving. Then, with an awesome flash of light, both monstrosities exploded.

2.

The dreams were disturbing. He wanted to help them, all of them, but he could not. He was being pulled away…wasn't he? Or was it perhaps that he himself was doing the pulling. He didn't like that idea. He wasn't a selfish man. Then he awoke.

He was lying amidst the wreckage of what had been his weapon of war. Now he would have to rely on his raw tools. For through his blurry vision, through the rocky wasteland that their explosion had created, the God was advancing. All around him the sky was a murky grey brown. It was not a colour Shabwan would have created. His foe had obviously healed far quicker.

'Fight me…' yelled Shabwan, hoping this might buy him a few seconds. 'Fight me like a man.' Veo laughed. He was not a man, of course. Shabwan knew that. Hauling himself to his knees he faced the advancing God head on. Veo had already filled his hand with poisonous energy. Clearly he was in no mood for talking. This was going to be done quickly and efficiently. But Shabwan was not ready to die just yet. He had a little more to give.

Lurching to his feet, he took a handful of magic of his own, it bubbled and brewed. Whatever divine power Veo was holding, it was no match. They moved towards each other, the God striding purposefully, a cruel sneer on his obscure wooden mask, the boy lurching as if drunk. Both had one glowing hand filled with power that had designs on the other. No more words were spoken, clearly the conqueror had nothing to say.

As they came close to each other, they swung their arms around in matching arcs. It was a fight of pure rage now, neither even tried to avoid the attack of the other.

Both landed their blows at the same time and the world went blank.

3.

On the ledge that overlooked Hardram, they stood and watched. The woman's words had seemed so easy. They had to stop Vericoos, they had to help Shabwan. But now they were looking at the only place that their friend could be, and what possible assistance could they offer? The chamber was thrashing around like a wounded animal. Above it, a black and red vortex of something, which resembled cloud but could be no such thing, swirled like a typhoon. Beyond it, another world flashed in and out of focus. Ugly screeches rang out punctuated by deafening roars.

Even three people who had taken stonk to its natural conclusion had never had such visuals.

Then it all went quiet. The chamber came to rest, spinning gently above the central point of the city. The cloud like things above remained but did not swirl. The noises that must have been coming from the other dimension seemed to calm and then stop.

'Look,' said Kayleigh and she was pointing, but not at the chamber. She was pointing over beyond the city, to the slow hills beyond. At first it just looked like a black stain on the green landscape but, as your eyes focused, it ceased to be one black mass and started becoming lots of little ones. 'People,' Kayleigh whispered.

But they did not have time to think about who they might be or what it might mean, for that was when it happened.

4.

Shabwan opened his eyes, but he might as well not have bothered. The effect was much the same. There was nothing to see. As he turned slowly in the nothing, however, he was proven wrong. Veo was here too. Together they were floating in an endless nothing. No longer did he possess the ability to create and his magic seemed to have deserted him too. Was this it then? Were he and the God doomed to float around for all eternity battling it out hand to hand?

Veo was moving. Not much, but enough to suggest he hadn't died. Had they both failed or had they both been successful? The former seemed more likely but then, they were still here. Wasn't the whole point that only one of them would escape from this place?

Then he saw the door.

After the grandiose of their battle it seemed like the most simple of things, but then, aren't the most important things always so? Veo had seen it too. For a moment neither moved. Then, with whatever force they had remaining, they flung themselves forward. Together they travelled through the air, like astronauts. There was nothing to gain purchase on; it was as if will power alone drove them on. As they neared the door they came together and fought.

They fought with nothing other than what they had, and that was very little. Battering and clawing at each other, they resembled two old drunks outside the Star in San Hoist. As they neared the door, it swung open invitingly, but they knew it did not welcome both. Veo's more muscular arm had gained a grip around Shabwan's neck and, strain as he might, the pressure was still increasing. In seconds it would snap. Without knowing why, he slipped a hand inside his pocket.

There was a knife there.

A knife had caused all this, perhaps it could end it. As he stabbed upwards and felt the knife cut through the God into where, Shabwan hoped like hell, his heart was. Veo twisted his arm and snapped Shabwan's neck. The two lifeless forms toppled through the open door which, graciously enough, closed after them.

Chapter 9.

In the Chamber, Again.

1.

Vericoos did not expect the calm. But then it came. For a while, as the conflicts had raged, the chamber had been the most volatile place in which to be, as it pulsated and lurched around. At first it had been a struggle to stay on his feet, then it had become a struggle to survive. And now it had stopped.

The three silver plaques on the doors now caught his attention. For a moment they glowed white hot, then they melted away into nothing. With an echoing click, the three doors unlocked and swung open. For a moment all he saw was black, then three figures appeared, growing larger by the second. This is it, thought the old sorcerer, I've done it.

But what he saw was not what he expected. Three Veo's did not emerge from the three chambers. Instead, stood in front of him like mummies awakening from a thousand year sleep, was one Shabwan, one Veo and...

2.

The romantic shook himself. He was back in the real world. Going through the door had not been a simple matter of just stepping through. Colour and sound had swirled around him, disorientating him as he'd spun like a top. Then he'd landed on solid ground. The colours and shapes, which had been flinging him around like a rag doll moments before, zipped into position to form the room of the chamber. Ahead of him was Vericoos, his friend Vericoos. Had he been successful? He turned his head, hoping against hope that he would see himself. He did not.

3.

The trickster saw Vericoos. He was indeed free, but he knew that this was only half the battle or, to be more precise, a third of it. To his right stood the boy. Panic rose in the God. What did this mean? Part of him had been defeated by this human? Impossible! It could not be. But yet here the boy was, looking back at him, seemingly equally as unsure what to do. He turned to his left. Perhaps the third would be the decider and surely there could only be one...

What he saw as he turned his head almost blew his mind out of his skull.

4.

As the two lifeless forms floated through the abyss together, they began to stir. Both had died...twice now, so stirring should not really have been an option, but who am I to judge? Stirring there most certainly was, and it soon became much more than that. As the swirling kaleidoscope through which they travelled organised itself into the interior of the chamber, Shabwan and

Veo stirred. They looked at one another for the briefest of moments, and then both God and human were sucked into one.

5.

Vericoos was not a screamer, it had never been his way. But what he saw drew, if not a scream, then as close as the old man was capable of from his dry throat. The thing that stood in front of him was neither Shabwan nor Veo…it was both. An unholy fusion of the two. The face was half wooden mask, half skin. The torso was huge and covered with scraps of material intertwined with the silver breastplate of the God. The half man, half God thing was still for a second.

Then all hell broke loose.

Vericoos would later try to remember exactly what happened and would fall well short. It was too much of a blur. All he really remembered was that one second there were three things stood in front of him, and then there was one. The three divisions were sucked in together and it all became a blur. Flashes of light broke out as if trying to forge one thing, the same way that the flashes had bound the three together as they'd attacked the Hoist. Each time the thin lines attempted to knit, they were flung back. The intensity in the room rose, a high-pitched sound scythed at Vericoos' eardrums. He raised his hands to block it. Then with a small pop, the lightning, seemingly so devoted to the task of making one from three, was gone. For a moment there was only white. Then there were two.

One Shabwan and one Veo now stood in front of the sorcerer, though neither were as he remembered them. For a moment he was in shock. All he had seen had proved too much. Then he realised that they'd done it.

Veo was free.

The fact that the boy had somehow escaped as well was a small problem. Very small.

As if reaching this same conclusion at the same time, the God and the sorcerer rounded on Shabwan.

6.

He was himself again but that was not all he was. And now he was going to die. He saw the combined energies forming between the God and the sorcerer, Vericoos, who he'd thought was his friend. This made no sense. After cheating death three times in the chamber, he was now going to get it for real just moments after his escape. It didn't seem all that fair to him. He had magic within him, but he knew it was not enough. Instead he turned his mind to its strongest bond. He saw Kayleigh's beautiful eyes flutter and saw his hometown melting under the summer sunset.

Then there was a click and a door opened once more.

7.

Lubwan strode forward, not disorientated like the divisions but tall and proud. He had a murderous look in his eye. Without so much as a breath, he unleashed a lethal bolt of energy at Vericoos who only just reacted in time.

Shabwan and Veo were now separated by the white hot line which the other two held between them. Their faces contorted as they tried to force each other back. The God and the human wasted no time; they too launched all they had at each other. The four beings were now connected by a cross of lethal energy, both divine and magical. The point where the beams met began to glow a darker shade as steam billowed up from it. From within came snarls and screeches. Shabwan closed his eyes, he could not begin to take in what was happening to or around him, but right now he had a simple objective. Kill Veo.

8.

The sky was swirling again, although the chamber was still spinning gently. Then the red cracks in it began to glow deeper and darker than ever they had before, and then came the roaring. It sounded like wind, but not a wind of this world. Kayleigh screamed, Shabwan was up there in that place, she knew it. But she could do nothing to reach him.

The pulses of dark red began crackling and huge rods of lighting began flashing from the dark clouds above. All of them connecting with the roof of the chamber. It seemed like the end, the end of all things perhaps, but most certainly the end of their quest. They had come *so* far and got *so* close.

She could not take her eyes from the chamber; she was willing her love to somehow travel into it. If she could not see Shabwan one last time, perhaps she could let him know that she was close.

As the four friends watched from the mountaintops, the chamber began to vibrate and the roaring intensified. Kayleigh no longer knew if she was screaming or not. There was one last intensely red flash then, in a ball of fiery flame and white light, the God Chamber exploded.

Lightning Source UK Ltd.
Milton Keynes UK
UKOW040657051212

203206UK00001B/14/P